# "Going over, Dad!"
# Dean yelled

Ryan realized that the boy was right. The mules were off and running, but the reins had snagged, dragging them inexorably toward the drop on the right.

They were within fifteen feet of the last mounted bandit, who was swearing at his mare, urging her out of the way of the charging mules. Ryan balanced himself against the rocking of the rig, firing once, seeing the man go down with blood blossoming on his chest, his arms flung wide.

"Dad! Foot's caught!"

Then the rig began to tilt, seeming to hang sickeningly on the edge of the sighing space for an eternity before the terrified team pulled it right off the trail.

**Also available in the
Deathlands saga:**

# JAMES AXLER

# DEATH LANDS®

## Crossways

A GOLD EAGLE BOOK FROM

# WORLDWIDE®

TORONTO • NEW YORK • LONDON
AMSTERDAM • PARIS • SYDNEY • HAMBURG
STOCKHOLM • ATHENS • TOKYO • MILAN
MADRID • WARSAW • BUDAPEST • AUCKLAND

As we move together into fresh woods and pastures
new, this one is for Liz. It comes with all my love
and it will always come with all my love.

First edition February 1996

ISBN 0-373-62530-8

CROSSWAYS

Teachers are to life what morticians are to death. They rip out your guts, drain you of your vital fluids and then turn you into what they think you should look like to face eternity. Or they just do what they can to make life feel like eternity.

      —*The Best Education Is No Education*,
        by Jean-Paul Godard, Vanquer Press, Paris

# Chapter One

Ryan Cawdor lay in the gateway chamber of the matter-transfer unit at the heart of Redoubt 47, in the wilds of what had a hundred years earlier been the state of Louisiana.

"Who could...?" he said slowly, his voice distorted, throbbing inside his skull.

Krysty Wroth's fingers squeezed his hand very hard, painfully. She was telling him something, shouting. But the jump was almost under way.

Almost.

A silhouetted figure stood outside the heavy door, someone tall and skinny, wearing black.

Ryan's grip on the present had almost gone, and he clung to consciousness by a ragged fingernail. Images floated through his whirling mind.

The massive dark brown armaglass door to the chamber was opening, closing.

Dark figure.

White hair.

Face close against his, with eyes that leaked bright blood. A skin like paper.

Old, immeasurably old.

Hissing words. "...what you did...."

As blackness finally swallowed him up and his eye closed, Ryan's last sentient thought was that his nostrils were filled with the acrid stench of decay.

Of death.

# Chapter Two

As usual, making the jump had plunged Ryan into the singeing deeps of nightmare.

He was in a frontier pesthole, standing in the scorching heat of the noon sun. It took only a moment for him to be aware that the scent of fresh-cut lumber that flooded his nostrils came from the wooden frame that surrounded him, a frame that was clearly a gallows.

Ryan's hands were tied tightly behind him with rawhide. The knots pulled so hard that he could feel blood dripping from purpled nails.

He wore his usual clothes, except for the long coat and the white silk scarf with the silver dollars sewn into each end. The holster on his right hip was empty of the SIG-Sauer, and the sheath on his left hip lacked the weight and balance of his eighteen-inch panga.

There was a crowd building around him. The sound of music attracted him, and he glanced to his right. A stubby white man and a tall, elegant black man leaned against the side wall of the Golden Eagle saloon. Both held long-necked banjos and were singing a song. The words weren't quite clear enough for Ryan to hear.

Something about a gun quicker than lightning?

The balcony of the Two Up gaudy was already lined with whores, dressed only in cotton drawers and chemises, with high-buttoned boots. All held parasols to shield them from the ferocity of the sun. One of them, a skinny blonde with sleepy eyes, saw Ryan looking in their direction and touched herself between her thighs, sucked her finger and blew him a kiss.

Ryan looked away.

There were three men on the gallows with him.

One was a stout sheriff with a polished badge who seemed to have eaten beans for his breakfast and kept making the air noisome with his farting.

Next to him stood a priest, sweating heavily in a black suit of good broadcloth. He looked to be in his mid-twenties, with a pale face and spectacles with gold rims that kept slipping down his beaky nose. He was holding a prayer book in both hands, but he had to keep wiping his fingers on the side of his pants to dry them. Ryan was irritated by the priest's nervous habit of noisily clearing his throat every few seconds.

The third figure was, Ryan guessed, the hangman.

He was immensely tall and skeletally thin, dressed from head to toe in black. On the index finger of his right hand the man wore a silver ring, shaped like a death's head, with a fire opal set in its brow. He wore a hood that covered his head, with slits for the eyes.

Ryan had glanced twice at the bizarre figure, blinking as he seemed to glimpse the red glow of fiery embers behind the eye slits.

The rough hemp noose tight around Ryan's throat was prickling at his skin, and he turned his head to one side to try to shift the discomfort of the large knot that the hangman had adjusted just below his left ear.

An urchin in the front of the swelling crowd stopped and picked up a rough pebble, hefting it at Ryan, who swayed to one side so that it missed his head. The child's mother, a rosy-cheeked matron in a gingham dress and poke bonnet, slapped at the boy, shrugging apologetically at Ryan.

"How long, Sheriff Nolan?" the priest asked, having cleared his throat.

The fat lawman reached into his vest pocket and plucked out a silver pocket watch, clicking it open and peering at the face. "Be noon in about five minutes."

"Time passes so slowly when one is being amused." The voice from under the enveloping hood was a sepulchral whisper, no louder than the rustling of paper.

"That is true, sir," the priest agreed, nodding like a rocking doll.

"Anything you want to say, Cawdor?" the sheriff asked. "You got a couple of minutes."

"I don't know why I'm here," Ryan replied.

"How's that, son?"

"I know it sounds stupe, but I'd be grateful if you could tell me why you're planning on hanging me."

Nolan threw back his head and laughed, the priest joining in with a nervous titter. "Well, now, that's a good one, ain't it, Reverend?"

"Indeed it is, Sheriff, indeed it is."

The noose seemed to be getting tighter around Ryan's throat, and he swallowed hard.

"You're here, Cawdor, to pay the blood price for the crime you committed."

"What crime?"

"As if you didn't know."

"I don't know. Fireblast, Sheriff! Stop this bastard game playing!"

"Now, son, you know very well that you must have committed a crime, otherwise we wouldn't be here to give you a neck-stretching party."

"To teach you to tango on air," the hangman whispered.

"To show the good folks of the town how we settle the hash of bloody bastards like you," the priest added quietly, clearing his throat.

"But why?" The rope was pinching harder, and Ryan found it hard to speak.

The hangman moved forward a couple of steps, to stand close to Ryan, emitting the odor of fresh-turned earth in an ancient grave. "This gallows has only been built for you, Ryan. Once you've hung a few hours we can take it down forever."

"What about my body?" As if that really mattered a damn, he thought.

Nolan answered him. "Cut down and dragged around town behind the lady mayor's stallion. Then stripped naked and slung on the manure pile behind the Clanton Livery Stables, so folks can see you're truly dead and gone."

"And then we can all sleep easy," the priest said sanctimoniously, holding his hands steepled together. "Is it noon, Sheriff?"

As if in answer, the town square was flooded with the deep sound of a church bell, tolling the fourth quarter of the hour, followed by twelve chimes.

Nolan farted noisily. "Best get it over."

He walked to the front of the platform and clapped his hands for quiet. Gradually the chattering died down. "You all know why we're here," he shouted. "So now, we'll do it."

The priest coughed nervously and stood at Ryan's side, resting one moist hand on his shoulder. The other held the small black prayer book, the pages fluttering like aspen leaves in a hurricane.

"Insomuch as it has blessed Almighty God to take this wretch into his keeping, we are gathered here today in his sight and in the face of this congregation to witness the prescribed ending for this evil doer."

"But what have I done?" Ryan said loudly.

His words were relayed through the crowd, now numbering several hundred, and were greeted with bellows of merriment.

"Tell us how blessed are the cheese makers!" shouted a fat old man in the middle of the mob, drawing more laughter from those around him.

The priest giggled and waited for the noise to abate. "The sentence of the court was that Ryan Cawdor should be brought to this place of lawful execution and here hung by the neck until he was dead, his body finally to be buried in an unmarked grave in the grounds of the prison where he was last confined." A studied pause followed. "And may God have mercy on his soul."

"No chance of that," the executioner breathed. "Not after slaying my brothers and my sister."

"Do your duty," the sheriff intoned.

"But you haven't told me my crime," Ryan protested hoarsely. The noose was shrinking, tighter and tighter, so that he could hardly breathe.

"Life is easy, but waiting is hard," the hangman whispered as he reached up to adjust the knot.

For a moment Ryan had an odd vision. He knelt naked in a shell hole between two masked men who passed a slim-bladed flensing knife back and forth in front of him, as though they waited for him to seize the bone handle and thrust it deep into his own chest.

"No," Ryan said. "I won't do it."

"I will," the hooded man stated, reaching to one side and throwing a long wooden lever.

Even as the trap jerked open and he started to fall, Ryan heard himself say "I want to be a living man."

There was a dreadful jarring sensation, as if his skull had been severed, the spinal cord snapping in two. Ryan heard a great roar from the crowd, but it quickly faded into silence, a silence so intense that he could hear the cold wind that blew between the worlds.

He knew that he still lived, that the gallows drop hadn't been long enough to break his neck and give him a relatively merciful passing.

His body revolved very slowly, but he couldn't breathe, his throat constricted, choking and strangling.

Ryan opened his eye.

Sheriff Nolan, the priest and the hooded executioner had all gone. The town, the saloon, the gaudy sluts and the watching throng—all gone.

The gallows had become transmogrified into a crooked hanging tree, a lightning-blasted sycamore with a jagged branch sticking out, almost at a right angle. Ryan glanced down, seeing that the toes of his dusty combat boots were only a couple of inches from the stunted grass.

But it might as well have been a couple of miles.

Slowly and agonizingly, he was dying, his body twisting in the summery breeze. He could smell juniper and sagebrush, and the scent of an opened grave.

The tall black-clad figure of the hangman stood just in front of him, hands clasped together, head to one side, as he considered Ryan's slow passing.

"Help," the one-eyed man whispered, the word barely breathed, almost inaudible, even to himself.

"Did you ask for help, Ryan?" he heard the feathery voice of the executioner ask.

"Please . . ."

"It pleases me not to please you but to please myself. And the memories of my family."

Either the sun was setting, or death was closing down all of the lines.

Darkness was spreading across the high plains country where Ryan dangled from the hemp noose. Shadows were lengthening across the sun-baked turf. He could see his own elongated shape, still slowly twisting.

"Show you mercy," the gloating hangman said. "I'll speed your passing. Feel the life flee your corpse. Hang on to you, Ryan, my arms around your neck in a lover's embrace." The voice was as dry and dusty as an ancient papyrus.

Now he was doing what he'd said, the pressure on Ryan's neck almost intolerable, as though a steel hand of fire was reaching up the inside of his spine and into his brain, squeezing out his immortal soul.

The hood was discarded, leaving a mane of snowy hair tumbling about the hangman's face, writhing against his skin like coffin worms. Mad ruby eyes glared at him.

RYAN OPENED his eye.

And screamed.

# Chapter Three

He was on his back on the floor of a gateway chamber as the armaglass walls changed from dark brown to the lightest and palest of pinks.

But Ryan could hardly see any of that, couldn't see any of his companions.

His range of vision was blocked by a leering skull, scant inches from his. The face was long and angular, the sharp cheekbones honed like an Egyptian mummy's, the skin dried and leathery. A mane of snowy hair tumbled across the high forehead, brushing against Ryan's cheeks, feeling like the caress of a hundred tiny desiccated worms. And the eyes, wide and blankly staring, brimmed with fresh crimson blood that leaked from the tear ducts and spilled down onto Ryan's face.

Ryan tried to scream again, but the creature had gripped him by the throat, iron fingers crushing his neck, making breathing impossible.

He knew who it was.

What it was.

"Melmoth."

Ryan, dying, heard the name, knew that it was the right one. But he hadn't spoken it and didn't know who had.

"Pull him off!" It was a woman shrieking out. Even as he slipped back into unconsciousness, Ryan felt that he recognized the voice.

KRYSTY WROTH, lover and friend of Ryan Cawdor, had been sitting in the gateway chamber in the bayous, holding Ryan's hand, watching the tendrils of white mist gathering near the ceiling, feeling her brain start to whirl as the matter-transfer jump began.

At the last moment Krysty had seen someone blunder into the octagonal chamber after the door had been closed, triggering the automatic mechanism. It had been a tall figure, in black, with a shock of white hair.

But Krysty had been too far along the road to darkness to do anything about the intruder.

Now she had come down, with the bitter taste of bile at the back of her throat, relieved that the nightmares that often haunted a jump hadn't clutched at her.

The woman had opened her bright emerald eyes, brushed back a wisp of her fiery, sentient hair and saw that all her friends were sprawled on the armaglass floor, unconscious.

Ryan, no longer holding her hand, lay flat on his back, feet moving slightly, heels rasping, and on top of him was Melmoth Cornelius, last survivor of the depraved family of genetically created vampires, the lingering spawn of the Genesis Project. In the last few hours, she, Ryan and the others had succeeded in slaying three of the four bizarre beings, destroying their bodies so that they could no longer rejuvenate themselves.

But Melmoth had been out hunting and had escaped their vengeance—or they had escaped his vengeance.

Now he was in the chamber at the end of the jump. His lean body covered Ryan's, and his long-nailed fingers were clasped tight around Ryan's throat.

"Melmoth!" she'd screamed.

But he hadn't moved, his face pressed into Ryan's neck as though he were nuzzling at the artery below the ear, sucking lasciviously at his blood.

Ryan's face was livid, swollen, his mouth open as if he were gasping for breath. His hands lay limp at his side.

"Pull him off!" Krysty shouted, fighting nausea, crawling on hands and knees and placing her hands on the shoulders of the tall vampire.

Someone was moving to help her.

Mildred.

Mildred Winonia Wyeth was an African-American doctor from the far predark past. She had been born in December of 1964 and had become one of the United States's leading cryonic scientists, specializing in the medical applications of freezing.

Ironically Mildred had been frozen in December of the year 2000, when minor abdominal surgery went awry. Days later the world went nuke mad, and only one person in every ten thousand survived. Europe, Russia and the Americas were totally devastated by the brief war that ended all wars.

Then came the long winters when the planet was pushed back to an almost medieval state, and all science and industry vanished forever. And the death count ran higher.

During the next ninety years or so, Mildred had slept dreamlessly on, sealed in her capsule, maintained in a buried medical fortress by comp-controlled machinery powered by tireless nuke generators.

Then Ryan and the others had come by, like princes in a fairy tale, and awakened her.

Mildred had come around from the jump. She blinked her eyes open and shook her head to try to clear out the cobwebs, the beads in her plaited hair rattling against the glass walls—walls that she noticed had changed color to a delicate shell pink, which meant that the jump had worked and they were elsewhere.

But Krysty was shouting for help.

Mildred looked around, her attention caught by Ryan, who was lying on the floor with someone trying to strangle him.

"Melmoth?" she whispered.

She lunged across to try to help Krysty, who was fighting to drag the vampire away from his victim.

The noise and scuffling woke Dean Cawdor, Ryan's eleven-year-old son.

The boy felt as if a mule had been dancing a slow shuffle inside his brain. He groaned, wondering whether he was going to throw up. Across the chamber he saw that Doc Tanner had suffered a nosebleed, as the old man often did during a jump.

But his dark eyes were caught by the strange tableau at the center of the gateway. His father lay unconscious, his face swollen and engorged with blood, while one of the vampires was trying to throttle him. Krysty and Mildred were both wrestling with Melmoth to try to drag him off Ryan.

"No," the boy yelled, his voice cracking, as he scrambled on hands and knees to try to help.

He crawled across the legs of the armorer to the group, John Barrymore Dix, one of the greatest experts on weaponry in the whole of Deathlands. He and Ryan had been friends for close to twenty years, both of them having ridden the powerful war wags with the legendary Trader.

Dean's jostling brought J.B. slowly out of the seeping blackness and he fumbled immediately for his spectacles, putting them on the bridge of his narrow nose. His right hand felt for his blasters, the 9 mm Uzi and the unusual Smith & Wesson M-4000 scattergun.

There was a fight going on in the chamber, with Krysty, Mildred and Dean battling to drag Melmoth off Ryan.

Doc slept on, undisturbed by the clumsy, ugly brawl that was taking place only a yard away from him.

Theophilus Algernon Tanner had been born in a small village in Vermont on a bitterly cold February day in 1868. In November of 1896, while a happily married man with two little children, he was a hapless victim of Operation Chronos, the time-trawling wing of the Totality Concept. A highly secret section of government,

Chronos had been trying to grab people from the past and bring them forward in time. There had been many hideously disgusting failures, and only one success: Doc Tanner, who proved to be such a difficult specimen that the whitecoats eventually pushed him nearly a hundred years into the future, into the heart of Deathlands.

The double experience of time travel had tipped Doc's mind a little off its gyro centers and he sometimes functioned as if he were missing a few cards from a full deck.

Now he lay there, still tipped into darkness by the swirling horrors of jumping from place to place, where your molecules, atoms and neurons were scattered through the ether and reassembled someplace else.

At his side, the albino teenager, Jak Lauren, also lay unconscious. Mat-trans jumps affected different people in different ways, and he lay deathly still, hands folded across his breast, a smudge of blood trickling from his left ear.

The young man and the old-timer, side by side, were oblivious to the fight that had suddenly developed.

A fight that stopped just as suddenly.

Krysty had grabbed one of Melmoth's slender wrists, trying to break the death grip that the vampire had on Ryan's throat. But it was as hard and cold as marble and didn't give a fraction of an inch. In desperation, the woman slid her hands down to the fingers with their curved horn nails. She levered her hand under the little finger of his left hand and jerked it back with all her power. There was a fragile little cracking sound, like a dry twig, and the finger snapped, dangling back and loose.

But Melmoth showed no reaction, not even moving when Krysty broke two more fingers of his left hand.

Mildred had locked her arms around Melmoth's white neck, trying to force him away from Ryan. Her fingers clutched at the side of the vampire's throat, probing for the carotid artery, intending to try to cut off the blood flow to the brain and render the white-haired butcher unconscious.

"He's dead," Mildred stated.

"Ryan? Can't be. We've got—"

"Not Ryan. Melmoth."

"What?"

"Dead."

J.B. had been trying to loosen the grip of the creature's right hand, also breaking a couple of fingers. "Yeah, he's already cold," he told them.

"Get him away from Ryan," Krysty said, half standing and pulling at the vampire, bracing herself as she dragged the stiffening corpse to one side of the chamber.

Ryan still didn't move, the skin of his throat marred by the bruises from Melmoth's iron fingers.

Mildred had knelt by him, her head on his chest, her hand on his wrist, checking respiration and pulse.

"Slow but steady," she pronounced. "Think he'll be okay."

Jak came around at that moment, jumping as the first thing he saw was the distorted face of Melmoth

Cornelius, inches from his own face, the bloodied eyes staring into his.

"What's he...? Dead?"

"Yeah," Dean said. "Nearly did for Dad."

"Dad dead," Doc muttered, starting the painful journey from dark to light. "Not dead, Dad? Who did Dad dead? Blues for Father Death." He opened a pale, rheumy eye. "By the Three Kennedys! It's wandering Melmoth, looking as though he sits now in the black ferry across the Styx."

"Bastard's chilled, if that's what you mean, Doc," Mildred said, straightening from the side of the one-eyed man. "And Ryan here came close to joining him on the last train west. But he'll make it."

Doc touched a gnarled finger to his nose, bringing it away streaked with blood, wiping it with the sleeve of his antique frock coat.

Between them, Krysty and J.B. eased Ryan into a sitting position. Already his face was resuming a normal color, and his breathing was steadier and less harsh, though the long scar that ran from the corner of his right eye down to his mouth still stood out brightly.

Gradually everyone in the chamber was making his or her own recovery from the rigors of the jump.

Dean looked down at Melmoth's shriveled corpse. "How did he get in? When I went under, he wasn't in here with us. Someone let him in?"

"No," Krysty replied. "Just as I slipped into the dark I was sort of aware of someone trying to get in. Must've made it in the last second or so. If he'd tried to open the door when the jump was already going on... Gaia knows what might have happened."

"Think there's probably a sec lock on it," J.B. said. "No way of testing it."

"Hey!"

Everyone looked around at Dean's exclamation. The boy was staring down at Melmoth.

"What is it, dear laddie?" Doc asked.

"The vampire's sort of...sort of rotting. Like dying's speeded up."

Krysty stayed at Ryan's side, but the others moved to join Dean, looking at the white-haired corpse.

"Dark night!" J.B. exclaimed softly. "You're right, Dean. Look at him go."

Alive, Melmoth and his brothers and sister had looked deathly pale and emaciated. Dead, he was shrinking away toward nothing. His ruby eyes had turned milky and were beginning to suppurate in their bony caverns. The skin across the honed cheekbones was so taut it was already splitting, opening up like tiny lips, showing the whiteness of bone beneath. The lips had peeled back from the slightly pointed teeth, cracking at the corners. The gums were receding, and several of the teeth were visibly loose in their sockets.

The vampire's fingers were curling into claws, the strong nails tearing deep gashes in the skin of the palms that wept a colorless ichor.

"Stinks," the boy said, pinching his fingers over his nose. "Can't we get him out of here before he rots into a puddle of dirty water?"

"Soon as Ryan comes around we can think about a move," J.B. told him.

"Air seems good, John." Mildred sniffed at it.

J.B. nodded. "Yeah. Fresh. Not the usual stale stuff. Mebbe a part of the redoubt's opened up."

Doc had picked up his beloved ebony swordstick, gripping it by the silver lion's-head hilt and tapping the ferule on the floor. "I would most certainly appreciate the chance to breathe in some cool and dry air. I think that we've had a little too much of the warm and damp recently."

Krysty looked up at the old man. "I have this idea that people tend to relish what they knew while growing up. Like you had in New England. Same for me. I wish I could sample the kind of air we had when I was growing up in Harmony ville. Like honey."

Ryan moaned quietly and lifted his right hand as though he were trying to knock away a persistent skeeter.

"Boss man's coming around," Mildred said. "Should be fine in a few minutes."

Ryan opened his eye.

# Chapter Four

"You think the jump killed him, Mildred?"

"I do, Ryan. We know that all four of them were sickly. That's why they wanted the boy and all of us—to freshen up their genes and revive their blood."

"And Melmoth got this far. Far enough to try and chill me. Then died."

"Looks that way. If Krysty hadn't come around when she did, he might've done it, too."

"Revenge from beyond the grave." Ryan looked down at the mutie creature. "Melting away like butter in a heat wave."

"Like they used to say up in the Yukon in the days of '49," Doc said. "We sell butter by the quart in summer and milk by the pound in winter."

"Hey, that's good," Dean said. "But what's a quart and what's a pound? I've never been good at all those difficult measurements. Rona never got around to teaching me."

The mention of the boy's mother brought her image to Ryan's mind. Remembering Sharona, Ryan wasn't that surprised that she never got around to teaching the boy much.

But she'd taught him plenty about survival, and in Deathlands that was worth more than all the history, geography, math and science put together.

Even so, everyone agreed, including Dean, that it was long past time for the lad to get himself a proper education. After all, he was to be part of the future, and the future needed every chance it could get.

It was just a question of finding the right place.

Good schools weren't all that common in Deathlands. In fact, schools of any kind were few and far between.

"SURE YOU FEEL all right, lover?"

Ryan nodded. His legs felt like wet string, and his throat was still crushed and painful. But he figured that this was likely to be about as good as he'd feel for a while. "Sure," he said. "Time to move."

Everyone drew their blasters, lining up behind Ryan, trying to avoid the small heap of festering liquid corruption that had once been Melmoth Cornelius.

"Triple red, people. Let's go."

He eased open the door of the gateway chamber.

THE ANTEROOM NEXT to the gateway was totally empty: no furniture, nothing tacked to the plain white walls.

The door that led to the control section of the mattrans complex was wide open. From where he stood, Ryan could see clear across the room to where the massive vanadium-steel sec door was solidly closed.

"Looks safe," he stated.

They stepped into the comp-controlled room, with its rows of desks and comp consoles. Everything looked perfectly normal. All but one of the ceiling lights glowed brightly, and all the monitor screens seemed to be functioning.

They all walked around, mesmerized by the dancing display of colored panels and whirling comp disks, the endless rows of buttons, switches, dials and knobs, the roaming sec cameras, mounted near the ceiling, their red eyes glowing fitfully, sending their images through the hidden conduits up to a control room elsewhere in the redoubt. The room probably hadn't seen human life for nearly a hundred years.

"If only we knew what all this did," Ryan said. "Then we could mebbe control our own jumps. Know where we were going and get there safely."

Doc sat at one of the rotating stools, spinning himself slowly. "Sadly all of that went down forever into the dark when the missiles flew and the blitzkrieg raged. And I for one do not lament the passing of the Techno Age. Humanity was already doomed, before the final war began. The bombs merely speeded up the process of decay."

"Cynical old bastard, aren't you, Doc?" Mildred commented, her broad smile taking the sting from her words.

"You're a mere chit of a girl," he replied. "What are you? Not even 150 years old. Wait until you reach past the two-hundred mark, and you may find yourself becoming a trifle cynical, Doctor."

"Enough," Ryan said quietly. "We'll go and take a look outside the sec door. No sign of anyone getting into here."

"Can I do the door, Dad?"

"Sure. Usual rules, everyone. Get ready."

He took his own place at the center of the dull metal door, kneeling, the SIG-Sauer cocked in his right hand. The others fanned out behind him, taking cover behind the desks. Dean went to the green lever at the side that was in the down, or "closed," position.

"Go," Ryan told him.

The boy threw the lever up, triggering the complicated system of gears that lifted the hundred-ton door off the concrete floor. There was the faint whine of buried machinery, then the door started to move slowly upward.

As soon as it had reached four or five inches, Ryan gave a hand signal to his son. Dean immediately steadied the lever in the central position, checking the ascent.

Ryan hugged the floor, squinting through his good eye, seeing more or less what he'd expected—an expanse of bare corridor stretching out both ways, lighted by long fluorescent tubes in the arched ceiling, and more of the ubiquitous security cameras in the angle between ceiling and wall.

No sign of life.

"Up another six inches."

Again, there was nothing to see. Ryan sniffed, tasting clean fresh air. Normally the air in closed redoubts was stuffy, flat and stale, having been recirculated around and around for nearly a hundred years.

"Another foot."

Once again the sec door rumbled higher, until Dean checked it with the control lever. Ryan was able to see some distance in both directions, but the curvature of the passage limited his view to about fifty paces to the left and right.

"All the way," he ordered, getting off the floor and moving slightly to one side.

"Hey, that air smells great," Krysty said.

"Sure." Ryan glanced back at her. "But it has to mean that parts of the redoubt have been broken into. So we step extra careful."

THEY TRIED LEFT first of all.

Most of the redoubts that they'd visited had been built to a similar pattern. Generally the matter-transfer section of the military complex was situated in the deepest part, as far away from the main entrance as possible.

It was no surprise to find that the passage, having wound to the left for about ninety yards, came to an abrupt halt in a wall of solid reinforced concrete. There had been no doors, elevators or cross corridors in that short length of the passage, and not a sign of anything living having penetrated that far.

"Back that way," Ryan directed, leading his friends along to the right.

THERE WERE TWO TURNOFFS, both blocked by sealed sec doors, each with coded panels to one side, with the full range of letters and numbers.

"Can't we have a go?" Dean asked eagerly. "Could easy hit the right combination."

Doc patted him benevolently on the shoulder. "I fear not, young fellow. Even if it's only a six-digit or -letter code, we could spend our entire lives here trying one combination every ten seconds and still not stumble upon the right mix."

"You sure about that, Doc?"

"Of course. Did I not spend some good time mastering Boolean algebra?"

"Numerical progressions and coding has nothing to do with Boolean algebra," Mildred said.

"Has it not? Ah, me, has it not?" Ryan noticed that Doc's pale blue eyes were twinkling, as they often did when he was teasing Mildred.

They continued along the passage, the watching lenses of the cameras following their steady progress.

"There doesn't seem to be any current of air," the Armorer commented.

"Doesn't need to be. If some part of the redoubt's been opened up, mebbe way above our heads on a higher floor, then that air would be utilized by the nuke-conditioning plant and pushed around to all parts." Ryan looked behind and ahead. "This is one of the best redoubts we've ever been in. Nearly all of the lights are working, as well as the cameras. Looks like it wasn't damaged at all during skydark."

"No cracks in walls," Jak observed. "Or ceiling."

That was also unusual. Most of the top-secret redoubts had suffered some sort of damage during the brief World Combat. Much of it was secondary, caused by the quakes and eruptions that the United States endured as the land was pounded by unimaginable nuclear forces.

"No sign of animals getting in." Mildred looked carefully at the high arched ceiling. "Not even a spider or a fly down in this part."

"Glad there's no vermin," Ryan said. "Don't mind most creatures, but I can't say I take to rats. Seen some real mutie bastard rats over the years."

"Remember that place in the Carolinas?" J.B. asked. "Where that fat baron with a residual third eye slopping around in the middle of his forehead caught us?"

Ryan nodded grimly. "Won't ever forget him. Baron Kagan. Tricked us to try and get at Trader. Holed us up in a cage set between the tidewater marks. Chained our hands to the walls. Cages got flooded every single tide turn. Water came right on up to our chins."

J.B. laughed at the recollection. "Wouldn't have been so bad in there if it hadn't been for all the blind eels and the giant rats."

"Eels weren't so hard. Learned from experience to open our mouths and stand real still. They got curious and stuck their heads in and you could bite them off, clean as whistling. The rats were tougher."

"Tell us, Dad," Dean said, almost jumping up and down with excitement.

"Big as cats. They somehow sensed that we were pretty well helpless. Particularly when the water was high, and they could swim at us and avoid our kicks."

J.B. carried on the story. "The little devils went for our ears, using their claws to climb onto our heads, pulling themselves up on our hair. What they were after most was our eyes. Very tasty that would've been."

"That's disgusting, John," Mildred said, pulling a face. "Disgusting."

"It would've been," Ryan replied. "But we found a way of dealing with them. We had to, or we'd have been blinded and the rats would easily have stripped all the flesh off our faces. No problem for them."

"So, what did you do, Dad? Bite off their heads, like with those eels?"

"Too big. And much too strong and active. Let a rat's head inside your mouth, Dean, and it'd be Brother Rat doing all of the biting and eating. No, we had to try and get a good grip on them with our teeth, and then take a breath and drop our heads into the filthy water."

"Drown them!" Jak exclaimed with immense satisfaction. "Hot pipe!"

"Wasn't simple." J.B. shook his head at the memory. "Hard to hold your breath when you had a huge mutie rodent wriggling and scratching and trying to take off half your face."

"But we made it." Ryan grinned. "Left the corpses floating so that their friends could come and feast. Made them less interested in us."

"Next evening Trader tracked us down and blew the cages apart. Baron Kagan regretted that he'd chosen to go against Trader and the war wags."

"What did he do?" Dean asked.

"Look, we're wasting time standing around here and jawing," Ryan said. "We should be moving on."

"Oh, Dad..."

J.B. answered the boy. "Trader stripped Kagan and staked him out. Got an iron bowl and strapped it around the baron's belly and balls. But first he put a couple of the biggest rats under it. Started a fire and laid some of the red-hot embers on top of the iron bowl."

"Wow! Triple ace on the line," the boy breathed. "Trader was the hardest."

"Had to teach the lesson that his people couldn't be touched without someone paying a big blood price."

"And the rats ate down into the baron to get away from the heat." Dean grinned. "Real good story."

Ryan nodded. "And now I think it's time that we moved on from here."

# Chapter Five

" 'Emergency Escape Stairs,' " Ryan read. "Haven't come across that in a redoubt before."

The sign was in blue, block-printed letters on a white plastic board. The notice looked remarkably unfaded, as sharp and pristine as the day it was painted, probably some months before skydark.

Beside it was a heavy steel sec door, with a simple push-bar release.

"Think that only opens from this side?" J.B. queried. "Best be careful we don't go through it and then find there's no way back here."

"Could be." Ryan examined it carefully. "Air seems fresher here. So it could be that whoever opened up the redoubt beyond this door couldn't find any way of getting it open."

"Take load plas-ex," Jak said, tapping it with his knuckle. "Triple solid."

"Implode might rock it." The Armorer considered the door. "Buried deadlock hinges. Gren might move it, but it's designed to jam solid if anyone tries to force it."

"Can I open it, Dad?"

"No!" Ryan spoke louder and fiercer than he'd intended, making the boy jump. He continued in a gentler tone. "You should know better than to ask that kind of question, son. The door could've been boobied on the other side. Trader used to say that a man who rushes in gets himself carried out."

"Sorry. I wasn't going to rush in and start trying to open it, Dad."

Ryan patted the boy on the shoulder, ruffling his thick dark curls. "I'm sure of that. Better to be blown up than be a stupe. If you're not a stupe, then you won't get blown up."

Doc cleared his throat. "Forgive me, gentles all, but are we going to stand here and chop homespun cracker-barrel philosophy with one another, or are we going to get the door open and move on into the redoubt?"

"We're moving on. J.B., let's check the door."

It hadn't been booby-trapped. At least, as far as they could tell from a careful examination of the lock, the door hadn't been wired.

"Everyone go back around the corner," Ryan ordered. "Flat on the floor, eyes closed, hands over your ears and your mouths open. Minimize any blast."

Krysty stared at him. "You saying that you think there might be a blast, lover?"

"No. I wouldn't be going to push the locking bar if I really thought that. But there's always that long-odds chance. Go on, now."

They all moved away as he'd ordered, leaving him alone by the sec door.

The round push bar was cold to the touch, and he nudged it experimentally, crouching over it and peering at the revealed part of the mechanism when the bar moved. Ryan saw nothing to make him suspicious.

He edged it a little harder. Nothing much seemed to be happening.

Ryan finally gave the bar a steady push, feeling it click as the lock was triggered. He winced at the tiny sound, but no flesh-rending explosion followed. The door was now ready to open, perfectly balanced.

"All right?" J.B.'s voice echoed and bounced in the odd acoustics of the tunnels.

"So far...." Ryan inhaled a slow breath, then wiped a trickle of perspiration from his forehead with the sleeve of his fur-trimmed coat.

If there was some kind of device linked to the door, it would be triggered now.

Ryan pushed the door open a couple of inches, seeing clear space all around the three sides. Nothing happened, and he could detect no sign of any problem.

He drew the SIG-Sauer and eased the sec door open a little farther.

"All right!" he shouted. "Come ahead."

Ryan heard footfalls behind him, but all his concentration was on what lay beyond the sec door.

As it opened, he could see more and more. A number of passages opened off, with what looked like the familiar kind of redoubt map standing at the center. The air was clean, this time with a definite current to it, blowing in his face, tugging at his hair.

Ryan held the door while the others filed through. He looked at the exterior lock.

"There's a small release button set into the bottom part of the handle," he said. "But it probably only works if the push bar's up on the other side of the door."

"Sure?" Krysty squinted at the impenetrable door. "Suppose you're wrong, lover?"

"Then we're stuck the wrong side of the gateway with no chance of getting to it. It's not the end of the world." He grinned at her, suddenly looking years younger. "On second thoughts, mebbe it *is* the end of the world."

"Check it," the Armorer said. "I'll go to the other side and we close the door. Test that button. If you haven't opened the door in thirty seconds, we know it doesn't work and I open her up again. And we have to consider our position."

Ryan nodded. "Sure."

J.B. vanished and the heavy door was swung shut again, the lock clicking home. Ryan pressed what he thought was the release button, and then J.B. carefully lifted the push bar, making sure it stayed up with the sec door locked.

Everything worked perfectly.

Despite the great weight of counterbalanced vanadium steel, Ryan was able to open it with one hand.

THEY STOOD TOGETHER to look at the map, which was an intricate maze of colors and coded numbers, all linked to a schematic plan below.

"We're here," Mildred said, pointing to a discreet green cross.

"And that's the gateway," Doc remarked, pointing at a section in pale pink marked Matter Transfer, which also carried the holographic message: Entry Absolutely Forbidden To All But B12 Cleared Personnel.

"Armory," J.B. said. "Quite a way off, up three levels, behind the guard section. Close by what looks like the main sec control area."

"Any food anywhere?" Dean asked.

"Yeah." Krysty tapped her finger on a green hexagonal area. "Dining hall and supplies. That's where it would've been. But it seems certain that the whole place was swept just before skydark. I'd be surprised if we found anything worth having anywhere in the whole redoubt."

"Entrance there." Jak pointed. "Two levels up."

Ryan was trying to work it out. "The way in and out of the complex looks like it's above us. Mebbe there's another set of those emergency stairs, but I can't see any."

J.B. had polished his glasses again, putting them back on to peer at the plan. He traced their route from the gateway. "Guess you're likely right, Ryan. It must—" He glanced behind them. "Over there. Short way along that tunnel."

The sec door was there.

Like the other one, it proved safe to use, and they left it tripped, ready to get back down toward the mat-trans section of the redoubt.

RYAN LED THE WAY UP the iron stairs, his boots rasping on the serrated treads of the steps. He guessed that there was probably a bank of elevators that they could have used to reach the ground level and the way out of the place. But he had a well-founded dislike and mistrust of elevators. At least nobody could jam a staircase with him on it. Or cut the cables and send him plummeting a thousand feet.

He looked up, seeing the silver-painted steps spiraling for at least another hundred feet. But that didn't give him much of a clue to how many floors that distance might mean, as all of the redoubts in the network were built to incredibly high-security defensive specifications.

The rest of the group was strung out below him.

The Trader had always insisted that any patrol should stick to the best pace of the slowest member of the unit. A situation where someone was being pushed that little bit beyond his or her limits meant danger for everyone.

Doc was the slowest.

"I don't suppose we might stop when we reach the top of the stairs, Master Cawdor?" Doc's plaintive voice bounced off the sec-steel walls of the shaft.

"I think we could take five after we get through the next door, Doc."

"Then you are truly a saint in human form, my friend."


THE THIRD DOOR was treated the same as the previous two, left open, ready for them to make their exit.

"One more floor and we should be up at ground level," Ryan stated, studying the new plan.

"Anyone smell anything?" Jak asked.

"What?" Krysty sniffed the air. "Can't pick anything up. What is it?"

"Cooking meat. Faint and far. Mebbe outside redoubt. Main doors could be open."

"Yeah," Dean said, turning his head from side to side, shuffling his feet with excitement. "Jak's right, Dad. Someone's roasting meat."

Nobody else had a good enough sense of smell to catch the elusive scent, but Ryan believed Jak and his son, though he didn't share their enthusiasm over the discovery. Not if it meant that a section of the sprawling military complex had been infiltrated and taken over.

It could mean trouble.


A WINDING CORRIDOR was marked on the plan as being only for Alternatively Abled Personnel.

"Wheelchairs," Mildred said.

"Cooking's stronger," Jak said when they'd gone about halfway up the gentle incline.

"Think I can smell it," Mildred stated. "Like a barbecue on a Pleasant Valley Sunday. Yeah, I'm sure of it. Can you smell it, John?"

The Armorer stood still, pushing his battered fedora back off his forehead. "Not sure. Mebbe I can only smell what you've said I should be able to smell."

"It's strong," Dean said.

"Must mean someone's inside the redoubt." Ryan rubbed at the stubble on his chin with his thumb and forefinger while he considered the implications. "Odds are, they're going to be hostiles. Get our shooting in first, if we have to."

The outer wall of the circling ramp was badly scuffed at about eighteen inches from the dark brown carpet tiles. And at one point they found that the white plastic handrail had been pulled loose from the wall.

"Must've had a lot of crips," Dean said.

"Not very PC to say that," Mildred chided. "Politically correct, Dean. 'Crips' is not a good word for people who are disabled in some way."

"But everyone calls them crips, Mildred." The boy shrugged.

"And everyone once called black people like me 'niggers,' Dean. Saying it doesn't make it right."

The anger was cold and unmistakable, making the boy drop his head and mumble an apology.

"ANOTHER DOOR," Ryan reported to the others as they reached the top of the winding ramp.

"This should be the level with the main entrance," J.B. said. "And even I can smell that meat roasting."

"Buffalo," Jak suggested.

Krysty laughed. "Now you're bluffing us, Jak. Granted it's meat, but it could be snake or gator or possum."

"Buffalo," he repeated stubbornly.

"Soon find out," Ryan said on the wide landing in front of the sec door. "Got to be real close to us."

The simple push bar worked smoothly, and Ryan inched the door open.

Now the cooking smell was almost overwhelming, and he found himself salivating so hard with anticipation of food that he spit on the floor.

"Here we go," he said. "Soon as the door opens, we all fan out on both sides and keep on triple red. Can't see anyone through the crack. Some smoke wreathing by."

"I'll set the sec lock in case it slams shut on us," J.B. said.

Ryan nodded. "Right!"

He pushed the door open and erupted into a wide, open area, with a ceiling at least forty feet above. Ryan moved right and flattened himself against the wall, while the others poured out, blasters ready.

A heavy pall of cooking smoke billowed a few yards in front of them.

A disembodied voice came from behind the smoke.

"Who de fuck're you?"

# Chapter Six

Ryan had drawn an instant bead on the voice, homing in on it toward the right of the mushrooming cloud of smoke. He held his fire for a moment.

"Who de fuck're you?"

The owner of the voice had silently moved several paces to his right. Ryan adjusted his aim, his friends doing the same thing.

Then, bewilderingly, the same voice came from two different places at once.

"Who de fuck're you?"

J.B. gestured with the Uzi, indicating that he could put it on full-auto and spray the whole area behind the dense white smoke.

Ryan shook his head, pointing for everyone to spread out a little more on both sides.

The smoke billowed around, rising in wraiths toward the high ceiling of the redoubt. From the design of that section of the complex, Ryan guessed that they were standing in the main entrance area, with the huge sec doors hidden somewhere beyond the cooking fire.

"Hear you. Gonna come get yer."

This time the voice was to the left.

"Guards of the Redoubt warn you to fuck off out of here, right now."

Ryan glanced at J.B. and held up two fingers of his left hand. Though the voices were identical to an uncanny degree, it was obvious now that there were at least two men behind the screen of smoke.

Since they hadn't yet opened fire, it was a fair bet that they weren't going to. A man who came to talk did some talking. A man who came to shoot did some shooting.

Well, that was what the Trader used to say.

"We don't mean harm," Ryan called.

He glimpsed someone moving and heard shuffling feet. This time both voices spoke from close together, in perfect unison, like a simultaneous echo.

"How do we know that, outlanders?"

"Because I don't tell lies. That meat smells real good, and we haven't eaten for a spell. Mind if we join you?"

There was a long pause, as though Ryan's words had to be translated before they made sense.

"Join us?"

"Sure. Why don't you show yourselves, and you can see us and we all know that there's not going to be any blasting."

"We could fuckin' blast you clean off Deathlands."

"Sure you could. But we don't want to play the game of who's got the biggest and strongest."

A giggle came from the smoke barrier. "Bet we got fuckin' biggest and strongest blasters."

"Sure you have. All we got is a 7.62 mm Steyr rifle, an Uzi machine pistol, a SIG-Sauer 9 mm automatic, a

Smith & Wesson M-4000 scattergun and about five
other big handblasters. Not much.''

Once again there came the eerie delay in a reply, but
just one voice this time.

''We won't play unless we got the biggest and bestest. Won't fuckin' play.''

''Not a game,'' Ryan said, keeping his voice as calm
and gentle as he could.

''Not?''

Doc interrupted. ''My dear friends, I hate to betray
any sense of urgency, but I worry that the meat could be
cooking a little too well.''

There *was* a taint of scorching overlaying the delicious odor of cooking.

''Buffalo's burning,'' Jak said tersely.

''How many of you?''

''Seven.''

''Any women?'' The dual voices overlapped so
closely that they nearly sounded like one man speaking. ''Haven't seen women in here for...'' There was a
long pause, then the voices split for the first time, riding over each other but not synchronized like the previous times.

''Fuckin' years.'' ''Can't remember how long.''

''We have two women. And they've both got good
blasters.'' Ryan was beginning to lose patience, and
considered making a fast flanking move to come in
through the smoke behind the speakers and wipe them
out.

''Truly?'' both men said.

"Just walk out and look. Or we'll come in through the smoke and show you."

"No. Guards of Redoubt in charge. Yes, we are. We'll fuckin' come out and see you now. Yes, we will."

Two figures, dimly seen, walked together, stepping slowly left and right and left, very close together.

The smoke pulled back like a theater curtain, revealing the Guards of the Redoubt to Ryan and the others.

They were identical twins, looking to be anywhere between the mid-teens up to the late thirties, with boyish features. They both wore green-and-brown camouflage shirts, with sleeves rolled well up, and pants, with highly polished combat boots.

They both had handblasters holstered at the waist, Smith & Wesson Model 29S, with the rare five-inch barrels, chambered for .44 Magnum rounds. But neither of the young men had made any effort to draw his blaster.

They were pale and soft faced, with straw-colored hair trimmed short. Their eyebrows were so faint they almost disappeared over bright blue eyes. Both of them wore identical Zapata mustaches, and both stood six feet tall.

Mildred was next to Ryan and she whispered to him. "Symptoms of bad rad sickness."

The moment she mentioned it, Ryan saw the signs for himself. They were common enough in Deathlands, particularly in some of the more notorious rad hot spots: purplish patches across the arms, particularly on the inside of the forearms; tight lines to the face and a general tautness as though they'd been dieting too hard; sores around the corners of the mouth; and threads of blood rimming the fingernails—those that remained.

"Outlanders, I'm Titus of the Redoubt Guard. This is my brother Mervyn of the Redoubt Guard."

"Yes, we are," said the brother on the left.

There was something about them that caught Ryan's attention, something above and beyond their obvious physical condition, something mental.

Their eyes were bright, but they didn't seem to reveal any intelligence behind them. And there was a deliberate slowness about the way they moved in sluggish unison.

"I'm Ryan Cawdor. These are my good friends, Krysty Wroth, J. B. Dix, Mildred Wyeth, Doc Tanner, Jak Lauren and my son, Dean. We're outlanders and seem to have gotten ourselves lost. Where are we?"

"How you fuckin' get in here?"

Ryan sensed that this was a potentially tricky one. He threw it back at the young man. "Well, Titus... By the way, what's your other name?"

"Other?" It was as though he'd been asked to solve the riddle of the sphinx.

"Do you have another name, after Titus?"

The blank face cleared a little. "Titus of Redoubt Guard. That what you mean, outlander?"

"No. Yeah. Yeah, I guess that's what I meant. How do you think we got in here?"

"That's a good one, Mervyn."

"Yeah, Titus, that's a good one."

"Seems we don't know the answer to that one, outlander. Tell us. Yeah, tell us."

"Through the door at the front."

Both foreheads wrinkled, and both men raised hands to stroke their chins. The idea of someone making their way into the redoubt through the front door was a thought too far.

"Someone told me the code."

"You know about three and five and two?" both men said together.

"Sure. Man called Trader told me, years ago. And two and five and three to close the sec door."

The brothers stared at each other. "How does he know that, Mervyn?"

"Don't know, Titus. He said that someone told him, didn't he?"

Titus's mouth opened wide, revealing a few rotting teeth and raw, bleeding gums. "Fucked if I remember, Mervyn."

"Biggest secret we was ever told by Pa and his pa. Back to days of first fathers and first mothers and children. These outlanders know it."

"Must be all right, Mervyn. Only us Guard knows it. Must be kin to us."

The worry lines vanished, showing the blank face again. "Sure they must."

Ryan picked up on it. "Distant cousins, is my guess, Mervyn and Titus. Now, how about some of that meat for your visiting cousins, huh?"

"Buffalo," they said together.

"Told you," Jak whispered.

"Nobody likes a smart ass," Krysty replied.

THE MEAT WAS FINE, the buffalo ribs just a little blackened around the edges.

The fire had been built more or less in the center of the concrete floor, surrounded by scorched beams of concrete. The smoke found its way to the ceiling, where the air-conditioning got rid of it.

The brothers sat cross-legged, each with a plate of the meat on his lap. Titus—at least Ryan thought it was Titus—had disappeared and returned with seven more plates, all dirty, and seven spoons, all filthy.

Ryan noticed that they were stamped with the U.S. Army markings.

"How long you boys lived here?" he asked, as he munched on a chunk of meat, wishing that there had been some vegetables or some bread to go with it.

"All our days," Mervyn replied. "Yeah, all our fuckin' days." It looked like Titus tried to speak at the same moment, but he nearly choked on a great chunk of the coarse-grained meat and ended up coughing and spluttering.

"How old are you?" Dean asked.

Both heads swiveled toward him like linked gun turrets, both pairs of eyes examining him curiously. "Don't know," they chorused. "Old as our teeth."

"You had family?" J.B. had been wrestling for some time with a particularly gristly piece of meat, and he finally abandoned the struggle and spit it onto his plate.

Titus and Mervyn looked at each other for at least a minute, as though they were communicating telepathically.

"You tell him how it was, Mervyn," Titus said.

Mervyn began to recite, hands folded in his lap, eyes closed, as if he were rattling off a tale that had been drummed into him years before.

"Skydark came and all ran from the redoubt. Many slept forever. After this came long winters when land slept. First father and mother with guard children came to redoubt from the small-house place. Found three-five-two after many days of counting and open came the great doors. Found two-five-three and closed. This was the power."

Titus echoed him. "Amen and this was the power."

"So it was. Guards forever. First father and mother slept. Children slept. Then came second fathers and mothers and children. After long winters they slept. But always guards. Yeah, always fuckin' guards."

"Don't say 'fuckin'' here," Titus said. "Say it the right speaking way."

"All well and this was home for many children and many fathers and mothers. Then came day of fire and white smoke in heart of Redoubt. Ever after, many fathers and mothers sleep younger. And less and less children borning."

There was a long stillness. Ryan wasn't sure if the saga was over as he looked at the others. "Skydark came and the place was evacuated. Local people from a nearby ville came here. Experimented for some time and stumbled on the number code."

"A short and simple one that wouldn't have taken an infinity of choices," Doc said.

"Right. Everyone lived here. Good protection once they mastered the outer doors. Looks like they never got deeper into the section toward the gateway. Then there was... A fire?"

"Could have been a nuke meltdown in part of the redoubt," Krysty suggested. "Account for the lack of babies and the rad sickness. These two look like they're the last of the line of self-appointed guards to the redoubt."

The words "guards" brought instant attention from the brothers.

"Guards of the Redoubt," they said. "We have the task of keeping the redoubt safe from enemies."

Titus suddenly looked sharply at Ryan. "You are enemies of the redoubt?"

"Course not."

"Enemies die," they chorused. "When shall that be? On the day of enemies? Who shall do it? The guards."

They gave themselves a round of applause, which Ryan and then the others joined in.

"You got sleeping places?" J.B. asked. "Be real honored if we could stay a night."

Ryan glanced at the tiny rad counter that he wore in his lapel, seeing that it was shading from yellow toward orange, lending credibility to Krysty's theory of a nuke leak. It was severe enough not to want to spend several

days in the redoubt, but one night should be safe at that
rad level.

"Showing highish," he said to the Armorer, who
checked his own counter.

"Yellow sliding toward orange," he said. "Probably risk staying one night."

Ryan nodded. "Why not? Have shelter and then
move on after dawn."

Titus and Mervyn exchanged stares, both nodding at
precisely the same second.

"We got plenty of beds," they said together. "You
friends of the redoubt, then you're all friends of the
Guards."

"Hot pipe," Dean said, clapping his hands together.
"Any more of that buffalo meat left?" He shook his
head at the response from Titus and Mervyn. "Well,
mebbe tomorrow?"

THEY ALL WALKED up a corridor for about a hundred
yards, straight into the domestic heart of the old redoubt, into the dormitories and living quarters of the
complex.

Titus and Mervyn strutted together, perfectly in step,
pointing out proudly where the washing facilities were,
as well as a room that was filled with racks of camouflage clothes like the ones they wore.

"No weapons?" J.B. asked.

"Got our blasters." Both tapped the butts of the
holstered Smith & Wesson Model 29s. "Father of fa-

thers said there was more, but they all got lost or broke.''

Mervyn spoke on his own. "Only got some small bits of ammo left now."

Titus slapped him on the arm. "Guards don't tell fuckin' outlanders shit like that."

"Sorry, brother."

He turned to Ryan. "We Guards of the Redoubt got plenty of ammo."

"Sure you do. Those are the sleeping quarters just ahead of us. You guards sleep in there?"

"Yeah, we do. But plenty of beds for all. Go look."

THERE WERE five long rooms, each with about twenty iron beds, each bed with its own small footlocker. The mattresses, sealed in plastic, were in a separate room farther along the white-painted passage.

Ryan had seen similar sections in redoubts that had only been partially evacuated during the days immediately before or after skydark.

Once Titus and Mervyn had shown them where they could sleep, the brothers seemed keen to head off on their own again.

But J.B. called after them. "Hey!"

"What?"

"You know where we are?"

A look of contempt crossed both placid faces. "Course."

"Where?"

Both freely waved a hand. "Here."

# Chapter Seven

There was no hot water, and the cold flowed from the taps with a grudging trickle, carrying with it the remains of myriad tiny insects.

"Looks like the boys aren't that hot on washing in here," Mildred commented.

"I was close to Mervyn and he was smelling kind of high," Krysty agreed. "Mebbe it was the heating system that went west and caused the rad leak."

Ryan looked around. "I reckon the best we can do is all take a rest as soon as possible. Then rise early and get out of the main gates. Find out where in Deathlands we are. Don't want to linger with the rad count high as it is."

"Taken its toll on the brothers," Mildred said, glancing over her shoulder to make sure that Titus and Mervyn hadn't come back. "They got all the signs of being inbred from the original folks that found their way into the redoubt. Way they look, I wouldn't want to lay too much jack on their being around in another three months."

"Triple creepy." Jak had let one of the taps run until the water flowed clear. He dropped his head to drink, his mane of white hair tumbling over his narrow, bone-pale face like spray from a winter waterfall.

Doc had been walking around that section of the redoubt, looking at the blank walls, testing the limits by finding the locked and coded sec doors that closed off other parts of the place. Now he had rejoined the others.

"Creepy is a better than adequate word to describe the siblings, my young fellow," he pronounced. "They are as strange a couple as I've seen in many a day's march, are they not? Gog and Magog of Deathlands. Old Brother Right and old Brother Wrong. Both Ossa and Pelion. Scylla and Charybdis. Are they not the topless towers of—"

Ryan patted the old man on the shoulder, getting a blank stare from the watery blue eyes. "Running off at the mouth again, Doc," he warned.

"Really? My dear fellow, then it would appear that apologies are in order."

"Never apologize," Mildred said, putting on a gruff voice. "It's a sign of weakness, pilgrim."

Dean came out of one of the cubicles, grinning broadly. "Shitter has a jet of water that gushes up and cleans your ass for you," he said. "So strong it sort of feels like it's going to push your ass clean out the top of your head."

Doc tutted. "The sooner that stripling gets a decent education, the better for him and for all of us."

"You're right, Doc." Ryan glanced at his wrist chron. "Enough, friends. Let's get some quality sleep."

But he and Krysty had things to do before they slept, finding the stillness in the farthest of the dormitories to be lovely, dark and deep.

RYAN RAN THE TOP of his tongue around his lover's nipple, making it stand up hard and hot.

Krysty sighed sleepily. "I hate to be a party pooper, but I'm feeling real tired. I think twice is going to be enough for tonight."

Ryan laid his head on her magnificent breasts. "Guess you're right. Out in a few hours to find . . . who knows? Just that it makes a good change to have a reasonable bed and reasonable security for a night."

"I know." She kissed the top of his head and stroked his cheek. "You could do with a shave."

"There were razors in the bathroom, still sealed in that shrink-wrap stuff."

"Cold water, lover," Krysty said, shuddering. "Mebbe wait until we get somewhere that's got hot water."

"No." He stretched. "If there's hot water, there won't be decent blades. Those predark whitecoats sure knew about putting an edge on fine steel."

Krysty ruffled his hair. "All right. Certainly make you a little less ugly."

"That wasn't what you said a few minutes ago." He grinned, his teeth white in the glow of the all-night sec lights.

"Then was then and now is now, lover." Suddenly she threw her arms around him, holding tight. "Be careful, Ryan."

"Always am. But why now? Why especially now? You got a feeling about the stupe brothers?"

Krysty half smiled. "I think of them as the smelly brothers. But stupe'll do. Yeah, there's a bad feeling. Like it's set on the back burner, but that doesn't mean there might not be trouble from them."

Ryan swung his legs out of bed. Feeling reasonably secure, he'd stripped off his clothes. He eased on his shirt and his underpants. "Well, I'll look out for the boys. I'm going to have a piss and a shave. Back soon."

A NARROW PASSAGE RAN alongside the dormitories, so Ryan could get to the bathroom without having to disturb everyone else.

At the last moment, his combat sense jarred a little by Krysty's feeling, Ryan had picked up the eighteen-inch panga, carrying it in its sheath as he walked through the night-silent redoubt.

The only sound as he walked past the open doors to the other large rooms was Doc snoring, like a buzz saw running at full throttle in the heart of a summer forest. The old man slept in a dormitory along with Jak and Dean. Mildred and J.B. were together in the third of the row of rooms.

Which left the last one, closest to the bathroom and the main entrance, to Titus and Mervyn.

Dean had gone sneaking around before retiring and come back to report that the brothers' dormitory was like an animal's den, filled with dried branches and skins of beaver, wolf and bear. The remnants of innumerable cooking fires were in the center of the room, which contained only two beds.

"Looks like all their kin lived there once," the boy had said. "Stinks so much their bodies might still be rotting away in there someplace."

The smell came wafting out as Ryan padded by.

But nothing moved.

SHAVING WITH COLD WATER was almost as uncomfortable as Krysty had warned. The steel blade seemed to catch and scratch, and the plastic one-use container of foam gave only a feeble dribble of watery white slime.

The air was cool, smelling strongly of the cooking fire. Ryan had glanced into the entrance hall of the redoubt, seeing the pile of glowing embers, which stood six or eight feet high, giving silent testimony that Titus and Mervyn tended not to remove ashes from old fires.

Beyond the smoking pile was an open space, littered with bits of unidentifiable scrap metal, animal bones and a ragged heap of damp material. And then there were the huge floor-to-ceiling sec doors, their paint dulled and scarred.

Ryan finished shaving, rubbed his hand over his stubble-free chin and dashed several handfuls of icy water into his face, blinking at the shock.

"Better," he whispered.

He looked up at himself in the discolored mirror, seeing the tight lines around his eyes and mouth. Not for the first time he could glimpse his father in the mirror.

Something moved behind him and he spun, facing the twin muzzles of the two Magnum revolvers held steady in the hands of Titus and Mervyn. They stood together in the doorway, less than twenty feet away, separated from him by another row of waist-high basins.

"Fireblast!" Ryan glanced at the sheathed panga resting on the third basin along the line to the right.

"Guards of the Redoubt present and defending," the brothers snapped, their voices in perfect unison. "Protect redoubt against outlander enemies."

"We aren't enemies. Been through all of that, haven't we? You agreed that we weren't enemies."

There was a mad chill in the brothers, their eyes narrowed with suspicion. They were fully dressed, and Ryan guessed that they probably hadn't even been to bed at all that night, waiting together in the semidarkness, whispering their plans to each other.

"You going to shoot me? Then go along and shoot the others in their beds?"

The question made them turn and stare at each other, and Ryan realized that Titus and Mervyn hadn't actually done all that much strategic organizing.

"We'll chill you all," Mervyn said, sounding and looking doubtful.

"Shoot me now and the noise of the shot'll wake the others, and they've got the weaponry to take both of you out of the game without raising sweat."

Titus giggled. "But you'll be dead."

Despite being a credible triple stupe, the man had put his finger unerringly on the one weakness in Ryan's argument. Posthumous revenge wasn't a great idea.

Though, as Trader had sometimes commented, it was ultimately better than no revenge at all.

"There's you and me in mirror," Mervyn said. "Haven't seen us in . . . lots of time."

The brothers stared vacantly at their reflections, smiling their identical idiot smiles, heads to one side at the same angle, the barrels of their blasters edging away from Ryan.

Lot of times you had no chance.

Sometimes you glimpsed a part of a chance.

Ryan took it.

He dived to his right, reaching for the hilt of the panga, his feet slipping on the wet tiles so that he nearly fell short. But his fingers just grabbed enough, pulling the knife off the basin, still sheathed.

But Titus and Mervyn reacted much more quickly than he'd guessed and the bathroom filled with the thunder of the big .44s, shattering glass and the ceramic basins.

Their speed of reaction had tugged away his only chance, and Ryan realized that bloody death could be only a few seconds away.

# Chapter Eight

Shards of splintered basin and slicing lengths of broken glass cascaded all around Ryan, cutting at him. He wriggled a little to one side, out of sight, covered by the central row of basins. The air was rank with the stink of gunfire.

Despite the racketing noise, the ricocheting bullets and screeches of delight from Titus and Mervyn, Ryan's combat mind was working like a well-oiled machine, calculating movement and action and time.

Obviously J.B., Jak and the others would hear the thunder of shooting and be out there to help him, but that was going to take at least several seconds.

Way too long.

The nickel-finished revolvers each held six .44-caliber Magnum rounds.

One of the things that Ryan did as second nature in a firefight was to count bullets. Titus and Mervyn had already fired eight shots between them, in that first crazed crescendo of flying lead. But Ryan had no way at all of knowing which of the psychopathic brothers had fired how many rounds.

Four bullets each?

Five and three?

Even six and two?

"Go that way!" It was impossible for the one-eyed man to tell which of them had called out.

A bullet missed his curled-up legs by a few inches, burying itself in the wall, gouging a huge hole from the crumbling concrete.

Five and four?

Six and three?

There hadn't yet been a pause long enough for either of them to reload.

The unsheathed panga was still no use against the pair of matched Smith & Wessons. Ryan reached out quickly with his left hand and scrabbled together a fistful of the larger splinters of broken glass, some of them several inches long, edged like razored steel.

A tenth round passed so close to Ryan's face that he felt its burning breath on his skin.

Five and five?

Six and four?

He came up into a fighting crouch, trying to watch both ways at once. This kind of combat situation was the one time that the loss of his left eye became a serious handicap. It sliced down his peripheral vision, making it immeasurably hard to look out for the brothers.

He tried to guess which of them would come at him first, be it from left or right.

The answer arrived a second later.

Titus from the left.

He appeared in a half-crouch, holding the revolver in both hands, pointing it at Ryan, his lips peeling back from rotting teeth.

"Got yer..." Titus gloated.

Ryan didn't waste time or breath on a reply. He hurled the handful of shattered glass into the man's face from close range, aiming at Titus's eyes, seeing the sparkling shards find their targets.

The twin staggered back, mouth sagging, pulped eyes carved open, blood bursting from his pale, unhealthy skin and dappling his shirt. "Fuckin'..." he began, squeezing the trigger of the Smith & Wesson, the gun bucking in his hand, the bullet ripping into the ceiling.

That made eleven rounds fired by the brothers.

One left.

Ryan wasn't sitting back admiring the partial success of his plan.

The instant the jagged splinters left his hand, he was moving after them, powering himself from the crouched position, jabbing with the sharpened point of the eighteen-inch panga, aiming at his adversary's thorax.

Titus screamed at the realization that he was blinded, waving his hands desperately to try to prevent the attack that he knew was coming.

It was easy for Ryan to dodge the flailing fists and thrust the panga home, a little to the left of the breastbone, twisting his wrist with savage power as the honed steel pierced both heart and lungs.

There was a great gushing torrent of bright crimson blood, which spouted over Ryan's hand and arm, pouring onto the floor among the broken fragments of the basins. Some of the copper water pipes had also been broken by the gunfire, and water flooded around Ryan's bare feet.

Titus staggered away, pulling himself off the panga, stumbling backward. Just as Ryan started to turn to face Mervyn, he found the other brother was already aiming his revolver at him, grinning wolfishly, seeming oblivious to his dying sibling, now on his knees.

"Guards win!" he crowed.

It was one of those moments when a man's life rested in the hands of the blind maniac gods of chaos and chance. One of the blasters still held a live round.

The other didn't.

As Ryan began to cock his wrist, ready to try a final desperate throw of the bloodied steel at Mervyn, knowing that if he lost the gamble it would be way too late, the index fingers of both the brothers tightened simultaneously on the grooved target triggers of the two Smith & Wessons.

Then came the boom of the explosion, the whine of the powerful bullet.

And the flat clicking sound of a hammer falling on a spent cartridge.

A bullet erupted from the barrel of dying Titus's blaster, as the man fell forward onto his face and lay still. The round had hit the door of one of the stalls, punching out a splintered hole larger than a man's fist.

"Twelve," Ryan said, checking his action with the panga. "All gone."

Mervyn squeezed the trigger on his empty revolver a second time.

And a third time.

"Guards have lost the fuckin' redoubt after all . . . all this time," he muttered to himself, puzzled, staring past Ryan at his dead brother. "You're no help to me, are you, Titus?"

Ryan moved closer, trying not to get cut by the sharp splinters on the blood-slick floor, where the water was already three or four inches deep.

Mervyn still seemed despondent rather than fearful, unworried by the approach of his own death. "Of all the guards of all the redoubts in all of Deathlands, you had to come and pick on this one," he mumbled.

For some reason that he couldn't place, the words seemed oddly familiar to Ryan.

But it didn't slow his advance.

Just as he judged himself close enough, he caught a glimpse of Jak out of the corner of his eye, the white-haired teenager already gripping a throwing knife in his right hand. J.B. held the Uzi at the lad's shoulder.

"Mine," Ryan said firmly.

Mervyn spotted the death thrust already on its way, and he reacted with surprising speed, trying to parry it with the empty revolver. The barrel glanced off the steel, deflecting the lunge, but the blade angled down and opened a deep-lipped cut across the man's wrist, making him yelp in pain and drop the useless blaster to the floor.

He took a half step backward, his feet crunching over the broken porcelain and glass, his muddy eyes wide with pain.

Ryan feinted toward his stomach, getting Mervyn to drop his hands, then swung the panga in a hissing circle of blood-slick steel.

He aimed at the angle of neck and shoulder, the blade cleaving flesh, jarring against the spinal column. Mervyn tried to pull away, nearly twisting the panga out of Ryan's hand, blood fountaining out from the severed artery.

Ryan got the knife clear, hefting it ready for a third cutting blow, but stopped at J.B.'s calm voice. "No need, bro. It's over."

It was.

The body slumped gracelessly to the floor, the fountain of blood slowing with the fading pulse until it became a feeble trickle that eventually stopped.

Now everyone was crowded into the doorway, even a rheumy-eyed Doc.

"You all right, lover?" Krysty asked, hesitating barefooted at the layer of crimsoned water that covered the broken glass. "They hit you?"

"No. Few minor cuts from splinters. They came up behind me as I finished shaving. They planned to chill us all."

"I fear that they were madder than the proverbial shithouse rats," Doc said.

"Looks like we'll move on and leave the redoubt a better, safer, cleaner place," Mildred added.

Ryan turned on one of the chrome taps, holding his hands under the running water, washing clean the dozen or so tiny cuts. He splashed more water in his face. To one side of him the broken pipes were still pumping out more water from the redoubt's huge central reservoir.

There wasn't much that could be done to check it. And they'd be leaving in the morning, anyway.

"Back to bed, friends," Ryan said.

"How about the bodies?" Dean asked.

"Just let them lie, son. They aren't going anywhere and they can't hurt us."

They left the washroom, where both of the bodies were already beginning to float sluggishly on the rising tide of water.

AFTER THE DISTURBANCE, and with the knowledge that the only threat to them had been permanently removed, everyone slept more soundly for the latter part of the night.

Dean woke first, lying on his back, looking around the semidark room, puzzled for a few moments, trying to remember where he was. The memory of the triple-crazy brothers came back to him, and he sat up in the bed.

The big room held two other sleepers.

Jak, his hair blazing like a distress flare, was at the far end of the dormitory, lying flat on his back, hands folded, looking like a carved image on a tomb.

Doc was on the far side of the room, also on his back, snoring.

Dean had been sleeping in shirt and pants, his combat boots standing on the floor by the side of his bed. He swung out his bare feet.

And yelped in shock.

The floor was eight inches deep in cold water.

EVERYONE HAD WET FEET, tucked into wet boots. One of Doc's worn knee boots had floated into the passage, intent on making its own way toward the main entrance area.

Several of the blasters had also gotten soaked. The Steyr rifle and the scattergun had been laid on the floor for the night, and both were covered in the rising flood by dawn.

Once everyone was up and dressed, they splashed toward the open area, where the brothers' cooking fire was a mess of drifting gray scum and ashes.

"Can't we turn something off, somewhere?" Mildred asked. "There's got to be a danger that the water'll eventually work its way down and down until it reaches the gateway section. Then we'll be in serious trouble."

"Main tanks in a place this size could easily hold several thousand gallons," J.B. commented.

Ryan sniffed, easing the rifle on his shoulder. "Could be worse than that. We know the water's coming through the broken pipes, out of the reservoir, somewhere locked away in the heart of the complex. Anyone considered whether that reservoir might not be automatically topped up from some external water source?"

"By the Three Kennedys!" The ferrule of Doc's swordstick rapped wetly on the concrete floor. "You mean that this flood will simply carry on and on forever? Until the rivers run dry? That is a bad thought, friends."

"Where will the water go, Dad?" Dean asked as he looked around. He pointed at the main doors. "Can't we get them open, then it can all run outside?"

Ryan smiled at the boy. "Worth a try, I reckon."

J.B. shook his head doubtfully. "Might be pointless, Ryan."

"Why?"

"We don't know anything about the internal structure of the redoubt. The water might already be flooding down half a dozen levels, toward the gateway."

Ryan nodded. "Mebbe. But you can see it's rising up against the sec doors. Let's open them and see what happens. And let's do it now."

# Chapter Nine

The control panel was battered and worn, some of the letters and most of the numbers completely illegible. Particularly, numbers two, three and five were wiped away.

"Water's a little more shallow here, Ryan," Krysty observed. "Over by the dormitories it was halfway up my boots. Here it only covers the heels."

"Some of it'll drain off soon as we get the sec doors opened." Ryan called across to Dean. "Ready on three, five, two to open them up."

"Long as the doors aren't at the bottom of a slope," J.B. said, grinning at his old friend. "Most of them that we've visited have been high up, so we best keep our fingers crossed."

While he stood there waiting, the Armorer was trying to wipe his spectacles clean, but was having problems finding any dry material.

"Go for it, son," Ryan said, standing at the center, where the twin doors met, his SIG-Sauer drawn in his right hand.

The boy peered at the controls, puzzling out which number was which, eventually deciding and quickly pressing the three numerals in order.

The massive single sec door from the mat-trans section usually opened upwards, but the double ones that connected the redoubt to the outer world usually slid sideways.

They all heard the noise of gears grating against one another, and it was several seconds before there was any visible movement. It crossed Ryan's mind that the family of guards who'd lived in the redoubt for most of the hundred years or so since skydark had to have been using the doors for all that time. And it was a peanut to a candy bar that the sec doors had never been serviced. After all that time it was amazing that they worked at all.

"Moving, Dad!" Dean called, his voice cracking with his excitement.

A sliver of daylight appeared, and Ryan tasted the freshness of the outer air. Breathing inside the redoubt had been unusually good, but it was still tainted with the smell of Mervyn and Titus and their cooking fires.

"Smells fine," he said.

The others were ranged on either side of him, all with their blasters readied, in case there was any immediate danger outside the sec doors.

The ash-covered water began to trickle through the narrow gap, running faster as the doors opened wider. All Ryan could see was an open space and bright sunlight.

"Hold it there, Dean," he called. "Let's just take a quick look outside."

He walked closer, peering out of the gap of about seven inches. It was possible to see through a wide arc outside. There was a trampled area, with scrubby undergrowth that looked and smelled like mesquite and sage. Beyond the open area there were trees, mainly conifers, and in the far distance was range upon range of tall mountains.

Ryan could also make out what looked like a boneyard, a stack of rotting carcasses, ravaged by vultures and other predators, standing twenty or thirty feet high. He figured the kills had to have been left there by Titus and Mervyn's kin. There was also a huge pile of speckled ash and partly burned branches—the remnants of hundreds of bonfires.

Beyond that there was no sign of life.

"All the way, son," he said.

The water flowed faster out onto the flattened area, finding its own level by running off in a new-made stream through the fringe of the trees.

"Still leaves some of the water pouring off someplace deep inside the redoubt," J.B. said. "Mebbe they got emergency storm drains to carry it off."

The sec doors slid remorselessly open, stopping with a sigh of compressed air. The gap was now wide enough for three big war wags to pass through side by side.

"Gaia!" Krysty exclaimed. "That air is wonderfully fresh. Reminds me of my teen times up in Harmony ville. Any idea where we are?"

J.B. slung the Uzi over his shoulder, where it rattled against the Smith & Wesson scattergun. He took out his minisextant and sighted at the sun, which was already a little way up in the eastern sky.

"Look at mountains," Jak said. Coming from the flatlands of the bayous, the teenager was always impressed when jumps took them into the high country.

The peaks were snowcapped, rising jagged and serene, highest toward the west.

"That one looks like a hooked bear claw," Mildred said. "I'd place a fistful of dollars on them being the Rockies."

Krysty was staring where the woman had pointed. "I may be wrong, but I'd place a handful of jack on us being within a hundred miles of Harmony."

She turned to Ryan. "You realize that, lover?"

"Could be. Old Colorado, mebbe."

J.B. had finished his calculations with the tiny comp-powered instrument.

"Not a bad guess, bro," he said.

"The Rockies?" Mildred asked.

The Armorer nodded, concentrating on folding up the fragile little sextant and stowing it once more in one of his capacious pockets.

"Yeah. Ryan was right about old Colorado. And you're right about Harmony, as well, Krysty."

J.B. had an astounding eidetic memory for a number of things, including weaponry. But he could also tell you where you were in Deathlands, simply from the digital parameters established by the sophisticated navigational aid.

"Where are we, my dear John Barrymore? It seems akin to Paradise."

"Nearest predark ville of any substance was called Glenwood Springs. Near as I can tell, we're a little ways north of there. Four or five miles. I think I recognize some of the mountains around us here."

"Then we're not that far from Harmony." Krysty clapped her hands. "We always said we'd visit my old home if we ever got close enough, Ryan."

He nodded. "Other thing that's important to remember is that the school we've been talking about for Dean is also up in these parts."

"Harmony first, lover."

Ryan looked directly at her. "No. Come too far to change on this. The school I've heard of that takes young boys as kind of lodgers..."

"Boarders, is the word you seek, old friend. Bed and board for the lad. Do him the world of good. Some Latin and less Greek and cold showers and a flogging every morning."

"Doc!" Ryan exclaimed. "No need to talk like that and try and put Dean off."

"It was a jest," the old man replied. "A small jest. Though I must confess that such a regime did me no harm."

"Why can't we go to Harmony first?" Krysty persisted. "All of us go. We could mebbe meet old Uncle Tyas McCann, though he'd be good and white-haired by now."

"How about your mother, Sonja?" Mildred asked. "Will she still be living?"

Krysty shook her head, tears welling in her bright green eyes. "Likely not. She was . . . not well when we parted. And we parted on poor terms."

"Where are the two places, exactly?" J.B. asked, taking in several deep breaths. "I'm certain it should be possible to visit both."

Ryan was stubborn. "No. I've set my heart on Dean getting something partway to a decent education. And that comes before everything. You can all go on to Harmony, and I'll meet up with you there."

"I'd like to see Harmony, too, Dad," Dean said. "Couldn't we just—"

"No, we couldn't just anything! Much more of this and I'm goin' to start becoming a bit angered. This school is for a year or so at the most. When we all come to take you away again, then we can all go to Harmony together. It'll be something for us all to look forward to."

"Oh, Dad, why can't—"

"Fireblast!" Ryan punched his right fist into his left palm. The shout of rage sent crows circling noisily into the air, like black tumblers, from the tall trees at the edge of the clearing.

"Sorry, Dad," Dean said, shuffling his feet in the carpet of pine needles that lay thickly around.

The fit of temper sidled away as quickly as it had come. "All right."

"Still nobody told me precisely where the school and Harmony ville are set," J.B. said.

Ryan considered. "From what I've heard of the school, it's on the back road to Leadville, off old 82."

"Harmony's that direction." Krysty closed her eyes as though she was visualizing a map. "We can go some of the way together. Harmony wasn't far from a small ville called Fairplay, high up at the head of a steep trail."

"That's above Breckenridge, isn't it?" Mildred asked. "I was taken up that way to ski when I was about thirteen. My father's brother, Josh, took me there. The skiing was all right, but it was triple snobby around there in winter." She slipped into a mock "mammy" voice. "Lordy, but yo din't see many of us pore nigras up there, and dat's de troof."

Ryan was already regretting his outburst of temper at his son and at Krysty, and was now looking for some way of trying to build bridges.

"My recollection of being around here with Trader is that there are backcountry trails south from Glenwood Springs, then heading east, up and over the high country towards Leadville. In summer you could get the wags over a dirt road towards Breckenridge. So mebbe we can go some of the track together."

Krysty smiled at him, the bright morning sunshine highlighting the vivid scarlet of her hair. "Sounds good to me, lover."

THEY CLOSED THE SEC DOORS to the redoubt, but only after a lengthy discussion between Ryan, Doc and J.B. about the leaking water.

Hundreds of gallons had come through the open doorway, bubbling past the pile of rotting deer carcasses, washing against both sides of a large, frost-splintered boulder, then trickling over the lip of the hillside and vanishing among the trees.

Doc argued that they had no way of knowing how much more liquid was going to flood from the broken pipes in the bathroom.

"It is not unreasonable to assume that there might indeed be some connection between the main tanks of the redoubt and some external supply. As long as it flows out one end, then it could, mayhap, keep gushing into the other end. It could go on until all of the water in Colorado has filled the redoubt from its top to its basement."

"And flooded the gateway," the Armorer said.

"I don't believe that the builders of these redoubts wouldn't have taken precautions in the case of flooding." Ryan shook his head. "Wouldn't make sense, would it?"

"These were the same people, or their superiors, who were responsible for the red buttons being pushed and civilization disappearing." Doc pointed a bony finger at Ryan. "Never, ever, underestimate the capacity of the government official for behaving like a headless chicken."

"So, you're saying we should go straight down and make a jump out of here?"

"No, bro." J.B. looked around. "We know where we are. For the sake of Dean and Krysty, we should make the most of this chance jump to explore some. If the redoubt floods completely, then is that so terrible?"

Ryan considered that. "I guess not," he said finally. "We know the locations of close to thirty gateways, and most of them are still functioning. We could always step it out and find another one for a jump."

"Never did too much jumping in the war wag days," J.B. said with a grin.

"Yeah," Ryan agreed.

Krysty had joined them as the argument reached its amicable ending. "So, we're going to do some walking?"

"Right," Ryan said. "Ace on the line, lover. We're going to do some walking."

ACCORDING TO THE ARMORER, the township of Glenwood Springs lay only an hour or so south of where they'd landed. It seemed reasonable to make it their first destination, so they set off in that direction.

It was a heaven of a morning. The sun climbed gently through a cloudless sky, the temperature was comfortably in the middle sixties, with a light westerly breeze.

They were still high up, high enough for breathing to be slightly affected. Doc called a halt after thirty minutes, panting and sweating. "Upon my soul! I had forgotten how thin the air can be up here."

"Reckon we're probably close to eight thousand feet," J.B. guessed.

Dean had wandered a little ahead, and he called back to them. "Hey, come and look at this!"

# Chapter Ten

At first glance it seemed as if they'd made a time jump. The holiday resort of Glenwood Springs looked just like it did before skydark and the long winters: the main streets with their stores and motels, the freeway scything through the town from east to west, running alongside the frothing Colorado River, with the railway line also following along the bottom of the deep gorge.

It was only when your eyes became focused that you saw that the ville was actually a ruin.

Most of the buildings were roofless, and no automobiles or trucks rumbled along the streets. Only a handful of people could be seen, moving slowly around.

The freeway had become riven and corrugated by quakes and the passing of time. By looking toward the east, it was possible to see where a big elevated section had totally collapsed, permanently blocking old I-70. The railway line was forked and buckled, and long stretches of the iron rails were missing.

Only the river remained, virtually unchanged.

"Must've been a nice ville once," Dean commented, sitting on a convenient rock and peering out over the urban ruins. "Might find some food down there."

"You ever think about anything beyond your stomach?" Mildred asked.

The boy considered that for several seconds. "No," he said finally. "Guess not."

THE TWO-LANE BLACKTOP that led from the redoubt vanished in less than fifty paces in a sheer scarp face, where the land had dropped away for a mile or more, taking all of the pavement with it. The friends scouted around for an alternate route.

"Plenty game here," Jak said as they picked their way along a narrow deer trail that seemed as if it would take them to the bottom of the valley.

They'd seen two separate herds of deer during the four miles or so they'd covered since leaving the redoubt. Ryan had been tempted to bring the Steyr to his shoulder and bag one for the pot, but he didn't want to risk drawing anyone's attention.

They passed a couple of children, a boy and a girl roughly eleven years old, and exchanged greetings with them, though the guarded faces told their own story of suspicion of outlanders.

"That long building must've been the hot pools and bathhouse," Mildred said, as they paused again. This time they were within a quarter mile of the edge of Glenwood Springs.

"I was here just the once, fishing with my father," Doc stated, lying back on the sun-warmed turf. "Must have been in '87 or so, when I was in my late teens. The thing I remember best is that the town seemed to be still in mourning for the recent death of Doc Holliday, part-time dentist and full-time shootist."

"One who rode with the Earps?" J.B. asked. "Dark night, Doc! You mean you were within a few months of actually meeting up with Doc Holliday?"

"I do indeed. It had been devilishly cold and they couldn't get him up the hill to the cemetery, so they buried him down below. Grave marker tells us that he died in his bed, which I believe to be true. Him being consumptive and all."

The conversation stopped and everyone turned to watch a six-wheel wag, its bodywork a patchwork of rust and green and blue paint, grinding its way into the ville from the north. Black smoke poured from its exhaust, and the engine was a cacophony of hideous metallic noises.

"Give it about twenty miles before the pistons come out through the side of the engine," J.B. said.

"Mebbe we can get hold of a wag to transport us to the school," Ryan said.

"To transport us to Harmony ville," Krysty added. "And what does 'get hold of' mean? Steal?"

"Probably," Ryan agreed. "Let's go and scout the ville."

THE HIKE FROM THE REDOUBT had taken longer than Ryan had anticipated, and it was close to noon when they eventually found themselves in the center of the ville.

Most of the damage to the buildings appeared to have come from the passing of time rather than any nuking.

"Could've used neutrons," J.B. suggested. "Just taken out all the life-forms and left most of the ville standing."

Ryan nodded. "Makes sense."

From above it looked as if the old resort town of Glenwood Springs had once held a population of around seven thousand. From street level, Ryan doubted more than a hundred people lived there.

Most of them looked like hunters and trappers, dressed in untreated skins and furs, despite the warmth of the day, hurrying by, often crossing the street when they saw the group of strangers. Most of them were armed with long-barreled muskets and bowie knives sheathed at their belts.

Ryan called to one of them, a limping man with a sallow complexion. "Good place to eat in the ville?"

"Only one place to eat in the ville, outlander." He looked at their array of weapons. "Do you a good trade deal for a few of your bullets."

"Where?"

"Ma's Place. Block down to the north along that blacktop. Past the Happy Trails store."

Happy Trails advertised itself in faded, sun-blistered lettering as being the Roy Rogers Emporium for all Western memorabilia. Its windows were long smashed in, and its empty doorway gaped like a toothless mouth.

Across the road from them was the wrecked front-age of the Sombrero Eatery, which still carried a faded poster in the unbroken corner of its window proclaiming that it was the hottest plateful in all Colorado.

Western Books was the last store on the opposite side of the wide highway. Like all the others, it had been smashed open and all of its stock long taken.

"Who in all Deathlands would want to steal books?" Mildred asked, shading her eyes against the bright sun to peer into the dark interior.

"Burn well," Jak replied as laconic as ever.

"The Nazis discovered that about one hundred and fifty years ago," Doc said bitterly.

"There's Ma's Place," Dean told them eagerly. "Boy, I can smell good food already."

It was food, but it wasn't that good.

"JUST SIT YOURSELVES DOWN at the big table. Plenty of room here right now. Not many folks care to eat their big meal at the mid of the day."

Ma was a three-hundred-pound transvestite who looked as if she hadn't shaved for a week, thick black stubble breaking through the layer of caked powder. She was wearing a short black dress with a hem and collar of yellow-brown lace that could possibly once have been white. Clouds of crimson sequins were scattered around the shoulders and bosom of the dress. Ma's shoes looked as if she'd rescued them from *The Wizard of Oz*. More red sequins decorated the high heels.

"You outlanders got some good jack, or are you aiming to trade with me?"

Her mouth was a tiny cupid's bow of scarlet, and her eyes dripped mascara down her dimpled cheeks. It was difficult to tell if Ma was wearing a wig or whether her hair had been dyed the coppery blue color.

"Trade," Ryan said, sitting at one end of the scarred and scratched table, pushing away a brimming ashtray and a plate smeared with grease and shreds of bacon rind.

"Bullets?" Ma asked hungrily.

"Could be."

"You guys got some 9 mill fmjs on you?"

"Could be," Ryan replied.

Now everyone was sitting around the table, with Krysty peering doubtfully out the filthy, fly-specked window. "We sure about this?" she asked the others. "Could always go and catch or shoot something."

"I'm hungry now," Dean insisted.

"I'll feed you all—much as you like of anything—for fifty rounds."

Ryan pushed back his chair, the legs grating on the worn linoleum. "We'll be going, thanks, ma'am."

"Thirty rounds?"

"Don't believe so." He looked at her. "We both know what full-metal-jacket rounds from predark are worth. One's worth more than a meal."

"Gimme ten rounds and I'll throw in beer."

"Getting closer."

"Seven. One each. That's my bestest and lastest offer."

Ryan nodded, sitting again. "What you offering?"

"Anything you like, stranger." She giggled and patted her meaty hands together.

"Food."

"Menu's on the board over there. And there's today's brunch special."

"What's that?" J.B. asked.

"Venison."

"How's it cooked? What with?" Krysty asked.

"Picky bitch!"

"Watch your mouth," the redhead warned. "I asked a fair question."

"Oh, did you? Well, it's cooked by being roasted, and it's served with whatever vegetables and bread we happen to have out in the kitchen. That satisfy you, lady?"

Dean was struggling to read the ill-scrawled menu. "Writing's hard to make out," he said.

Ma looked at him as if he were something she'd just spotted on the bottom of her Dorothy-red shoes. "Well, kiddo, you wanna catch up on your reading and writing. I can read the board easy enough. It says meat and fish and deer." She looked sideways at Krysty. "And all of them's roasted."

"What is the soup of the day?" Doc asked.

"It's whatever flavor's in the pot, old-timer. Last time I looked it was kind of vegetable with peas and corn and tomatoes in it. Doubt it's changed since the day before yesterday. Not without someone telling me."

"We'll have the deer," Ryan stated. "With vegetables and bread and some beers and a pitcher of water."

"Let's have the bullets first," Ma said, gloating. "No pay, no eat."

Ryan stared at the immensely fat transvestite. "After the meal," he said. "No good, no pay."

Grumbling to herself, Ma lumbered off into the kitchen, through a battered pair of bat-wing doors, returning in a couple of minutes with a dozen dark brown bottles of beer that she banged, foaming and frothing, on the table. In her other hand she held a wooden platter of bread with some rancid unsalted butter.

Meat'll be along later," she informed them, scowling at Ryan.

"Fine," he said.

"NEVER PLAY CARDS with a man called Doc, and never eat at a restaurant called Ma's Place," Mildred said, after they'd been waiting for nearly a half hour. "I knew the first bit of the old saying was true after trying a few hands of strip jack with that old goat. Now it looks like the second part of the saying's true, as well."

There were no other customers, and no sign of life in the street outside the eatery.

"We could go some other place," Dean suggested.

Ryan sniffed. "No. We've waited long enough here. Can't be too much longer. We go elsewhere and start this business all over again. No thanks, son."

There had been a coil of black, greasy smoke from the kitchen a few minutes earlier, which had promised much.

And delivered nothing.

There had also been a rapid burst of Spanish from what sounded like a young girl, then the deeper voice of Ma, followed by the meaty thump of a roundhouse right finding its target. A flurry of tears followed.

"Won't be long, strangers," Ma called, poking her head above the door. "Figure you're all getting a mite hungered."

"We were mite hungered before got here," Jak said. "Now all very hungry."

"Take care, you white-head freak. Boy gets too sharp and he cuts hisself."

Less than five minutes later Ma waddled into the room carrying the seven helpings of meat with the promised assortment of vegetables.

She dumped the platters in front of each of the party, then started back toward the kitchen.

She stopped in the doorway when Ryan called her. "This it?" he asked.

"Sure it is. Roast venison and sweet potatoes and honeyed cabbage with peas and carrots. What the fuck does it look like, outlander?"

"I'm not that sure. Meat looks like parts of it have been flame-grilled and parts haven't seen any heat at all. And it looks more like horse than deer to me. And the vegetables look to be either over- or undercooked."

She pointed a hand at him, the fingers sticking out as if they were contained in an inflated red glove. "Best not use such details as an excuse for not completing the trade, mister!"

Ryan didn't answer her, and she disappeared into the kitchen.

THE FOOD WAS AS AWFUL as it looked.

"I can only eat about a quarter of the meat, Dad," Dean moaned. "The rest's either raw or burned."

"My carrots were quite pleasant," Doc offered. "But I confess that the rest of the so-called 'special' meal falls rather short of adequacy."

"I think the potatoes were actually past their eat-by-if-you're-starving date," Mildred said. "I might have eaten worse, but I can't remember when."

"Beer's warm." Jak sipped at a second bottle, leaving it unfinished. "And flat."

Krysty glanced at Ryan, sitting next to her. "What do we do, lover?"

"Easy. No eat, no pay."

"Ma doesn't look the sort of man, or woman, who'll listen to a reasoned argument," J.B. said as he polished his glasses on a torn napkin.

At that moment the door flew open and Ma erupted into the restaurant. "I heard that, you shitters!" she screamed. "Well, you pay me or you'll all get to eat this!"

She held a sawn-down 12-gauge.

# Chapter Eleven

Nobody made a hasty move, all of them watching Ryan to see how he was going to play it.

He sat still, both hands on the table, pushing the nearly full plate away from him, his one chillingly blue eye fixed to Ma's flushed face.

"You think this is worth any payment?" he asked mildly. "Really?"

"Sure. You did a deal, *compadre*. You had the food, and I want the bullets."

"Seven rounds of the 9 mm full-metal jackets? Was that it?"

"Yeah. Should make you trade double for the trouble." A broad smile stretched across her face. "Double trouble. Get it? Double for trouble."

Ryan was fighting against his anger, struggling to conceal the red rage that was seeping over his brain.

"The food was shit," he said.

"Takes a shitter to know shit, sweet one," Ma said with a snigger, pointing the gaping barrels of the 12-gauge into Ryan's face. "Ain't that the truth?"

"You're sowing seeds of blood," Doc warned, "and you'll reap the harvest."

"Shut up, you triple-old stupe!"

Ma turned to Ryan. "Instead of just a few miserable bullets, I'll take that pretty automatic you got on your belt, One-eye."

"All right." Ryan had it all under control now, his ice-cold combat brain offering him alternative plans of action, showing which was the best.

"Take it out of the holster, slow and easy. Or the wall behind you gets to be decorated with your blood and brains. Place could do with refurbishing."

Ma was smiling broadly at her triumph, the scatter-gun locked on Ryan's face.

His right hand reached down, feeling the butt of the SIG-Sauer, taking it out slowly and beginning to lift it toward the top of the table.

"Good, good," Ma whispered. "Real good. Keep the hardware coming."

At the far end of the table, J.B. stood suddenly, sending three plates of food crashing to the floor, knocking over the pitcher of water.

Ma was taken by surprise at the noise and half turned, her little sunken eyes flicking toward the Armorer, the barrels of the blaster wavering from Ryan for a crucial moment.

Ryan had been ready for J.B.'s action. He had sent him their secret hand signal that meant "stage a diversion," seconds before beginning to draw the automatic.

He brought up the SIG-Sauer and squeezed the trigger once, at the same time powering himself backward out of his chair at the end of the table.

As he rolled, the thunder of the shotgun rode over the flat crack of the 9 mm SIG-Sauer. He felt the warm blast pass over his head, the pellets smashing into an old lithograph of a mountain man's encounter with a grizzly on a narrow mountain trail.

Ryan did a back somersault and came up with the blaster in his hand, aiming at Ma.

But he saw immediately that he wasn't going to be needing a second round.

The bullet had struck Ma through the rolls of fat below her chins, drilling up and backward. It distorted and tumbled as it went, breaking the lower jaw away from the upper, splintering a mouthful of rotten teeth. Some of the shards of splintered bone exited through the side of the cheek, just below the staring left eye, ripping the flesh to scarlet tatters.

The full-metal-jacket round had continued its inexorable progress, tearing at the back of the right eye, forcing it out of its socket in a hideous parody of a wink.

Its power still not spent, the bullet carried on upward, scouring out the brain pan. It exploded through the top of Ma's head, lifting off what was revealed as a wig, splattering the ceiling with blood and brains.

In death, her fingers tightened on the triggers of the shotgun, as Ryan had guessed they might, and the blaster had gone off, the twin charges roaring over the top of Ryan as he tumbled backward on the greasy floor.

Ma took two clumsy, tottering steps, then dropped the scattergun, arms hanging limp by her side, head tilted to the right. She caught her heels in a crack on the linoleum, falling full-length on the floor with a resounding crash.

Everyone around the table was on their feet, blasters ready for action.

Ryan looked down at the corpse. "Food wasn't even worth that one bullet I gave you," he said.

THE BAT-WING DOORS to the kitchen eased open. Seven blasters moved their aim, centering on the frightened face of a little Hispanic girl, looking no older than twelve, with a dark bruise just below her left eye.

"Ma's Place is closed," Ryan said. "Best go quietly on home."

The child nodded and backed out of sight, leaving the doors to swing themselves shut.

"Jak, Dean," Ryan said. "Take a quick look out back and see what you can pack into a couple of bags for food. Might be some meat or cheese or fresh fruit. Grab what you think might come in useful for us."

Glenwood Springs seemed so deserted that there was a good chance that nobody would have heard the shooting. But it would be only a matter of time before someone stepped into the eatery and stumbled over the corpse. And the outlanders would instantly become public enemies number one.

Dean reappeared, carrying a hessian bag. "Mainly fruit," he said. "Peaches and apples."

"Anything else in there?" Ryan asked, busily reloading the spent bullet from his blaster.

"Big pan fat starting smoke," Jak told him, carrying another sack of food. "Turn it off?"

"No."

"Set place on fire next ten minutes," Jak said, his ruby eyes opening wider as he started to grin. "Course. Fire cover chilling." He handed the food to Doc. "Go back and help fire."

"Have a look out the front door," Ryan told J.B. "Anyone looks like they're coming in here, either put them off or put them away. Whatever's needful."

"Ryan!" Mildred exclaimed. "You can't just kill someone because they happen to want to come eat at Ma's Place. It's plain murder."

He looked at the woman, surprised at her comment. "You been with us long enough to know which way the needle pricks. We get caught in here and the whole ville could turn into an instant wasps' nest, with us caught smack in the middle. Better by far we walk away clean."

"The girl might tell," Dean said.

Ryan nodded. "I thought on that. Decided she was probably too frightened to tell anyone anything."

"Otherwise she'd have been dead," Mildred said.

Ryan nodded. "Yeah. Otherwise I'd have gunned her down where she stood. If that had been the only choice to keep the rest of us living."

"Fat's ready to blow," Jak said, appearing in the batwing doors. "Back opens into alley. Walk along out of sight. Then past row ruined houses. Come out by broken bridge over Colorado. Best we go now."

The dirty kitchen stank of the simmering fat that sat in a large iron pot, with a haze of dark smoke wreathing above it. Jak had placed some old clothes near the stove, as well as a pile of kindling. The wood-framed building would go up in minutes once the fire started.

Ryan led the way through, holding the back door open for everyone, pausing to watch and make sure the fat was going to do the business for them.

The smoke thickened like a living serpent, roiling over the ceiling, lapping toward him. There was a dull whomp and Ryan ducked, closing the door behind him as the inferno of dark yellow flames erupted.

He ran quickly along the alley, past the rusted ruins of a predark automobile and a battered bicycle frame. The stores to his left were all derelict, and the houses that sloped away from him on the right were all clearly long-abandoned.

There was no sign of life.

"Wait." Ryan peered around the corner of the street, looking toward the desolate broken bridge and the silent rail lines. "Let's move it."

They moved across the makeshift bridge that had been thrown together parallel to the old crossing, deciding that it would be wise to be as far off as possible once the fire started in earnest. The companions walked together on the north side, along the redbrick ruins of the old hot springs.

"Stop looking around, Dean," the Armorer snapped.

"Mebbe the fire hasn't worked. It's got to be an hour since we left the place."

"It's six minutes," J.B. said, checking the time on his wrist chron. "There. Don't look around!"

Ryan stopped and stretched theatrically, glancing over his shoulder, across the weed-grown interstate toward the row of stores. He saw the darkness of smoke and the brightness of flame, heard the faint distant shouts as the locals of the ville became aware of the growing inferno in their midst.

"Burning like a paper house," he said. "Guess we can all look at it now."

It was spectacular.

Even as they all turned to stare, the fire cascaded through the shingle roof, sending the flaming wooden tiles floating into the still air.

Already a few men were trying to organize a bucket brigade from the river.

"Might as well piss on Mount Vesuvius," Doc said. "I rather think that the wretches will be exceedingly lucky to save anything out of the entire block."

"It was all empty buildings," Ryan said.

"Not that it would have made any difference if they hadn't been," Mildred said bitterly. "It wouldn't have changed your plan, would it?"

"Yeah, mebbe it would," Ryan replied, stung by her criticism. "If there'd been folks living close by, I'd have raised the warning myself to give them time to get clear."

She applauded him ironically. "Well, hurrah for you, Ryan Cawdor. Winner of the Nobel prize for humanitarian of the year. Children spared while you wait. Bar mitzvahs a speciality. Discount for groups."

"That time of month, Doctor?" Doc said mockingly. "Or did you get out of your little bed the wrong side this morning? Must be some explanation for your being more ill-tempered than you usually are."

"Enough," Ryan said. "Best thing we can do is get across there quickly. Make a lot of noise about arriving to help put out the fire."

DOC HAD BEEN RIGHT.

The whole block that had Ma's Place at its center was razed to the ground, reduced to smoking ashes in less than a half hour, with only the half-dozen brick central chimneys standing at the center.

"Like Jennison Gravestones," J.B. said. "What they called that sort of scene in the Civil War. After the man responsible for many of them. Specially around Kansas, bloody Kansas."

Ryan and the others had weighed in with a will, working flat out once it became obvious that no power on earth could save the buildings.

"Probably that prevert let his fat catch fire one time too many," said an old toothless woman, sucking on an empty corncob pipe. "Don't see no sign neither of that poor little girl who worked for him. Probably both in the ruins."

A few of the locals asked Ryan and the others what they were doing in Glenwood Springs, and received the stock answer that they'd been trading but their wag had fallen apart a couple of days earlier. Now they were stranded on foot, heading over the pass toward Leadville.

Was anyone, by chance, going that way?

The smoke-dark crowd of forty or fifty people considered the question.

"What did you want to go to that dead-alive craphole for, mister?" barked a trapper.

"Heard of a good school for my son," Ryan answered, following Trader's rule of telling the truth unless it seemed more convenient to lie.

"And we thought we might stop by Harmony, as well," Krysty added.

"Be Nick Brody's school," one of the deer hunters said. "Heard it was good for book learnin'."

"What we need," Ryan said, smiling pleasantly. "Where exactly is it?"

The man scratched his soot-smeared nose. "Now, that's a fair question. Not many folks go that way. Trails are all broke down. Doubt there's a man or woman been beyond Leadville—what used to be Leadville—these long months."

His partner, a thin little man with a pocked face who looked as if someone had once made a hearty attempt to scalp him, nodded. "Even more true of Harmony. Bad things up there. Nobody takes the old high trail to Fairplay and beyond."

"What kind of trouble?" Krysty asked.

"Bounties up there, so they said." The man rubbed at his puckered forehead. "Gang of swift and evil bastards. But there's only been whispers. Haven't heard of anyone actually going all the way up to Harmony for... Like you said about going beyond Leadville, Ezekial. Not for months."

A third man pushed to the front of the small crowd. He was extremely tall, and wrapped in a buffalo-hide jacket and pants that smelled as if they hadn't been within a country mile of any sort of curing process. They were still caked with dried blood and reeked of urine and dung.

"The name's Lemuel. I'm driving a mule team up to Leadville," he said. "Got to deliver a piano to the old opera house up there. The Tabor place. Going in an hour or so. Aimed to eat at Ma's, but I'll have to pass on that." He looked at Ryan. "Point is, I could take a couple of you folks up with me."

"Only two of us?" Ryan queried.

Krysty tugged at his sleeve. "You and me. Got to get to Harmony, lover. Find out for sure what's going on up there. Mebbe some of my kin could be in danger. My mother..."

Ryan ignored her, speaking instead to Lemuel. "Any other wags or teams we could hire?"

"Probably some around the ville that you could take if you wanted. Population's dropping. Livery stable's got animals going cheap."

"Ryan!"

"What, lover?"

"If he'll take two, then it has to be you and me. Find out what's happening."

He shook his head. "Doesn't make fighting sense. If there's bad trouble in Harmony, we have to be together. Then we could need a fast run out of the place. Might not be time to get Dean up to this Brody school."

"You're going with the boy and leaving me behind with the rest? I don't believe you, Ryan."

"He's right," J.B. said. "Only sensible plan. Ryan can drop off the boy and meet us all at Fairplay. That way we have a united attack."

"I need to get to Harmony, so butt out, John!"

"It's been years and years, lover," Ryan said, trying to calm her. "What's with waiting another day? Two days more at the outside?"

Krysty was suddenly close to tears. "I left on such bad terms. We'd fallen out and we never...never got to say goodbye to each other. I want to see Mother Sonja again and tell her that I love her. That I always loved her."

"You can do that, Krysty." Ryan put his arms around her, and she began to pull away. But he held tighter and Krysty melted, sobbing, into his arms.

"I have to see her, Ryan."

"Sure thing. But if Sonja's in deep shit, then it'll take us all to get her out of it. Agreed?"

"I guess so," she said, then thanked Doc as the old man passed her his precious swallow's-eye kerchief to blow her nose and wipe her eyes. "I guess you're right."

Lemuel had watched the emotional scene without saying anything. Now he coughed, hawked up some dark brown phlegm and spit it onto the sidewalk. "You comin' with me or not, mister? Another blaster or two could be useful up that trail. But I ain't waiting while you argue the toss. Just up sticks and leave."

Ryan nodded. "Sure, sure. Me and the boy's coming with you on the wag."

"And you help me unload it the other end? That's a part o' the trade."

"Yeah. Why not?"

He turned to Krysty. "Meet you up in Fairplay, or somewhere on the trail. Look out for me."

"When?"

"Fireblast, I don't know, do I? Guess it'll likely be two or three days.

"J.B., you sort out a couple more wags and get the teams for them."

The Armorer touched his finger to the brim of the fedora. "Sure thing, bro."

Dean had been standing apart from the others, waiting to see which way the bones fell. Now he moved to stand by his father. "That mean I got to say goodbye to everyone? Mebbe for a year or so? That's like forever."

J.B. shook his head. "Wrong, Dean. When you get a little older you'll know that forever is ... forever."

# Chapter Twelve

The upright piano had been manufactured by Gothstein of Toronto, Ontario, Canada.

Ryan knew that because it said so in a convoluted golden Gothic script, just above the keyboard. It was made of mellow beech, ornamented with inset maple and had obviously been constructed some time before skydark.

He was sitting on the rear of the wag with Dean, squeezed in by the piano, perched behind Lemuel; who was whipping up his team of eight mules.

It was difficult to know which smelled worse, the man or his animals.

The tearful farewells in Glenwood Springs had been intense and hasty.

Everyone had hugged Dean, telling him again and again that they'd be up to see him and that the year would race by, and think what a different person he'd be when next they saw him.

The boy had borne it well, only crumbling and sobbing when Doc stooped over and embraced him.

"Don't want no education," he cried. "Don't want none of that stinkin' thought control they give you in schools. I do all right without it."

"But you'll do so much better with it, dear boy," Doc said, tears glistening among the silvery stubble on his chin. "Wisdom is power. The pen is mightier than the sword."

"Next time we face a gang of stickies, I'll keep the Uzi and you can have a drawing pencil, Doc," J.B. called, trying to lighten the moment.

"I know what you mean," Dean said. "Know I'm a real stupe with no book learnin'. Never had time when I was with Rona. Just had to keep moving the whole time."

Ryan had placed his hand on the lad's shoulder. "Right. And that's just what's happening here with us, son. No time to stop and breathe. No time to look at a book or smell a flower or just go for a walk for the joy of it. That's what Mr. Brody's school should give you."

"What if I hate it?"

Jak had grinned. "Then send word. Shout loud and we hear. Might take time, but we'll hear. And come."

There had been a final round of hugs and handshakes, then Dean had scrambled up into the bed of the ramshackle wag, followed by his father.

A crack of the whip and a stream of curses in Spanish, and they were off, driving up the long road that ran south and eastward from Glenwood Springs.

Ryan had agreed with Krysty and J.B. to meet up somewhere around the little ville of Fairplay in two or three days.

Now he waved with his son until the little group of friends had finally blurred into the distance.

DEAN FINISHED EATING a ripe peach, chucking the stone out of the back of the rig into the rutted track. He had the resilience of youth and was in good spirits now, an hour out of the ville.

"Will there be lots of boys in the school, Dad?"

"Probably."

"No stupe girls?"

"Don't know."

Ryan raised his voice above the rattling of the wag and the clattering of the ironbound wheels. "Lemuel?"

"Yo?"

"There girls at the Brody school?"

"Wouldn't know. It's set off the main trail a distance. Believe they got their own gardens and farm and crops. Keep themselves to themselves." He spit a stream of tobacco juice off to the left, smothering a tiny cluster of Deathlands daisies. "Heard Brody had been ill, but that was a good few weeks ago. Probably fine by now. Whoa up, you bastards," Lemuel shouted, lashing the lead mule with the long whip.

"He's good with that whip, isn't he, Dad?"

Lemuel heard Dean and laughed. "Take the balls off a skeeter at twenty paces with it."

"Can I try?"

He laughed louder. "I think not, young man. Likely pluck your own eye out with it." He paused. "Then you'd look even more like your father."

"Dad?"

"Yeah."

They had eaten the rest of the fruit that they'd stolen from Ma's Place before it burned down, though they'd left the lion's share of it with the others, down in the ville.

The sun was sinking beyond the snowcapped peaks away to their right.

"I was with Rona once at some frontier pesthole where they was showing some old vids. Real triple old in flickery black and white. Know the kind of show I mean? On a sheet strung off the rear of a wag."

"Yeah. We used to come across them back in the war wag days with Trader."

"You ever see one of the vids about a couple of pre-dark comics?"

"Don't know."

"One was real fat and the other was real thin. There was no sound with it. No talkin' at all. Only they had to deliver a piano like this one, up this triple-steep flight of steps. And it kept breaking away and clattering all the way down again. They had funny kind of round hats on." Dean laughed. "Hot pipe! It was one of the funniest things I think I ever saw. Rona laughed a lot at it, as well."

The description rang a small bell in Ryan's memory, but he couldn't put a name to the twosome. "Have to ask Doc or Mildred," he said thoughtlessly.

The boy looked at him, his eyes widening, his mouth beginning to tremble. "I'll have to wait a long time to ask them, won't I, Dad? Real long time."

"Yeah. But I reckon there might be one of the teachers up at the Brody school that'll know the answer."

"Will they know everything, Dad?"

"Most everything that's worth knowing."

"When will we get there?"

Ryan shook his head. "Don't know precisely. We had to get around that landslip an hour back. Slowed us down some. Lemuel? When do we get close to the school?"

"Tomorrow evening, if we make good progress. Next morning on if we get slowed again."


"DID YOU REALLY LOVE my mother?"

The sun had vanished and a cold norther had sprung up, bringing a dusting of snow for a half hour. Lemuel had unharnessed the mules, helped by Ryan and Dean, and succeeded in getting them feed and water. The animals were notably ill-tempered, and both father and son took several painful kicks.

Apart from carrying the piano, Lemuel was also well stocked with general supplies, including ample food for the three of them.

They had sat around a crackling fire at the edge of a huge and impenetrable forest to the west of the trail, by a narrow stream that raced into a deep beaver pool. There was a skillet brimming with fatback and beans, two loaves of fresh-baked bread, all of it washed down with some bottles of locally brewed beer.

"Better than..." Dean began, wiping his mouth on his sleeve, stopping when he caught the sudden turn of

the head and angry glare of warning from his father. He
realized that he'd been about to reveal the unsavory fact
that they'd been eating in Ma's Place around the time
that the eatery went up in flames, taking its transvestite
owner with it.

"Better than what, young fellow?" Lemuel asked,
picking at his teeth with a splinter of peeled pine.

"Better than lots of meals I've eaten in lots of other
places," the boy concluded lamely.

"Me too," Ryan agreed.

Afterward they got ready for the night. Lemuel un-
packed some gray blankets. "Best all sleep under the
bed of the wag," he said. "And I got some drinkin'
whiskey to help get off good and sound. Either of you
want some?"

"No thanks," Ryan said. "Boy's a little too young
for it. You don't think we should post a guard?"

"Why?"

"Talk back in the ville of some serious trouble with
a gang of killers up around Harmony. Fire could have
been seen for twenty miles or more on a clear night like
this."

Lemuel considered it, rubbing at the side of his nose,
where a ragged scar showed that someone had once
tried to break a bottle in his eye and narrowly missed.

"No. Fire's still bright enough to keep off most
predators. Bears and wolves likely won't risk it. Anyways, the mules are good guard dogs. Near as good as
geese. Nobody and nothing'll get close enough to harm

us. We can all get to sleep with quiet minds and restful hearts."

Within a quarter hour, the skinner's heavy breathing told Ryan and Dean that the liquor had done its stuff.

There was a ten-cent moon in a dollar sky, glinting through ragged tendrils of high cloud.

Ryan had been about to drop off himself when Dean asked him the question.

"Did I love your mother? Did I really love Sharona? Is that your question, Dean?" It wasn't the first time the boy had asked, and his insecurity tugged at Ryan's heart.

"Yeah. I know you and her didn't have too much quality time with each other. The fighting kept you apart after you got married in that chapel in the valley."

In fact, love and marriage hadn't had very much to do with it, Ryan thought.

Nothing to do with it.

She had been the wife of a particularly evil baron, and Ryan had literally only spent a few minutes in her company.

During a half dozen of those minutes, twelve years ago now, he had coupled with her. Not made love. It had been more like a pair of wild cats rending at each other's flesh, fueled more by hatred than by anything approaching love. In all of Ryan's many sexual encounters since his early teens, there had never been one so powerful and revolting, and memorable, as his time with Sharona Carson.

"Well, did you truly love her, Dad?"

Ryan was lying on his back, between the rear wheels of the creaking wag, looking up through the spokes at the star-spangled velvet of the Colorado sky.

"So many bridges crossed since then, son," he said.

"Does that mean you didn't love her after all?" The disappointment rang clearly in the boy's voice.

"No. Doesn't mean that. I was just thinking back over the long years when I didn't know you existed. I'd thought that Sharona was likely long dead."

"Lost years, Dad."

At that moment Ryan came suddenly to the brink of abandoning his plans for his son's education. He regretted all the wasted time when he and Sharona and the boy had been roaming Deathlands, their paths never crossing. It was almost four years since she'd died of rad sickness, trusting a friend to track down Ryan and deliver the boy up to him.

"Yeah. As far as your mother goes, Dean, I did love her at the time."

"Much as you love Krysty?"

Ryan hesitated. "No. I can't lie to you about that. Krysty's special. The best."

Dean smiled at him, his teeth white in the moonlight. "I knew that before I asked you, Dad. But I'm real glad that you loved Rona. Means a lot to me."

"I know it."

Lemuel muttered in his sleep, turning over, the empty bottle clinking, his stinking coat crackling as he moved, releasing more of its foul miasmic stench.

"Best get to sleep, if you can breathe," Ryan said. "Could be a long day tomorrow."

"Yeah. Guess so. Good night, Dad."

Ryan reached out and squeezed the boy's small hand in his. "Good night, son."

Beyond the circle of red-orange light from the dying fire, death waited.

# Chapter Thirteen

They passed the ruined site of the township of Basalt around ten in the morning, heading steeply up an even more narrow and dangerous trail, some of the time traveling alongside what Lemuel told them was the Fryingpan River.

"Leads up toward Turkey Lake."

"You wouldn't see many turkeys at this height," Ryan said.

The skinner slapped his leg, roaring with laughter. "Got me there, outlander. Turkey comes from the water being a kind of a mix of blue and green. Some good reader and writer said that this was something to do with a turkey, and the name's stayed ever since the long winters."

"Blue and green," Ryan said, puzzled at the odd naming. "Fireblast! It was called Turquoise Lake, not Turkey. Turquoise. Mix of blue and green."

THEY WERE MAKING good time through the tundra. The higher they climbed, the colder it became and the more they could see the tens of thousands of acres of virgin forest stretching below them.

Breakfast had been just after dawn, with a pink mist hanging between the ridges of rock ahead of them. More bacon and more beans and more bread, washed down with a coffee sub that was at least hot and sweet.

Dean returned to the wag, scrambling over the tailgate, after hopping off the side to take a piss. "Think we're going faster than if we'd been walking, Dad?"

"For sure we are."

"You looking forward to seeing Harmony, Dad?"

"Krysty never talked much about it. Some about her mother, Sonja, who taught her how to use the special Earth power of Gaia. And she often mentioned her uncle, Tyas McCann. Not much else beside that."

Dean took a deep breath. "Air tastes good up here."

"Should be healthy for you. And there's not been too much predark rad sickness or bad hot spots in the high mountain country of the Rockies. Most of the nuking around here was short-term, ground-zero stuff."

"Look. There's a moose. Use the Steyr and kill it, Dad. Good roasting meat for tonight if we haven't reached the school. Go on, quick, before it reaches that grove of larches."

Ryan reached instinctively for the rifle, slung across his shoulder, then checked himself. He watched the big animal lope across the bracken, its hooves kicking up splashes of silvery water at every step. "No. We got plenty of food. Never kill for the sake of it or the fun of it."

BY NOON THEY'D REACHED a point where the trail had been cut across the face of a steep cliff, where the old road had been carved away by an ancient landslip.

They had bare rock to their left, and a drop of a couple hundred feet to a hanging valley below them on the right side of the wag.

"Only wide enough for one wag," the boy said, peering doubtfully over the side of the rig. "What happens we meet another wag coming down?"

"Just hope he's smaller than us," Lemuel replied, grinning at Dean. "No, there's a few spaces cut out of the rock, for passing. No problem."

"Be a good place for an ambush," Ryan said. "Get much trouble like that on this trail?"

"Not much. Way back in the old days there was still some mining up here and there used to be big trains with oxen or mules. They used to get whacked so often they carried up to twenty shotguns with them. That was then."

"And this is now," Ryan said automatically, concluding the common Deathlands tag.

"Yeah. This is now."

THE BULLET SPARKED off granite in the trail, a yard or so in front of the lead animal, making it whinny with shrill fear. It reared up, bringing the wag to an instant, jolting halt.

"Hands away from blasters, amigos!"

The voice came from their left, somewhere behind a tumbled mass of rock that broke down into loose scree.

Dean had drawn his blaster, regardless of the warning, looking around for a target.

"Kid wants to see another birthing day, he'd best holster that cannon."

"Put it away, like the man says, Dean," Ryan warned. "Got us coldcocked for a moment."

Lemuel had reined in the team, cursing under his breath in a mix of English and Spanish. He scanned the area, trying to figure out if the ambusher was alone.

"Let's all see if we can stretch right up and scratch them clouds, amigos."

Ryan had eased his position a little, giving himself easier access to his SIG-Sauer and the panga, raising his hands above his head, his face poker-still.

Lemuel hitched the reins around the big brake handle, spitting onto the track, then slowly put up his hands.

"And the kid!"

"Put them up, Dean," Ryan said, then, dropping his voice, added, "And keep triple-red ready."

The boy finally, grudgingly, lifted both his hands to shoulder height.

"That's good." A piercing whistle was answered from around the next bend in the road.

"Got company," Lemuel whispered. "Best sit quiet unless we get a chance at the fuckers."

Ryan agreed with him. The man who covered them with a rifle still hadn't shown himself, not taking any unnecessary risks. The clattering of hooves told of at least a couple more of the robbers.

Two of them appeared leading a spare horse, presumably for the rifleman.

Ryan studied them carefully, trying to gauge the quality of the opposition. That had been one of the first things that Trader had ever taught him.

One man was short, one-armed and wore a wide-brimmed sombrero trimmed with silver conches. He held a Harrington and Richardson .32-caliber revolver, with wooden grips and a blued finish, in his good right hand. He had a hunting rifle slung over his shoulder. Sitting on a pinto pony, he looked relaxed and shared a joke with his swarthy companion.

His companion looked to be of mixed blood, wearing cotton shirt and pants like an Apache. He rode a bay mare, barebacked, and seemed of average height. Like his partner, he appeared to be in his mid to late teens. He, too, had a rifle on his back, and casually held a little vest-pocket Walther Model 9 in his left hand, the 6-round, tiny .25-caliber blaster looking like a child's toy.

"It's okay, Joey-boy!" he shouted. "Got 'em colder than a Thanksgiving turkey. Reckon they seem like real sensible folks. Not lookin' for trouble."

The third man finally revealed himself, precisely where Ryan had located him. He was a good ten years older than the other two, with a stubbled beard and slitted blue eyes. He wore a checked shirt and jeans. The rifle was a Winchester bolt-action type. J.B. could probably have spotted precisely what the model was, but Ryan's knowledge wasn't that specialized. All he noticed was the professional, easy way the man handled the blaster.

He slid down over the scree, keeping his balance, his eyes never leaving the three people in the rig. Once he reached the trail he walked toward them, pausing when he was by the lead mule.

"You heading for Leadville, skinner?" he asked Lemuel.

"Could be."

He wrinkled his nose. "Damnation! How long's that coat been dead? Takes a man's breath away."

Lemuel didn't say anything, his fingers opening and closing as though he were squeezing a coil of steel between them.

"What's he carryin', Joey?" shouted the man with the little automatic.

"Yeah, what're you carryin', skinner? Apart from a kid and a one-eyed crip?"

"Piano."

"Well, now, I reckon there's a few saloons and gaudies and drinkers within fifty miles of here that might pay a few handfuls of prime jack to have them a real predark piano. It *is* predark, ain't it, skinner?"

"Can I put my hands down? I got bad cramps in my shoulders from the cold. You got three blasters on us."

"Sure, skinner."

He spoke to Ryan and Dean. "You two can relax some. No harm's comin' to any of you, if you don't get triple stupe. But we'll likely take the rig, skinner."

Ryan lowered his hands, letting them settle comfortably in his lap, inches away from the butt of the SIG-
Sauer. Dean did the same. The sides of the wag were
high enough for Ryan to feel fairly sure that they hadn't
seen his own handblaster, but assumed he just carried
the Steyr.

"Do I get the wag back when you're finished with
it?" Lemuel asked, his right hand fondling the stock of
the long whip.

"Sure you do," Joey said reassuringly. "We'll ar-
range that in a while. Now, you'd best get down off the
wag."

Every one of the six people on the trail knew that the
bandit was lying. Ryan had seen the half turn of the
head and the nod to his companions, the nod returned
from both of them. Life for the trio of prisoners was
now something to be measured in minutes.

Maybe in seconds.

The bandits would open up as soon as the three of
them were clear of the rig, so that the shooting wouldn't
harm the valuable piano.

"Ready," Ryan whispered to Dean.

"Mebbe those fellers might say something about
losing their piano," Lemuel said, pointing with his left
hand farther up the trail, past the three robbers.

It was the oldest trick in the book.

All of them turned to look, taking their attention
away for a vital half second.

The wag driver was fastest, with Ryan a nanosecond
behind him, followed by Dean.

The whip cracked out with uncanny accuracy. Lemuel had picked Joey, with the rifle, as the danger man, and had gone for him. The steel tip of the lash caught him a fraction below the right eye, slicing open a fold of his cheek as neat and deep as a straightedge razor.

The man screamed in pain, dropping his rifle. He fell to the ground as both hands darted up to try to stem the flood of hot crimson from his gashed face.

The noise startled the horses, as well as the mule team, making them all buck and rear.

The result was total chaos.

Ryan had drawn his SIG-Sauer, leveling it at the bandit with the Harrington and Richardson, reasoning that the bigger blaster was the bigger threat. At less than forty feet, it was a safe enough shot.

But at the very moment that Ryan squeezed the trigger, the mules jerked the rig forward. The reins had fallen to the dirt, and the wag began to slew toward the sheer drop into the canyon on the right.

Ryan's shot caught the pinto pony through the top of its head, above the eyes, so that the skull exploded into the man's face, splattering him with blood, brains and splinters of bone. His shrill scream matched the dying animal's, and he went down with it, trapped by its legs.

The third of the robbers fought for control over his horse, snapping off four popping shots with the little automatic. It was extreme range for shooting, and from the back of a rearing animal a hit was a thousand to one.

But Lemuel's luck was out and the long shot came in. One of the .25-caliber Walther rounds hit him through the throat, above the collar of his coat, knocking him back on the seat. He'd just dropped his lethal whip and was fumbling under the layers of clothing for a hidden blaster.

Lemuel tried to shout, but blood flooded his lungs, choking him. He coughed, dowsing the rear pair of mules with a fine scarlet spray.

The smell of the raw blood spooked them even more, and they bolted. One of the leaders caught Joey with its shoulder and he went down, the front wheels of the loaded wag rolling over his stomach and thighs.

"Going over, Dad!" Dean yelled, his voice cracking as he fired twice at the man on the bay mare, missing both times.

Ryan realized that the boy was right. The mules were off and running, but the reins had snagged, dragging them inexorably toward the drop on the right.

They were within fifteen feet of the last upright bandit, who was now swearing at his mare, urging her out of the way of the charging mules. Ryan balanced himself against the rocking of the rig, firing once, seeing the man go down with blood blossoming from his chest, his arms flung wide.

"Dad! Foot's caught!"

Then the rig began to tilt, seeming to hang sickeningly on the edge of the sighing space for an eternity before the terrified team pulled it right off the trail.

# Chapter Fourteen

As soon as the wag, with Ryan and Dean waving good-bye, had vanished from the outskirts of Glenwood Springs, J.B. suggested they should start looking for transport to follow up the southeasterly trail.

But they quickly came across three problems.

One was that parts of the ville, mainly along the Frontage Road, had suffered badly from an earthquake and few of the buildings in that sector had more than a shell left. Which cut down the options of locating a rig.

Secondly, as the weather had deteriorated, becoming colder, with a short flurry of snow, all of the wild horses and mules that had been feeding quietly on the lower pastures around the ville chose to kick up their heels and trek west out of town, moving parallel to the Colorado River, the ruined railway and the buckled interstate.

But the third unexpected problem was far more dangerous to the five companions.

They'd split up to facilitate the search, and Krysty and Doc had paired up, moving along the side roads, past what looked like a park.

"That might perchance be worth a little investigation," Doc said, pointing with the tip of his swordstick at a rusted wrought-iron sign that had toppled sideways, but was held up by a spreading fig tree. It read, Rio Rancho Bar-B-Q Eats and Livery Stable.

Krysty grinned at the old man. "Sounds a better bet than Ma's Place, Doc."

"Of blessed memory," he said, crossing himself.

There was an overgrown entrance drive, between two rows of fallen picket fencing. The pavement was broken up and covered in weeds, though it still showed occasional smudges of white paint where cars had been parked.

The front of the building was designed to look like a nineteenth-century ranch, constructed from pitched logs with deep-set windows and rifle slits. But as Krysty and Doc drew nearer to the entrance, they could see that this was all a crude facade and that behind the exterior was a single-story concrete building in poor repair.

The doorway gaped like an unfilled tooth, and the row of shattered windows stared like blinded eyes.

"Some outbuildings around back," Krysty said. "Barn with its roof still in place."

The park was quiet, with only a gentle wind blowing through the fluttering leaves of some stately aspens that had seeded themselves at the rear of the restaurant. There were some peculiar shapes in what had to have been the back garden, mostly buried in yellow-flowering creeper and poison ivy, which Krysty finally realized were just the rotting relics of plastic picnic tables and chairs.

Thunder rumbled somewhere to the north of Glenwood Springs, where a bank of dark purple chem clouds threatened a serious storm.

"Long way off," Krysty said.

"I do most fondly hope so. I would not like to think of Ryan and the poor dear lad caught out in the open in inclement weather. I shall not feel totally happy until this year has crawled by and we are reunited once more with Master Dean."

"I'll feel happy when we meet up with Ryan again," Krysty said, running her fingers through her fiery hair, feeling the tightness of the curls.

"Up by Fairplay. One of the things that amazed me, when I was trawled back to the days just before predark, was the way that snowy, remote Colorado had become infinitely fashionable Colorado. Little hamlets that one passed through, like Vail, becoming the abode of the briefly rich and famous."

They were only a few paces from the barn, with one door swinging gently back and forth, when Krysty held up a hand, silently drawing her Model 640 Smith & Wesson double-action .38. Doc raised an eyebrow, pulling out his own Le Mat, thumbing back the scattergun hammer.

"What?" he whispered.

"Someone in there," Krysty stated. "I can feel it. Someone frightened."

"Mayhap I should go on ahead and attempt to seek out this person, while you wait here, Krysty?"

She smiled. "I don't think so, Doc."

She raised her voice. "Come on out, whoever you are. We won't hurt you."

Nothing happened. A tawny bird, with a red breast, took off noisily from the aspens, fluttering north.

"We're coming in. If we do, then someone might get themselves chilled."

"Don't . . ." said a small, quavering voice.

Krysty glanced at Doc. "I got a feeling I know who's hiding in there."

She called, "Come out, child."

The door opened wider and a young girl emerged into the daylight, blinking, hands held up in front of her as though she feared a blow. There was a deep bruise on her face.

"By the Three Kennedys!" Doc shook his head. "The serving wench from Ma's Place. Did you guess that it was her, Krysty? Quite amazing."

"Don't shoot me like you shot Ma."

"We won't."

The little face had sharp, foxy eyes and a pinched mouth. "They don't know you shot Ma, folks here. They think she died in the fire. And me. They get real hanging cross if they know truth."

The underlying message was all too clear.

Doc had holstered his pistol, but he half raised his cane. "You impudent little minx!"

"You can hit me, but that don't hurt. Been hit by Ma, then you been hit by best. One way stop me goin' and tellin' everyone in the ville that you butchered poor Ma."

"And that's doubtless a handful of jack, is it?" Krysty asked gently.

"Could be." She grinned confidently, sticking her tongue out at Doc. "And you better be nice to me, you old fart."

"What?"

"Or you get to dance on air from the hanging tree by river. Yeah, you better be real nice. Maria say kiss my feet, and you better get on your belly and do like I say. Or one word from me..."

Doc's knuckles were white on the silver lion's-head hilt of the swordstick, and his mouth opened and closed like a stranded fish at the girl's rudeness.

Krysty was barely keeping her iron self-control, glancing casually around the garden to make sure that they weren't being watched by anyone.

She spoke to Doc. "You know what Ryan would do if he was here, don't you?"

He nodded, his face like flint. "For once I believe he might be right."

"What you talk about?" the girl asked, edging closer to them. "You don't whisper secrets or else..."

"Can you do it, Doc?"

"In cold blood? Or even when I am angered, as I am now?" He hesitated. "I fear that I could not."

"Mebbe I can." Krysty drew her blaster and pointed it at Maria. "Don't make a sound or you get to go meet Ma again. Understand, child?"

"Sure," she replied, her eyes wide with sudden terror at the realization that her cunning plan was built on shifting sand. There was a faint tinkling sound, and a dark pool appeared in the dust between her bare feet.

"Turn around, quickly," Krysty ordered.

"You shoot me in back of the neck." Her voice was almost inaudible with fear.

"Turn around and lift your hair off your nape. Do it!" A harsh note of command had entered Krysty's voice.

"What is nape?"

"Off the back of your neck," Doc said, doing his best to sound kind and reassuring.

Maria did as she was told, standing in front of Krysty, looking toward the barn, her body trembling.

Krysty brought up the .38, pointing it at the back of the girl's skull.

She sighed, then reversed it and brought it down butt first with a dull thud on the back of Maria's neck, sending her sprawling into the dirt, instantly unconscious.

Doc tapped the ferrule on his cane on a loose stone. "Well done," he said quietly. "I admit that I had thought you were about to . . ."

Krysty smiled grimly. "No, Doc. There's things that Ryan and I are real close about. And there's things where there's a chasm between us."

"Won't hold her for long."

"We could tie her up." Then she had second thoughts. "No. Do it properly and she'd likely die. Might deserve that but . . . Tie her loose and you might as well leave her free."

"Talking's time, Krysty."

"You're right. Have to abandon any idea of finding transport. Meet the others as quick as possible and head out of town on the same trail as Ryan."

"On foot?"

"Have to be. Take what food we got. Going to be a tough hike, Doc."

He shrugged. "What will be, will be, my dear. If it's to be done, then it will be as well to get it done quickly. Let us go unite ourselves with the others."

IN LESS THAN thirty minutes they were all together, walking fast out on old 82, following the route taken by Ryan and Dean.

Jak had been all for going back and quietly strangling Maria, unable to believe that Krysty and Doc had spared her. "Don't you learn anything?" he asked.

"Life is precious, Jak," Krysty replied, defending their actions.

"Our lives!" he said angrily. "She comes around quick and gets mob after us. Be lot more dead than one girl. Real stupe, Krysty. Real stupe, Doc."

By late afternoon the albino teenager was in better spirits, leading the way south and east. He climbed a spur of rock to peer back down the track behind them.

"Nobody coming. No posse pursuit. Mebbe hit her hard enough to put on last train to coast."

There had been a number of marmots, almost as large as domestic dogs, popping up out of burrows as the five friends strode along, and Jak had managed to kill one with a shrewdly thrown knife. He took out another one when it came sniffing inquisitively to see what was happening.

"Least we got meat," he said, skinning the animals as they followed the road.

EVENING CAME SOFTLY, almost unnoticed.

One moment they had been walking at a steady rate up a steep section of the trail, with woods close in around them. Only a couple of minutes later, so it seemed, twilight had come and gone and they needed to stop for the night.

Jak and J.B. collected plenty of wood for a good fire, setting it blazing as they cooked the butchered meat.

"Wonder how far ahead of us the others are?" Krysty said musingly.

Jak pointed ahead and a little to the left. "Thought saw pinprick of fire," he said. "Could be them."

They all stared into the clinging blackness, but could see nothing.

Krysty found it vaguely reassuring to know that they were, at least, on the same stretch of trail.

Though she slept restlessly, plagued by anxiety dreams.

# Chapter Fifteen

Falling.

The wag rolled sharply to the right, the first pair of mules already shrieking like tortured humans as the trail vanished from beneath their hooves and they began to plummet over the edge.

Dean's face was taut with panic, yelling for his father to help him, to free his trapped foot.

And all around was death and injury.

Lemuel lay sprawled back across the seat, blood flowing freely from the wound in his throat.

Joey, leader of the bandits, moaned on the trail, his face bleeding, his body crushed by the wheels of the heavy rig. One of his companions called for someone to free him from where he was trapped under his dead horse.

The piano squealed in protest as the wag began to twist and flex and bend, the weight of the mules pulling it over the sheer edge of the steep drop.

"Dad!" Dean's voice was high and thin, his eyes on his father's face.

Ryan was hanging on with his left hand to the top of the piano, saving himself from plunging over the wrong side of the rig. He could see the taut cord that had caught his son's ankle, trapping it between the piano and the back of the seat, where Lemuel's corpse was slumped sideways.

The problem was that his razor-sharp panga was sheathed on the left side of his hip, and he was holding the SIG-Sauer in his right hand. There was no way that he could holster the blaster and draw the panga without going over the edge.

There was screaming bedlam all around him as he made his lightning decision.

He steadied the automatic and fired.

The first round frayed the cord and tore through the wag bed, knocking out a splintered hole. The second shot hit the rope with an ace on the line, severing it with a loud twanging sound.

"Get out!" Ryan yelled, trying to work his way around the bulk of the upright piano, held on the ravine side of the wag, the side that was already beginning to dip sharply down, ready for the big plunge.

He glimpsed Dean flying out the safe side, though he didn't see him land.

The world was spinning.

With a desperate acrobatic twist and lunge, Ryan hurled himself off the tailgate, landing clumsily on his back and shoulder, the impact making him drop the SIG-Sauer. Out of the corner of his eye he caught the last of the wag as it slithered ponderously over the brink.

Ryan would never forget to the end of his days the noise as it fell, a noise that seemed to last forever and ever.

The mules, helpless, cried like children at their rushing doom, and then came the sickening crash of wood, flesh and bone, and the hideous jangle of the piano as it smashed to pieces among the sharp-edged boulders, spilling its last chords in a thunderous finale.

After the echoes had bounced their way into stillness, the morning was almost silent.

Ryan fumbled for his blaster and stood, brushing dirt off his coat and pants. He saw that Dean was also on his feet, gripping his own 9 mm Browning Hi-Power.

And their attackers?

Joey had finally stopped moving, thick clots of dark blood oozing from his open mouth, crushed to death by the iron wag wheels.

The bandit that Ryan had shot in the chest was also dead, lying spread-eagled in the rutted dirt, one hand clawed shut on a fistful of barren dust.

Which left the one survivor.

Trapped beneath his dead horse, the one-armed man had stopped wriggling, staring up at Ryan and Dean. His revolver had vanished, and his elegant sombrero had become trampled and bloodied and muddied.

"Let me go, mister. I can't do you no harm. I just went along with them."

"Man carries a gun and rides with coldheart killers, then he shouldn't look for any other ending," Ryan said. "You die with the company you kept." He shot the young man cleanly through the forehead.

JOEY'S HORSE HAD FLED back up the trail, the sound of its clattering hooves fading slowly in the immense silence. Ryan stooped to slit the throat of the fallen bay mare, once he'd seen that it had shattered its fetlock in its fall.

"Shame," he said. "If that horse had stayed around and the little mare hadn't crippled herself, we could've been a good spell on our way to the school well before dark."

"We leaving the bodies here, Dad?"

"I guess so. We could heave them down the ravine after Lemuel and the piano. Not much point, though. Leave it all like it is. J.B. and Jak should be able to read what's gone down here. They'll see our tracks heading southward, clear as day."

The boy brightened, looking around him. "Wow, that was a triple-bright light, Dad. Shooting out the rope that got my leg caught was...well, it was the greatest. I thought for a bit that we was all done for. But you was so cool and in control. You *knew* we'd be all right."

"You should learn to say 'we *were* done for,' not '*was* done for,' Dean."

He didn't reveal to his son his own mind-numbing fear that they had all been going remorselessly to hell with the piano.

IT WAS ONLY WHEN they were forced to resort to walking that they realized how fast they'd been going with the mule team.

"How long've we gone?" Dean asked, kneeling by a tiny stream that dashed its way across the tracks, cupping his hands to drink from the icy clearness.

"Since the ambush?"

"Yeah."

"Hour." He checked the chron. "Well, call it about an hour twenty."

"That all?"

"Sure is. After you with the water." The boy wiped his mouth on his sleeve and straightened, allowing his father to take his place by the bubbling stream.

"Seems longer. If I look back down the trail, where it bends in that sharp sort of fork, I can still see the dead horses and men." He moved to the unmarked edge of the trail, staring down. "And I can still spot the broke-up wag and mules. Doesn't seem very far away from us."

"Mildred has an old predark saying about how times passes quickly when you're having a good time. I guess the downside of that's true, as well."

THEY DIDN'T SEE another living soul, but they found mute evidence that Joey and his two desperadoes had been working their business a little higher up the trail.

The weather was changeable, and as they came around a snakeback turn in the trail, there was a drop in the temperature, the sky grew darker and hailstones began to patter down, bouncing off the rocks.

And there, lying at the side of the trail, was a dead donkey and the bodies of an old man and a girl, barely into her teens. It was only when they drew near enough to peer more closely at the naked girl that they could be certain of her sex.

The man, who, they presumed, was probably her grandfather, lay huddled on his side, a small black hole just in front of his ear, the silver hair scorched by a powder burn. His clothes were in disarray, all of his pockets turned inside-out.

Someone had slit the girl's throat, and it was obvious from the bruises and congealed blood around her mouth and between her thighs that she had been brutally used before being slaughtered.

Her face was turned to the sky, her eyes wide open. Dean noticed that hailstones were striking into her staring eyes and winced with horror. Looking around, he saw a kerchief that had been ripped from the old man's pockets and he unfolded it and placed it over the girl's face.

"We can't bury them, can we, Dad?" Dean said, answering his own question. "Course, we got no spades. Nothing to dig with." When he turned away from the bodies, Ryan noticed a new hardness to Dean's face, as though the experience had aged him.

ONLY A FEW MINUTES of daylight remained when Ryan spotted a small, neat sign, set in concrete, off to the left of the Leadville trail. Nicholas Brody School, Twelve Miles, was all that it said, in rectangular yellow lettering.

Ryan knew that road signs, even before the long winters, had always been fair game for any trigger-happy drunk motoring by. But this sign was virginal and untouched.

"We make it tonight?"

"No way, Dean. This part of the Rockies got grizzly and wolf running wild, as well as cougars. And it used to be a breeding ground for muties, back in my war wag days. No, we'll find somewhere for the night. Start fresh in the morning. That way we'll both make a better impression."

DEAN SLEPT BADLY. He had lain awake for two or three hours, working over in his mind the fact that this was probably the last night he'd spend with his father for at least a year.

There had been a gas station on the same side of the road as the sign for the school. The pumps were long gone, hacked off their squat bases for the scrap-metal content, and the cash office had all its windows smashed. But it still retained its flat concrete roof, stained by nearly a hundred years of Rocky Mountain winters, and all four walls.

As Dean had lain there, aware of his father's steady breathing at his side, he had caught the eerie sound of a wolf pack on the hunt, their keening rising and falling, ending in the exultant, unmistakable noise of their making a kill.

They sounded as if they were only a mile or so away, but distance was difficult to judge among the snowy peaks.

Finally, sleep had come.

But it was an unquiet, uneasy sleep, disturbed by gibbering phantoms.

The dream that finally jerked the boy awake, sweating, crying out, had him in a schoolroom. Then there were rows of desks but no other pupils, a blackboard covered in arcane squiggles that made no sense at all to him and a teacher.

A bunch of columbines sat on his desk, and a stuffed lark stood on a shelf behind his head.

The teacher was elderly, his clothes disheveled. He had white hair and had cut himself shaving, with dried blood mottling his chin.

He beckoned to Dean, indicating a box that lay across the desk, about four feet in length. As the boy drew nearer, he was aware of the smell of corruption and he stopped.

"Come on, son," the teacher said with a kindly smile. "You want to learn, don't you?"

"So my father'll be proud of me," the boy replied. "Yeah, I do."

"Then come and we'll carry on with the biology lesson." The teacher picked up a metal pointer with a needle-sharp silver end. "Come closer and you can see what I'm doing."

Dean dragged his feet, the sound harsh, like flints rubbing together, approaching close enough to see that the box had its lid open, but not quite close enough to make out what it contained.

"Come, come. Let me point out to you the main features of the human anatomy."

Now Dean could see what was in the box—the naked body of a very beautiful girl, about thirteen years old, with long blond curls.

"Here is her nose and her mouth, for scenting and eating," the teacher said, jabbing at each part of her face with the metal pointer. "And these are for seeing."

He tapped hard on the open, staring eyes with the silvered end of the pointer, which clicked loudly, as though it had made contact with steel.

"No," Dean said in a calm, conversational tone. "Don't do that, you cruel bastard."

Suddenly he screamed, "Don't!"

The yell woke Ryan, who held his son tightly, until the shaking and the fear had passed and the boy was sleeping quietly again.

# Chapter Sixteen

That second night saw Krysty, Doc, J.B., Mildred and Jak not far behind Ryan and Dean.

They had passed the ruins of Basalt, about twenty-five miles from Glenwood Springs.

The walking wasn't all that tough, despite the occasional hard detour to get around an earth slip, but the altitude was a problem for them all.

Particularly for Doc.

He had a nosebleed late on the first afternoon and a couple more during the second day. The last one was so bad that Mildred made him sit down and rest, his back against a fallen boulder, his head tilted, while she tried to staunch it with his kerchief, which had been soaked in meltwater.

The blood came out in lumps, rather than in a trickle, splashing on the trail, staining his boots, and it took nearly a quarter hour to finally stop the flood, by which time the old man was looking even more pale-skinned than usual.

"Ready to go," he said.

"Fine," Mildred said, holding his wrist. "Soon as your pulse stops fluttering and gets someplace close to normal, we can all get on our way."

"I swear that I do most sincerely pity the poor devils who found themselves your patients, Dr. Wyeth. I have often wondered whether your mysterious freezing 'accident' might not have been contrived by a cabal of your colleagues and patients. Had I been one of them on that December day in 2000, I would happily have passed the ice myself."

"Just stop talking and take it easy, will you? That was a bad nosebleed."

"Lack of acclimation," he said. "Give me another few days and I shall be a cross between a young gazelle and spring-heeled Jak himself."

"I don't honestly think we've got all that many days, Doc," Krysty said gently. "Should meet with Ryan either tomorrow or the day after. Then comes the hard time. Things could easy slip downhill from then on."

"How far Fairplay from here?" Jak asked.

Krysty shook her head. "Not sure. I was only in my teens when I left Harmony. I'd guess around fifty miles or so. We'll go some higher than here."

"Take us three days, this speed," the albino commented, looking at the mountains around them.

"Then we'll meet him in two or three days, Jak. One way or another, we'll meet up."

J.B. BLINKED his eyes open, aware of someone moving close to the dead ashes of the previous night's fire. His right hand felt for the Uzi until he caught the glimpse of the dawn light on the flaming hair.

"Krysty?" he whispered, reaching for his spectacles from their hiding place beneath his fedora, where they'd been protected from the night chill.

"Yeah. It's all right." She knelt by him, keeping her voice low to avoid waking the others.

"You see or hear something? Or feel something?"

"Not sure." She sat, tucking her knees up under her chin and hugging herself. "Sure is cold at this height."

"Yeah. Heard Doc get up to take a leak a couple of times. His teeth were chattering so rad-blasted loud I thought he'd wake everyone up."

Krysty laughed softly. "Poor old Doc. He does his best to keep up."

"And he's good at finding some reason why we should stop for five. 'My dear friends, I fear that I have a pebble in my boot.' Or, 'I think that the ladies look a touch fatigued. I would not be averse to helping them by taking a short break.' You know the kind of stuff?"

Krysty smiled again. "You got him there. Never admits he wants to take a break because he's an old man and he can't cut it the same anymore. Kill him to own up to that."

"Hope I'm in such good shape when I get to be 250 years old." The Armorer had been polishing his glasses while they talked, and he squinted through them before he perched them on the end of his sharp nose. He looked around him. "Still some way off full dawn," he said.

"Yeah. Sorry I disturbed you. I don't sleep well without Ryan at my side."

"He'll be fine."

"Come on now, J.B., that's just a knee-jerk reaction. Ryan's not a god or a superman, like something out of a pulp novel or a comic. He's flesh and blood and bone, and he's not indestructible. I know it and he knows it."

"Only delivering the kid to a school for a spell. Shouldn't meet up with the old man with the scythe on a simple errand like that."

"When I was about fourteen, in Harmony ville, there was a girl called Penny Teller. She was walking across the street carrying a pencil. The hem of her dress was unpicked, and it snagged and she tripped. As she fell the pencil went clean into her eye and into her brain, and she was dead in ten seconds. Don't try and cheer me up making jokes about dying, J.B., please. I've seen more than enough of it."

"SOMEONE'S FIXED the highway up," Dean said. "Been graded recently."

"Not only that. The edge is marked with a line of round stones. Seems like someone's taken a lot of trouble to make the road to the school look good and neat."

"How far did the sign say?"

"Twelve miles. Only gone about a mile so far."

It was a predark blacktop, but it showed little sign of chronic deterioration like most of the stretches of highway throughout Deathlands. This was smooth with hardly any breakup or buckling, and most of the vegetation at the sides had been trimmed back.

There was a dense forest of Colorado blue spruce on the right side of the trail, with some scrubby mixed conifers stretching out on the left. The road wound from side to side, rising and falling, then rising again, making it impossible for them to see any great distance ahead.

By Ryan's guesstimate they'd gone about half the twelve miles when they spotted a larger notice, standing proud and foursquare on the left side of the road.

"Not very friendly," Dean said, reading it.

" 'Warning. Proceed at your peril. This road is private and goes only to the Nicholas Brody School. Unless you have business there, turn back now. This means you! Woods are man-trapped, and anyone invading is hostile and is likely to be attacked without warning and killed. Stay on the road until challenged. But only if you have business. If you don't, then turn around and get out!' "

"No excuse for going on and getting chilled after that," Ryan commented.

"Long as you can read."

It was a fair point from Dean. In Ryan's experience, only about one in eight of the population of Deathlands was functionally literate. Trader himself had been unable to read or write, though he had always tried to conceal that from people.

"Right. Man who wrote that notice doesn't sound like the kind of person would listen to many excuses."

"Think it's Nick Brody, Dad?"

"Seems a fair guess. But I don't—"

"Then he sounds a triple-tough mother, Dad. Not the sort to take shit. Not Nick."

"Mebbe. But listen, Dean."

"Yeah? What is it, Dad?"

"Might be best to call him Mr. Brody. Not Nick. Show him some respect right from the start. Might be he'll like you to call him Nick, but it's best to start off on the right foot. Know what I mean?"

The boy nodded, the wind ruffling his dark, curly hair, his eyes fixed piercingly on his father. "Whatever you say, Dad."

"Let's step it out. Should arrive there ready for a noontime meal, if we get it right."

"THERE'S SOMEONE watching us, Dad."

Ryan stopped, his hand feeling for the butt of the SIG-Sauer. He cursed himself under his breath for letting his attention wander. His mind had been filled with thoughts of saying farewell to his son, and he had let his combat sense sleep as they walked along the road—the road that they knew carried dire warnings for trespassers or outlanders.

"Where?"

"Ahead and to the left. Caught the flash of sunlight off a glass on the edge of the spruces."

"Can't see it."

"It's there, Dad."

"Believe you."

"What do we do?"

"Keep walking. Not much point in turning back when we've come this far. Can't be more than a couple of miles from here to the school. Must be set among the trees over there," he said, pointing toward the north.

The place where Dean had seen the glint of light was about four hundred yards ahead.

Ryan took that side of the blacktop, the rifle across his shoulder, his right hand never far from the butt of the SIG-Sauer. Dean was beside him, on the other side of the road.

They had closed to within a hundred yards, and there was still no sign of any action.

"Dad?"

"Yeah." Ryan's nerves were stretched with the tension of knowing that something was likely to happen at any moment and not having any idea what that something might be.

"If anything happens, least we're together."

"That's some consolation, Dean. It truly is. But I don't think anything's going to happen."

It was almost a replay of their run-in on Lemuel's wag with the three killers.

A blaster was fired from out of the spruces, the noise muffled by the trees, the bullet kicking a chunk out of the pavement a yard or so in front of Ryan's feet. It ricocheted off and whined into the distance.

"Far as you go," a man's voice called.

# Chapter Seventeen

"Wag's smashed to shit on rocks. Mules all dead. Can only see one body."

Jak had shaded his pink eyes against the sun, now setting low on the western horizon. He stood perched on the very edge of the deeply rutted trail, staring into the shadowed drop to the deep ravine on the right.

"Who?" Krysty asked as she joined him, her legs feeling oddly stiff, as if her knees had become filled with ice.

"Mule skinner. Recognize coat. Was coyotes there but run off when saw me."

The bodies of the three men and two horses behind Krysty were also showing signs of having been raided by predators. A pair of raw-necked vultures had flapped reluctantly from the feast as Krysty and the others appeared around the bend in the track, one of them with a long string of gristle and flesh dangling from its yellow, hooked beak.

All of the men and both the pinto and the bay had lost their eyes, plucked neatly from swimming sockets. Much of the soft tissue of the men's faces had also gone, rendering them unrecognizable, though it was obvious from their clothes and their builds that none of them was Ryan or Dean.

"How long?" J.B. asked, studying the scene of slaughter with a professional interest.

Mildred had knelt and slipped her hand inside the collar of the plaid shirt on one of the corpses. "Cold. Several hours. Think that this all is Ryan's work?"

Doc had sat on a seat-sized boulder, wiping sweat from his forehead with his kerchief. "Where he walks, death steps in his shadow," he said quietly. "Flowers die and the little children weep in the streets."

"For Gaia's sake, shut it, Doc!" Krysty snapped. "Ryan doesn't bring death, but it sure seems to seek him out."

He half bowed to her. "Mea culpa, my dear lady. The blame is mine, and you are quite correct. It is just that I am tired, and I had not looked to end the day at the center of a charnel house. And I'm old and foolish."

"Going for the sympathy and self-pity vote, Doc?" Mildred asked interestedly. "Not like you. Must still be the effects of the altitude."

J.B. and Jak had finished a hasty look around the slaughter scene.

"Way I read it," the Armorer began, "and correct me, anyone, if they think I'm wrong. Wag stopped here." He pointed with the muzzle of the Uzi. "Deep ruts. Ambushed. Probably shots fired from cover to stop them. Then there was talk after two men arrived on horseback. Leading a third animal that isn't here.

Though there's hoof marks leading up the trail to the east. Must've gotten away."

"Can't tell who started it. Ryan or Dean or driver shot pinto through head. Another bullet took him out," Jak said, pointing to one of the corpses. "Wag rolled over that one. Last one chilled was trapped by horse."

J.B. nodded at Jak's re-creation of the scene, walking to the gouged ruts that showed where the rig had finally toppled off the trail, pointing at the marks.

"Shooting spooked the mules. Something like that. Could be the bandits shot Lemuel. Just before it went, you can see two sets of prints. Small ones are Dean's. Stake my life on that. Other marks are probably Ryan jumping for it, landing awkwardly and rolling over. Just here."

"And afterward?" Krysty had walked past the bodies of men and beasts. "These are their prints, aren't they? Heading on up the track."

Jak joined her, stopping for a quick glance. "No doubt," he said. "Both up and walking good. Almost certain not wounded. Fine."

"We should go on a little farther and then find somewhere to camp for the night." The Armorer looked around at the carnage. "Hope we don't find any more corpses."

THE BODIES OF THE GIRL, the old man and the donkey were only a little farther up the trail.

The vultures were there again, one of them standing its ground when its fellows flew away, beak jutting out as it squatted on the girl's chest, its crimson eyes glaring at the human invaders.

"Fuck you," Mildred said, drawing her Czech target revolver and shooting it through the skull, sending it toppling over in a flapping bunch of feathers.

"What in God's name is happening on this benighted mountain?" Doc said. "There is death rampant wherever one looks. What villains committed this crime?"

J.B. answered him. "My guess is that these bodies are a little older than the three men and the animals. Way I read it—" he peered at the trampled hoof marks and boot prints "—way I read it those three guys did this. Raided the old man and took their funning with the girl. Then they were moving down the trail when they ran into Ryan and Dean and the wag, and found themselves all buying the farm."

"Serve them right," Krysty said. "And Ryan and Dean passed by here?"

Jak had walked a few steps farther on, checking the ground. "Been hailstorm. Ground marked. But here's Dean walking and...over here's Ryan. Both moving up."

"Could they not have paused to inter these two wretched cadavers? It is so unseemly and beastly to lie here like discarded rubbish."

Mildred had been checking the bodies. "Difficult to be sure, but I put their passing an hour or so before the three men down the trail." She straightened. "The girl was raped and then butchered. You said why not bury them, Doc? Look around. We got bare rock and thin ground cover. Bracken and then the trees. Unless Ryan had been carrying picks and shovels, they could have taken a week over grave digging.''

The old man blew his nose on his kerchief. "You are correct, my dear Dr. Wyeth. As you so often are."

"Why, thank you, Doc."

"But it makes scant difference to my sickness of spirit and despair of the soul. To see such scenes makes one realize that Deathlands is damnably well named."

"STAND WHERE YOU ARE and keep your hands away from any of those pretty blasters!"

"Do like he says, Dean. And don't make any sudden movements. Stay loose."

"Sure, Dad. Think he's from the school?"

"Could be."

The voice came again from the shadows beneath the blue spruces. "And cut the gabbing."

Ryan half turned toward the hidden speaker. "Name's Ryan Cawdor. This is my son, Dean. Come up here to enroll him in the Nicholas Brody School."

"Oh yeah?" Mocking laughter echoed from the opposite side of the trail, near where Dean was standing. "You don't have the look of a fond parent, outlander. Do he, Joel?"

"He looks to me like a hired killer, Ahab. That's what he looks like to me."

"You coming out so we can all get on, or do we stand here all day?"

There was a silence after Ryan's angry shout.

Far above them a bald-headed eagle circled effortlessly on a thermal. Ryan looked up at it, wishing the standoff could be quickly resolved. He was feeling tired, ready for the possibility of some food and a hot bath.

"How old's the kid?"

"Eleven."

"Where do you come from, stranger?"

Ryan waved his hand in a circle. "All around," he replied. "Can we get a move on?"

"Now, now," Ahab tutted. "Could be it's all right and we'll escort you to Mr. Brody. Only, you seen the signs?"

"Have to be blind to miss them."

"Sure. We keep this place tighter than a duck's ass. Been word about that there's some sort of gang in the region. Farther the far side of Leadville."

"Toward Fairplay?" Ryan asked, thinking of the rumors they'd heard about Harmony.

"Yeah. You know anythin' about it?"

"Like you. Heard the word."

After another short silence a man appeared from the trees on Ryan's side, carrying a Browning 71 rifle, the replica of the famous Winchester 71. He was casually dressed in a light blue shirt, and black jeans that were tucked into work boots. He wore a sun-bleached Stetson.

Ryan was immediately struck by Ahab's professional air of casual competence.

If he was one of the sec men for the school, then it meant Brody ran a tight establishment.

"Come on out, Joel. Think we might have us a live one here, after all."

The screen of scrubby bushes parted and the other guard appeared, similarly uniformed, carrying an unidentifiable remake rifle.

"You best give us your blasters... What did you say your name was?"

"Ryan Cawdor. My son, Dean. And I don't give up my blasters to anybody."

Joel and Ahab exchanged glances, both of them obviously trying to calculate the odds on pushing the issue, both deciding that the odds weren't that great in their favor.

Ahab nodded and grinned. "Guess this wouldn't happen if you weren't genuine. Best come along with us, Mr. Cawdor. And you, Dean, and you can meet up with Mr. Brody. He's always pleased to welcome new pupils, isn't he, Joel?"

"Sure is. Yeah, he sure is."

DOC HAD ANOTHER VIOLENT nosebleed that brought their day to a premature end only a short distance beyond the bodies of the old man and the girl.

There was a pocket of old, tired snow not far off the trail, and Mildred used some of it, packed into the swallow's-eye kerchief, to staunch the flow. But Doc was knocked back by the incident, sitting and resting his back against a weathered tree, seeming dizzy and disorientated.

"Little Rachel once had a bad nosebleed. Was it El Paso? Or Carlsbad? I disremember the place, but there was a beautiful swimming pool, the water limpid and sparkling. My dearest daughter was about to plunge in when I noticed that her neck, chest and stomach were covered in blood. For a moment my heart stopped in midbeat until I realized it was only from her adorable little pixie nose. She jumped in and the blood clouded the water, until I couldn't see her at all. Not at all."

Mildred was sitting with him while J.B., Jak and Krysty scavenged for wood for a fire.

She held his hand, feeling him trembling. "Be fine soon, Doc. Altitude is a son of a bitch to get used to. Soon have a blaze going and you can relax. Eat some fruit. Catch up on sleep. You'll wake up tomorrow like a new man."

He looked at her, his pale blue eyes unusually solemn. "That is not what I wish for, Mildred. I beg you not to tell the others. Communicable despair, don't you know? But most nights I go to bed, I pray the Lord my soul to take."

"I don't get you, Doc."

"There is not a night of my life that I don't wish to be taken in my sleep. So that I can rejoin my beloved Emily and my two little dear ones. But every morning I awake and it is all the same. I am here and now, and they are there and gone."

"I sometimes feel the same about my folks, Doc. The thought that everyone I ever knew has been dead for at least twenty or thirty years. Most of them would have died in the nukecaust, anyway. But I get over grieving." She paused. "Most of the time."

"I try to send my poor prayers across time and space to Emily," Doc said shakily. "Tell her that the breeze she feels is my breath upon her cheek. Tell her that I am waiting to join her. Not to grieve me gone. But it's all..."

His mind wandered again, and the sentence flowed away in the late-afternoon sunlight.

"THERE IT IS."

An area of forest had been cleared and they had passed through cultivated fields, some with horses and cattle, one with a large herd of pigs. Then they came upon a massive vegetable garden that had to have covered twenty acres.

And beyond it, set on a rise in the ground alongside a crystal lake, was the school.

"Looks like a fort, Dad," Dean observed.

"That's because it is a fort, young fellow," Ahab said. "Self-contained with its own well and storerooms. We could withstand a siege for a month or more."

The school looked as if it had originally been a stone farmhouse, then had been extended with some concrete blocks, the whole thing finally covered in fresh adobe. There were slits for rifles and heavy shutters of steel that could be closed quickly and bolted from the inside.

A large flagpole was set in the center of a courtyard out front, with a flag flying from it.

"That's not the Stars and Bars, is it?" Ryan asked, shading his eye.

"Stars and Stripes, Dad." Dean grinned. "Even I know that, and I haven't even started at school yet."

A few figures worked out in the fields, a couple of them rounding up some goats. But the main building seemed completely deserted.

"Where are the children?" Ryan asked.

"Most at lessons in the classrooms," Ahab replied. "This time of day."

"Those are Mr. Brody's students, as well," Joel said, pointing with his rifle. "He believes in some active outdoor work to keep the body and mind both healthy."

"Don't fancy shoveling goat shit, Dad," Dean muttered. "Not what I call learning."

"You do what Mr. Brody tells you to do, son. He knows best about education."

"He sure does, Mr. Cawdor," Joel agreed. "And that goes for everyone who works here."

"But you'll be seeing all of that for yourselves," Ahab said.

"Looking forward to that, aren't we, Dean?" He saw that the boy was staring at the range of buildings. "Aren't we, Dean?"

"Oh, yeah. Sure are, Dad. Sure are."

# Chapter Eighteen

Ryan had received a decent education as a young boy in the ville of Front Royal, at the instruction of his father, Baron Titus Cawdor.

But the few hours he spent with Dean in the Colorado school of Nicholas Brody stretched his confidence almost to the breaking point. He was constantly worried that one of the teachers would spring some question of history or geography or reckoning at him and reveal his ignorance. Knowing that grammar was a particular weakness of his, as Krysty was ceaselessly pointing out, he took great pains with every sentence, trying to avoid any foolish mistakes, trying to think through what he was going to say before it slipped from his mouth. He examined each word with the suspicion of a timber wolf scenting poisoned bait.

Ahab and Joel left them at the heavily fortified front gate, iron-studded with a vanadium-steel inset for added strength. It would have taken a heap of implode grens or a small nuke to have broken it down.

They were turned over to an older man, wearing the same casual uniform, who led them wordlessly through a large, airy entrance hall and along a short corridor toward a reception room where Ahab had told them they'd meet Nicholas Brody.

On the way they passed two half-glassed classroom doors, and Ryan peeked into both of them as they walked by.

One had a mixed class of six or seven children, looking to be about twelve. They sat at desks, staring attentively at a blackboard where a long-haired male teacher was pointing to a map of Deathlands.

The second room had about the same number of older children, around fifteen, mostly boys, who were writing busily in notebooks while a middle-aged woman in a white blouse and a tweed skirt walked up and down between the desks, dictating from a large, dark blue textbook.

Dean was too short to see through the glass in the doors and walked happily along behind the sec man.

Ryan felt a familiar chill in his guts at the sight of the classrooms, and he wondered whether this really was such a good idea after all.

NICHOLAS BRODY WAS a very large man with a neat beard who spoke in strangely convoluted speech patterns, with a slight hesitancy that never became a stammer.

"So this is another seeker at the well of knowledge, is it?" he said, shaking hands with Dean. "Another apostle to carry the sword at sunset against the swamping print death of the universe. Welcome, thrice welcome, Dean Cawdor."

Despite his slightly off-putting way of talking, Ryan took an instinctive liking to the man and felt more relaxed about leaving Dean. The boy also seemed to like Brody and laughed at some of his more obscure pronouncements, though he obviously didn't understand them.

Brody handed them both a prospectus of the school, telling them how many children were there and how they were divided into groups or "houses."

"I base it frankly and openly upon what used to be the classical English public school system," he said, "which offered the finest education in the history of the world—apart from a strange belief in the powers of freezing showers, cold toilet seats and a flogging every morning. We have disposed of those aspects here at the Nicholas Brody School."

"We play games?" Dean asked.

"Sir," Brody prompted gently. "I and my male staff are referred to as 'sir' and female members as 'ma'am.' That does not apply to the members of the security service. And we do indeed play games."

Ryan was glad that his son hadn't breezed in calling the man "Nick."

RYAN WAS OFFERED A BED for the night, as well as supper. "I assume that you will join myself and the members of my peripatetic team of pedagogues in burying our snouts in the trough of sustenance. You may then bid a fond farewell to young Dean in the morning and leave him to us." He patted Ryan on the shoulder.

"That may be done in conditions of privacy as our experience is that it can be a touch emotional with watering of the glim ducts on every side. At least the lad's mother is not here. There is a Mrs. Cawdor...?"

"She died about five years ago."

"My condolences. Rest assured that the boy will be well treated here. If you have any questions...? Of course, you may visit us at any time. Any time at all, even if there be a mystical conjunction of the planets and a solar eclipse, linked to a revolt among Brazilian sheep shaggers. It matters not a tittle or a jot, Mr. Cawdor. Come when you wish."

RYAN AND DEAN HAD a little time together before supper when they were in the dormitory that the boy would share with five other lads of about the same age.

The furnishings were spare but solid. Ryan sat on one of the firm beds. "What do you think?" he asked.

The boy sat facing his father, looking suddenly younger and much more vulnerable. "I think it'll be all right," he said finally.

"I like Brody. Seems a straight arrow kind of a man. You back him and he'll back you."

Dean nodded. "I like him, though he talks funny some of the time."

"You don't mind wearing the uniform?" This was simply a light colored shirt and dark jeans. There were blouses and skirts for the girls. "Seems comfortable."

"Guess so. How do I get it?"

"Brody said you'd have to see the housekeeper, Mrs. Miggens, in the morning and she'll provide you with everything you need. Clothes and pens and books and stuff."

"How are you paying for all this, Dad?"

Ryan smiled at him. "That's for me to know and you to guess, son."

"Must be a shitload of jack."

"I wouldn't use too many expressions like that, if I were you, Dean."

"Sorry, but..."

"Don't worry about the jack. I've been careful over the last few months. Took it where I found it."

"Stole it, Dad?" Dean sounded shocked.

"Let's just say that Mr. Brody is content with the arrangements for payments, and so am I."

"Fine."

"You got any questions, Dean?"

There was a long pause. Somewhere outside the room an electric bell rang twice.

"Must mean supper," the boy said, standing.

RYAN WAS SHOWN to a seat at the head table in the dining room, with the members of staff of the school. He found himself settled between the middle-aged lady with the tweed skirt and a young man with slightly slanted eyes.

He saw Dean led by Brody to one of the pupils' tables and introduced to the boys on either side of him.

But he was distracted by the woman touching his arm. "I'm Natalie Davenport, and I have the singular delight of pounding mathematics into these eager young skulls."

"Ryan Cawdor. That's my boy, Dean."

The man on the other side joined in. "Chris Akemoto. I do what I can with the sciences. How old's your son?"

"Eleven."

"Good age to come here. Give us a year and you won't recognize him."

Natalie smiled. "Probably what Mr. Cawdor fears, Chris. But we are not like the Jesuits."

"The who?" Ryan asked, feeling the ground turning to water beneath his feet.

"They were a strict religious order. Their boast was that if they were given a child at, I think it was ten, then he would be theirs for life. We make no such claim."

Nicholas Brody had taken his place at the head of their table, and he tapped a spoon on a water glass. Everyone, staff and pupils alike, rose to their feet, Ryan a mere half beat behind everyone else.

"We welcome a new pupil, Dean Cawdor, to our community. We will all make him welcome and offer him the hand of friendship. Let us pray." Ryan closed his eye and bowed his head. "Merciful Lord, bless this our home and these our endeavors. Let us render to no man evil for evil. Strengthen the fainthearted. Let us learn justice and loyalty. And let us relish this our supper. In the name of the Father and the Son and the Holy Ghost, now and forever, amen.''

"Amen." Ryan joined in the chorus, squinting from beneath the lowered lid to watch Dean, seeing that the boy had taken his part in the small ritual.

TO RYAN'S GREAT RELIEF, the conversation around the top table wasn't at a high intellectual level. Quite the reverse. The staff was far more concerned with the institutionalized trivia of who had done what and said what. Through it all, Natalie had endeavored to bring Ryan into the talk whenever more general topics arose, and he felt that he had been able to avoid letting Dean down.

But Chris Akemoto had been largely silent. He spoke little through the main course, which was buffalo stew, the coarse-grained meat well cooked, with a rich variety of fresh vegetables, waiting until the dessert was served, which was thick slices of delicious steamed treacle pudding covered with creamy custard.

Then he leaned across to Ryan, pitching his voice low so that nobody else could hear. "You said you were a general sort of a trader, traveling all over the place, Mr. Cawdor."

"Sure."

"Forgive me, but I think the key word in that story is the word 'Trader,' isn't it?"

"I don't understand, Chris." Though he did, resisting the automatic reaction, when threatened, to reach for the butt of the SIG-Sauer.

"I recognize you. God knows, I have reason to! You were once the right-hand man of the infamous Trader."

# Chapter Nineteen

Twenty-four hours later Doc was still not well enough to travel up the trail toward Leadville.

He had become feverish and restless, sleeping patchily during the night and even more restlessly during the day. There had been another nosebleed, though not so severe as the previous one, and he had twice thrown up food.

The fruit and supplies that they'd raided from Ma's Place were almost gone, and J.B. had asked Mildred to kill a couple of the hairy marmots that proliferated around the open hillside. The pop of her ZKR 551 was quickly swallowed up by the vast space around them. Now their dog-size carcasses were roasting under Jak's care.

Krysty was becoming uneasy at the delay, even though she recognized that the old man was doing his best. He'd made a couple of tries at carrying on, but each time his wobbling legs and spinning head had let him down, and Jak had helped him to lie down again in the shade.

"I am so sorry," he kept repeating weakly. "I realize what an anchor I am upon this expedition. If only I could go outside the tent and be some time, like good

Captain Oates." He saw bewilderment on the faces of his friends. "He was a gallant gentleman who went with Scott to the Pole. Suffered terribly from frostbite and slowed down his companions. Blizzards and whatnot. Said he was going outside and would be some time. They all knew he was walking to his death. Wish I could do the same."

"And that saved all lives?" Jak said admiringly.

Doc coughed. "Well, not exactly. In fact, in a manner of speaking, it didn't. You see, they all died."

"Then there's not much point in your going for a short walk off a high cliff, is there, Doc?" Mildred said, patting him on the wrist. "So put that stupe idea straight in the 'forget' file."

LATE THAT AFTERNOON, with the sun sinking slowly into a dazzlingly beautiful sky of orange and red, Krysty and Mildred walked a little way up a side trail.

"Think he'll be all right?" Krysty asked, the last bright rays from the west setting her hair ablaze.

Mildred stopped and looked at her. "Now, are we thinking about Dr. Theophilus Tanner or might we be worrying more about Ryan Cawdor?"

"Both, I guess. No, Doc's more pressing. If any man in Deathlands can look after himself, it's Ryan. Shouldn't run into trouble just taking his son to school."

"I think Doc just needs a break. God knows, I feel a need for a rest sometimes. Just to be able to sit back someplace where there's no chilling, killing and no switchblade knife. Don't you feel that, Krysty? I know you do, 'cause you've talked about it before, haven't you?"

Krysty nodded. "Place with good grass and clean water and no cold heart calling to you from the shadows? Me and Ryan and Dean, and our friends coming to visit? It's my dream, Millie. But every day that passes makes it seem more like a dream that's never going to come true."

THEY CAME ACROSS an odd physical occurrence.

An earth slip had severed the track off the main highway, probably very shortly after skydark. Then, some time in the past few years, there had been another slide from higher up the mountain and it had repaired the great gash in the slope, making it possible to walk along it.

"Shouldn't stay out too long," Mildred said. "Like to keep an eye on Doc."

"Will he be well enough to walk on tomorrow?"

The woman shook her head, the plaited beads in her hair whispering in the evening stillness. "Who knows? Let's hope so."

"Hey," Krysty said, "there's a house up yonder."

It was a two-story building, made mainly from wood, with a sharply peaked roof, set into the hillside. A double garage stood at the side. Unusually none of the windows appeared to be broken, and apart from a few missing shingles near the chimney, the roof was intact.

"Let's go take a look." Krysty was excited. Because of the speed of the nuke war and the unbelievable death toll it exacted, it wasn't unprecedented to find an isolated property untouched since the long winters. But there was always a thrill, with the uncertainty of not knowing what might be found.

A MAILBOX WAS PERCHED crookedly at the end of a short circular drive, its paint stripped back to bare metal by a hundred Colorado winters.

"Any letters?" Mildred asked, opening it herself to find it held only a few shreds of dust-dry paper. "Nope. Bugs got here first."

"If it's safe, we could bring Doc up here for the night. Lot better shelter for his old bones than lying out on the cold, cold ground."

"Why not? Best take a look-see for ourselves first. There's some cords of wood stacked against the wall."

Krysty nodded. "Place like this, when we've heard word of various swift and evil bastards around, not to mention stickies, it's best we go in on double red. I'll take the front door and you slide around the back."

"Fine."

"Watch yourself."

Mildred gave her the thumbs-up, drawing her revolver from its holster.

Krysty watched her friend walking slowly around the side of the property, giving her a few seconds before making her own move toward the front door.

While she waited, she concentrated for a moment, drawing on the power of the Earth Mother, trying to see if there was anyone close by. She picked up the vibrations from Mildred but nobody else that she could detect.

The 5-shot .38 Smith & Wesson was gripped firmly in her right hand as she walked toward the front door of the house.

The setting sun glinted off the solar panels in the roof, blazing like fire. She paused and looked behind her, seeing what a fantastic view the house had across the Rockies.

Two steps nearer and Krysty jumped as a sec light came on, flooding the drive with its brilliance. She froze like a rabbit trapped in headlights, waiting for a hail of bullets to tear her apart. But nothing happened.

As she reached the door, the light clicked off.

The brass handle was cold, streaked with ancient verdigris that felt slightly sticky to the touch. It turned and the door swung silently open, showing her a hallway with two rooms opening off it and a staircase to her left.

Krysty held her breath for a moment before slowly letting it go. The place was fully furnished and it appeared that nobody had been there for the best part of a hundred years. She reached out her hand and pressed a wall switch and the interior lights tripped on, dazzlingly bright.

"That you, Krysty?"

"Yeah. Come ahead, Millie. I don't think we've got any company here."

"Back door's open. Kitchen through there's neat as a new pin. Everything stacked away on shelves, pots and pans all ranged in order. Like someone just walked out."

"Rest of the house looks like it's just as trim. Let's take a look around."

"You don't feel anyone here?" Mildred asked nervously, rubbing her left hand across her forehead.

"No. Whoever lived here's long, long gone."

But for once Krysty's intuition had let her down.

RYAN'S IMMEDIATE REACTION to the accusation from Chris Akemoto had been to totally and blankly deny it. But there was such unquestioned confidence in the young man's voice that he guessed there was little point.

And it could easily have made a very difficult situation much, much worse.

To be spotted as the right-hand man of the notorious Trader might, literally, prove fatal. The old man's ideal for an enemy was for him to be dead. But over the years enough people had escaped, brimming with hatred for Trader and his men, to make it a potential hazard.

Ryan knew how distinctive he looked, even though Deathlands was filled with men with an eye missing—or a hand or a leg or an arm or an ear.

But Akemoto didn't seem the sort of person who could be bluffed.

It was time to bite hard on the bullet and be ready to move fast and kill quietly.

"I rode with the Trader for years," he said. "Sorry, but I don't recall having crossed trails with you."

Out of the corner of his eye, Ryan noticed that Dean was deep in eager conversation with the boys on either side of him, looking as though he'd known them all his life.

"More of the treacle pudding, Mr. Cawdor?" Natalie Davenport asked from the other side.

"No. No, thanks."

Once she'd turned away, Chris Akemoto continued. "Remember me? Why should you, Mr. Cawdor? I was a child of eleven years old when my parents were butchered and Trader came into my life."

"Your parents were chilled by Trader? Or by his people from the war wags?"

Akemoto shook his head. "No. No, you misunderstand me. I'm obviously not making myself plain."

"I thought that's what you meant."

"No."

"Where was all this? Gives me a decent clue to hang a memory onto."

"My mom and dad ran a small grocery store out near Memphis. Little ville called Yesteryear. One of the postnuke villes. They had some hard times and grief, being from Oriental stock, but all that passed. Me and my brothers and sisters learned how to give back better than we got, and gradually things became all right. Became good."

"This rings a small bell. Wasn't there some kind of rebirth of the Klan?"

Akemoto placed a hand on his arm and Ryan noticed that the young man was trembling with emotion. "That's it! You remember. It started in the east. Some said they came from old Georgia. But they were intent on riding off anyone who wasn't a white Anglo. They came to Yesteryear."

All around them, the meal was coming to an end. Spoons were laid on empty plates and Nicholas Brody rose to his feet, clapping his hands for silence, offering a quick prayer.

"There will be tea in the staff room, Mr. Cawdor, if you would care to join us?" Natalie suggested.

Chris leaned across. "I promised to show Mr. Cawdor the grounds after supper. Before full dark. But I'll bring him back in fifteen minutes or so."

IN THE EVENING COOL, alongside the limpid water of the lake, he carried on his story.

"My parents wouldn't move and most of the good folks in the ville supported them. Until the night of…of the burning. Trader had arrived, and your war wags were camped by a creek a half mile west. He'd bought plenty of provisions from our store."

It was seeping back to Ryan. A well-stocked general shop, run by a couple of friendly Orientals. And lots of kids running around helping to fill the big order for the wags.

"The Klan came that night," he said. "And they burned you out. I remember. Your parents were shot and their bodies thrown in the flames. And you kids escaped by..."

"The storm cellar of the Reverend Mr. Dexter. True Christian. We heard Mom and Dad's screams. I still hear them."

They walked on in silence, while Akemoto regained control.

"The leaders of the Klan made a big mistake. They thought Trader would be on their side."

Ryan grinned. "Big error. Nothing Trader hated as much as hatred. The Imperial Wizard, or whatever he was, rode up the next morning, bold as brass with a dozen of his thugs. Asked for help in finding you kids. Said..." He hesitated, his brow furrowing as he struggled for the memory. "'We got the mongrel and his bitch. Might as well clean out the whole litter.'"

"And Trader hanged him," Akemoto said. "Him and all his crew. From a line of live oaks by the creek."

"I remember." Ryan saw in his mind's eye the row of kicking, strangling corpses that gradually became still, heard the squeaking of the new hemp ropes above the bubbling of the stream. "Yeah, I remember."

"Then Trader took a day off to rebuild the store for us and left a hatful of jack to restock it. Place is running still, with my older brother and two sisters there. Any time you're near Yesteryear..."

"Thanks, Chris.... Can I call one of my son's teachers by his first name?"

"Sure can. What I wanted to say, swinging down all the years, was . . . Thanks."

They walked back to the brightly lit school through the gathering gloom.

# Chapter Twenty

Mildred browsed around the first floor of the isolated house, while Krysty slowly climbed the stairs.

"We'll only have a quick look," she said, pausing halfway. "Best get Doc and the others up here as soon as possible. Before dark. Start a fire and we can all have a really good, warm, secure night."

"I saw some cans on shelves in the kitchen," Mildred said. "Depends on what they are, but some of them might still be usable and safe."

There were three rooms opening off the landing, and Krysty checked them all.

The first was a bathroom, with thick towels folded neatly on a chair. But when Krysty tried to pick one up, it crumbled into powdery dust between her fingers.

There was a dry smell in the house, a smell of stillness and antiquity.

The second of the doors was half-open, and Krysty pushed it all the way, revealing the sterility of what had obviously been a guest bedroom. A faded watercolor of Glenwood Springs hung on one wall, and a floral duvet covered a narrow double bed.

Krysty went to the last of the rooms, where the door was closed.

"You all right?" Mildred's voice floated up from downstairs. "Some of the electrics still work. Must be the solar panels, but they sure built them to last."

"Yeah, I'm fine. Just going into the last of the rooms up here to—" Her voice stopped as though it had been sliced off with an ax.

"Krysty?" There was a note of worry in Mildred's voice.

"I'm fine. But I was wrong. The owners of the house are still here."

THEY LAY SIDE BY SIDE, wizened hands locked together, on a large bed beneath a picture window that looked west toward the setting sun.

The flesh had long, long gone and all that remained were the dark brown sinews that held together the loosened bones. She had been blond or gray, and he had been mainly bald. Strands of their hair had flowed together on the pillow, just as the juices of their decaying corpses had flowed together, staining the bed and the carpet beneath it.

She wore a pantsuit and sneakers. He was dressed in casual pants and a shirt beneath a patterned sweater. His feet were bare bones.

Mildred stood in the doorway. "Looks like they picked the time and place of their going." She walked to a glass-topped table that held a ceramic doll and picked up an empty bottle of pills, peering at the label. "Yeah. They knew what they were doing, all right. Is there a note?"

"Haven't seen one."

They found it in the living room in an envelope propped up by a photograph of a smiling couple, blinking into the sun on a ski slope, arms around each other.

To Whom It Might Concern was printed neatly on the outside. Krysty picked it up and weighed it in her hand. "I don't know whether we should open this."

"Let's see what the others think. Sun's well down. Be good to move those poor remains out of the room and bring in some wood. They left a fire ready-laid in the hearth, and we don't know how long the electricity'll hold out after all this time."

ALL OF THEM were fascinated by the house.

Jak brought in wood while J.B. got the fire going. Mildred and Krysty shared the task of bundling the desiccated corpses in the stained sheets and carrying them out back, laying them in a garage that held a large crimson wag. Krysty checked, but the engine was seized up solid as granite. They carefully remade the beds, using the fragile sheets and blankets from a closet on the landing.

Doc sat on the sofa, his knee boots resting on a piece of old towel he'd found in the kitchen, so as not to make the material muddy.

He was holding the envelope that Krysty had shown him. "What is the consensus of opinion on this?" he asked. "Should we read it or not?"

"Not," Mildred stated firmly.

"Read it," Jak said, crouching in front of the hearth and coaxing the fire into reluctant life.

"Yeah, sorry, Millie, but I don't see why not. It's a keyhole into the past. Don't get chances like this all that often. I say read it." J.B. avoided Mildred's eyes.

"Why do you think, Krysty?" Doc asked.

"I don't have strong feelings. One thing's for sure. It can't hurt the folks who wrote it."

They knew now that they had been a Mr. and Mrs. James Tickell, and that he'd been an orthodontist. They had three children, all in their twenties, who had left home and lived in Boston, New York and Albuquerque.

Doc tapped the envelope on the arm of the sofa. "Then I will open it."

The fire was beginning to blaze, and Krysty had brewed some coffee from a sealed, airtight tin she'd found in the larder. She handed out the mugs, everyone sighing and breathing in the wonderful aroma.

The only sound then was Doc's fingernail ripping open the envelope and extracting a single sheet of white paper. "Not very long," he said.

Krysty sat on the floor, tucking her feet under her. Jak leaned back against one of the padded chairs, while Mildred sat in another. J.B. stood with his mug in hand, by the window, looking out at the last speck of deep, deep red on the western horizon.

Doc began to read in his fine, orotund voice. "It is signed by both of them at the bottom. It begins,

" 'May God forgive us, but we can see no point in trying to carry on. The phones and radio and TV are all down, as they have been for several days. Ever since the skies darkened.'

"Interesting that they used that phrase 'skydark' so soon after the nuclear holocaust."

"Go on, Doc," Krysty said.

"Very well.

" 'We know now that the world has ended. The world we knew and loved is gone forever and we are alone in it. The road is blocked both ways, and no plows have come through. They will never come again. The last news was of the ruin of the great cities, which must mean the deaths of our beloved children. Some sort of radiation sickness is gripping us both. We are finding our nails and teeth are becoming loose and our gums bleed. We know enough to realize that the future is short and bloody and bleak. Best we do what we have decided now, before it becomes impossible. This way there can still be affection and dignity. A time and way of our own choosing.'

"Oh, dear."

He stopped and blew his nose loudly. Mildred wiped tears from her cheeks with her sleeve.

"This sort of thing must have been repeated thousands of times," J.B. said. "Perhaps millions. Once they realized there was no hope at all..."

Doc tucked away his kerchief and sipped his coffee. "There is just a little more.

"'As soon as I finish writing this, we will go upstairs and take the drugs, perhaps washing them down with our last bottle of good brandy. No point in leaving it behind. It is a pity, but I do not think that I can write any more. God bless America and God bless you all. Try to understand and to forgive. May those who come after remember us in their prayers.'

"And then they've both signed it."

"And they went up to the bedroom and drank the brandy and took the pills. Lay down together and held hands and slipped gently away from the horror that life had become." Krysty shook her head. "Best way out."

Mildred sighed. "Brave and intelligent. If they'd waited another day or so..."

Doc stood and moved to the fire, crumpling the letter and the envelope and throwing both onto the flames, where they were consumed in seconds.

MILDRED PICKED OUT some food she thought was safe, mainly in freeze-dried or package form. A number of the cans had blown and split, but some of them still held firm and smelled all right when opened.

So supper was a mixture of several kinds of soup with some added beans and canned carrots. And some reconstituted potato that tasted passingly edible when mixed with powdered milk and water, and well-spiced with salt and pepper.

Afterward they all sat around drinking more of the exquisite coffee. "Forgotten just how good it used to taste," Mildred said. "In fact I'm sure it never used to taste quite this good in my previous life."

"Everything's relative." Krysty added a little sugar to the dark brown brew, savoring the flavor. "Compared to most coffee subs, even mule piss is better."

Conversation faltered, everyone touched by the tragedy of the owners of the house, and they agreed to retire early and make a good start after dawn.

Mildred and J.B. had the main bedroom, opening a top fanlight window to air it.

Doc was allowed the bed in the spare room, which he went to early.

Krysty picked the sofa for herself while Jak scavenged in the garage and found a camp bed with an inflatable mattress. It revealed a very slow leak but it held up enough for him to have a reasonable night's sleep in a corner of the living room, close to the window.

KRYSTY STARTED AWAKE once in the middle of the night, reaching out automatically for Ryan's comforting hand, feeling the cold shock of desolation when she realized where she was, and that she was alone.

For some time she was unable to slide back into the warm comfort of sleep, and she found herself thinking of the tragic ending of the owners of the beautiful house. And how that same tragedy had to have been repeated countless times, as J.B. had said, all through Deathlands.

A phrase she'd heard Doc use came to her. Something about people leading lives of quiet desperation.

With that doleful thought she finally fell asleep once more, not waking until dawn light broke through a gap in the dark brown velvet draperies.

And she could smell the glowing embers of the night's fire and the wonderful scent of fresh coffee coming from the brightly lit kitchen.

EVERYONE HAD SLEPT pretty well, and Doc, in particular, seemed a new man, back to his old form. He sang an old song in a hearty voice as he helped Jak prepare breakfast for everyone.

Mildred had given her approval to some sealed foil packages of scrambled eggs with ham and peppers, and Jak and Doc served them piping hot from a pair of skillets. They'd opened some cans of dough that they heated in the electric oven, finding that they came out as crescent-shaped rolls, soft and buttery.

And more coffee.

The only major failure was some self-bake pecan pie, which turned into foul-smelling sticky cardboard.

"Think it would be possible to actually live up here and get the house going again?" Krysty asked.

J.B. considered the question for several seconds. "Need reliable transport. Come the winter you could be locked in here for three or four months. Doubt the electrics would cope if they were used too much. Heating would be difficult with only one fireplace. And you wouldn't be able to grow too much fruit and vegetables at this altitude and on an exposed scarp like this. Plenty of game. But, on balance, it'd be rad-blasted hard."

It was an unusually long speech from the sallow little Armorer.

"Guess in those technodays the road would have been swept clear, and you could get groceries and stuff delivered from Leadville or Glenwood Springs," Krysty said. "And all kinds of repairmen the other end of a phone."

"Die here in winter." Jak had just had a hot bath upstairs and come down with his long white hair plastered to his skull and shoulders.

"I'll do the washing up," Mildred said. "Maybe we should be going."

"The hot-bath idea seems admirable." Doc laughed. "Though I see little point in washing the plates. It has been a century since anyone came this way last. And it will probably be another hundred years before anyone returns. By then I think that the old house will be a mass of tumbled timber."

Mildred stared at him. "You can live like a pig in muck, Doc, but I was raised not to leave dirty dishes around. There's plenty of hot water from the boiler to the fire if we all want hot baths."

The thought of that was too tempting, and they agreed to postpone their departure for Leadville and beyond until after lunch, by which time they would all have used the deep tub and be ready to face the trail once more.

"Ryan'll wait for us up at Fairplay," Krysty said. "Like we arranged."

# Chapter Twenty-One

After an excellent and sustaining breakfast, Ryan had a last brief meeting with Nicholas Brody.

The big bearded man was alone in his study, and as Ryan entered the room, he was doubled over his desk with a horrendous coughing fit. He had a white handkerchief pressed to his face, and Ryan thought that he glimpsed a dappling of crimson before the headmaster quickly put it back into his pocket.

"Are you all right? Should I get someone?"

"No, no, no, my dear fellow. Something I ate must have slipped down the wrong way. Foolish of me. Do forgive me for that histrionic impersonation of the Lady of the Camellias." Seeing Ryan's puzzled expression, he added, "A fine book, my dear Mr. Cawdor. Perhaps we can introduce it to the boy. He seems to have settled in wonderfully. His dormitory prefect said he slept well and was no trouble at all. Excellent."

"Just looked in before I left to make sure all was all right about Dean."

"Better than all right, I think, Mr. Cawdor. The lad is obviously bright. We have been observing him. He is the most self-sufficient eleven-year-old I think I've ever known in my long career as a pedagogue."

"Not many eleven year olds have lived like Dean has. Not many chilled as many people as he has."

"Chilled many? Oh, I see. It is a joke, Mr. Cawdor. Slightly ghoulish, and not perhaps in the very best of taste, but none the worse for that."

Ryan realized he shouldn't have mentioned that fact. But he was going to get away with it.

Brody was laughing, managing to smother the onset of another coughing fit.

"One thing, Mr. Brody."

"Yes?" He paused. "If it's the teaching of intrapersonal relationships and human hygiene, I think you can rest assured that we handle this with great sensitivity and—"

"Not that. I'm heading for Leadville, then on across the tops to the next valley along, up to the head of that to Fairplay. One of my friends comes from Harmony, near there. Heard stories of trouble."

"I fear so. We too have heard such tales. Which is why our highway was being patrolled with more than usual zeal."

"Any details?"

"How long since your companion was in Harmony? Does he visit often?"

"She."

"I'm sorry?"

"The particular companion we're talking about is a lady. And she hasn't been back for many years. Her mother lived there, but she has lost touch."

Brody steepled his fingers. "Alas and alack! That this happens so frequently in Deathlands." He peered out the window. "The sun seems to be showing us his merry face today."

Ryan pressed on. "What kind of trouble was it?"

"Ah, yes. We heard of a gang of bounty hunters and general bandits. The odd part of the tale was that there were norms and muties riding together."

"We ran into three killers on the road here from Glenwood Springs. They'd slaughtered an old man with a mule and a girl."

Brody sighed. "And did the perps of this evil act sleep last night in the bosom of Abraham?"

"You mean did we chill them?"

"I do, indeed."

"We did, indeed."

"They might have been a rotten branch off that same corrupt tree, Mr. Cawdor. Take the greatest of care. We would not want our newest pupil to suddenly become an orphan."

The two men shook hands and parted.

Ryan was shown down the corridor to where Dean waited for him.

The boy was looking out a window, across the lake. He turned and grinned at his father. "Hot pipe, Dad!"

"What is?"

"You've saved me from doing English grammar with old Coco Copeland. The boys reckon he's a real bastard."

"Watch the language, Dean, please."

"Sorry. Anyway, you've got to go now, haven't you, Dad? Give my love to all the others."

Dean was being unnaturally bright and perky, with a forced smile pasted uneasily on his face.

Ryan nodded. "I'll do that. Remember, if there's serious bother, a message will eventually find me and we'll all come running."

"Sure, sure. Thanks, Dad. But from what I seen so far, I don't mind it too bad."

Ryan put a hand on the boy's shoulder, and the defenses crumbled and the floodgates opened.

It took several minutes for them both to recover some degree of self-possession and wipe their eyes and blow their noses.

"Sorry about that, Dad," Dean muttered. "Promised myself I wasn't going to—"

"Me too, son, me too." Ryan took a deep breath. "Right, I'm going now."

"And I'll go and do grammar. Then Krysty won't have to moan at me again." Dean's voice trembled, and Ryan turned away quickly, opening the door into the passage.

Ryan knew that Dean had led a hand-to-mouth existence with his mother, Sharona, for several years. He'd faced a lot of adversity in his short life, and now he had a chance to settle down to a regular life for a year or so, in relative peace and quiet. He'd gain some education and acquire some life skills. Ryan couldn't deny his son that, though it tore at his heart to leave him behind.

"In a year, if not sooner," he said, and closed the door firmly behind him.

AHAB AND JOEL WERE both back on duty, and they escorted him for a couple of miles along the road away from the school. As Brody had said, it was a fine morning, with a few bunched clouds to the northwest that held the possible threat of a storm later in the day.

They recognized that Ryan wasn't in a talking mood, and the three of them walked along, mainly in silence.

At the crest of a rise in the trail, Ryan turned and took one last long look at the buildings. He thought that he might have glimpsed a little figure waving something white from a second-story window, but he couldn't be sure.

"LEAVE YOU HERE, outlander," Ahab said. "Get back to our patrolling."

"Thanks. Guess I feel all right about leaving my son in the school. Seem like nice kids and teachers. And Brody himself. Real bad cough he's got, though."

The sec men exchanged glances. Ahab answered him. "Worries us, as well. Head was supposed to be seeing some top doctor back east . . . could have been Kansas City way. But he never went. Some days he seems fine, but on cold, wet days it can grip him."

Joel nodded, whistling between his teeth. "Days when there's a blue norther. Bad as well."

"Brody told me a bit about this gang of norms and muties," Ryan said.

"That's what we heard," Ahab agreed. "Pickin' on some of the frontier pestholes and taking them over. Suck them dry and move on. Like fuckin' locusts they are."

"Think twice about coming our way," Joel said. "Need sharp teeth to bite us off."

"You know a ville called Harmony?" Ryan asked.

Ahab looked puzzled. "That up Nebraska way?"

Joel shook his head. "No, that's the place beyond the divide, couple of valleys over east. You know that swank old ski place, Breckenridge?"

"Oh, yeah. Head of the valley there, isn't it? Beyond, what do you call it?"

"Fairplay," Ryan suggested.

"Right on the money, stranger. Fairplay. Harmony's beyond that. Is that the ville you're heading for?"

"Yeah. Meeting friends there."

Joel patted the Steyr rifle on Ryan's back. "Need that and some more like it if that gang sees you."

Ryan nodded. "You're right."

After shaking hands with the two men, he turned eastward and began the long, lonely walk back onto the main trail.

MILDRED WAS LAST of the companions to enjoy the deep tub, brimming with hot water. She poured in the contents of one of the many bottles of subtly colored, scented foaming oils.

Each successive bath seemed to take longer for the water to heat properly, and Krysty was beginning to get edgy at the delay.

J.B. and Doc reassured her.

"Ryan'll likely spend a little time at this school before he leaves Dean there. We know they were both safely through that ambush. And we've got a place fixed for a rendezvous." The Armorer had been reading through a pile of magazines from the predark days and he picked up another *Reader's Digest*. "He'll be fine, Krysty. You'll see."

Doc had been listening to some classical music on headphones. Now he took them off and smiled at her. "Worry not, dear madam. The bullet has not been cast nor the blade forged that bears the name of Ryan Cawdor. Another couple of days and we shall all be reunited together once more. Will we not?"

Krysty had been reassured by that.

All of them had noticed that the electricity had begun to fail. Several lights had gone out, though replacement bulbs from a bag in the garage had kept some going. The microwave oven and stove had both ceased to work—in the case of the former, with a loud bang and shower of orange sparks that had nearly taken Jak's hand off when he tried to heat a mug of coffee.

"Come on, Mildred!" Krysty shouted up the stairs. "Be dark before we get going. In fact it's getting dark already."

"Only a little after two," J.B. said, checking his wrist chron. "But it does seem gloomy."

"I'll take look," Jak offered, getting up from the corner, where he'd been flicking through a book on handblasters.

He went out the front door, where the security light failed to snap on, then walked around the far, northern flank of the building. He stood there for several seconds, then returned briskly to the front door.

"Big storm on way," he called, as soon as he was inside the house again.

"Snow?" J.B. asked.

"Probably. Sky like lead. Wind's rising. Whole mess coming this way."

Everyone except Mildred, who was still relaxing in the tub, rushed out to look.

Jak's description had been accurate. The sky was dark, slate gray, with heavy clouds squatting over the mountaintops a few miles away.

"Moving this way," J.B. said.

Krysty stamped her foot. "Gaia! Mebbe if we get out now we can outflank it. Looks from its path like it might not reach farther up the trail."

Doc looked doubtful. "I do most earnestly comprehend your reasoning, my dearest Krysty. To be reunited with Ryan is the wish of all of us. But that—" he pointed with the tip of his cane at the approaching storm "—to be exposed on the hillside in the teeth of that—"

J.B. finished the sentence. "When we can sit it out in warmth and comfort and safety. Seems like close to suicide to run against that. It's going to be a real triple-big blow, Krysty. Real big.''

Nonetheless, Krysty insisted that Mildred complete her bath and get dressed as quickly as she could.

"I'd finished soaking, anyway,'' she replied, somewhat pettishly. "Though I don't believe I had anywhere near as long as anyone else. Including you, Krysty.''

"We have to try and get going. Please. I'm getting more and more worried about what's happening to Ryan.''

RYAN WAS FIFTEEN or twenty miles east of them, striding steadily toward the township of Leadville. He'd seen no further signs of human life, though the forest seemed to teem with activity. A pack of thirty or forty gaunt coyotes snarled at him until he unslung the rifle and shot the leader, sending the rest of the animals scattering. He also saw moose, and once a black bear lumbered quickly across the highway, about eighty yards ahead of him. And there were enough deer to keep a man going for years.

At a sharp turn in the road he looked back and down, wondering how far the others were behind him, or whether they might have passed by while he was at Brody's school and be ahead of him.

Staring behind, Ryan was able to see the huge storm that looked as if it would cut the trail about ten miles below him. The silver lace of lightning crackled around the tops of the clouds, and he could see at the base that it was either snow or unimaginably heavy rain.

"Hope they're free of that," he said aloud.

EVERYONE WAS PACKING and ready to go. The land around the house was almost invisible in the gloom, and they could all hear the rumblings of thunder.

"We can do it," Krysty said, opening the front door, staggering a little in the wind as she looked out at the first whirling flakes of snow.

"No," J.B. stated. "We can't." And closed the door again.

# Chapter Twenty-Two

A little after midnight Krysty stood by the picture window of the isolated house, gazing out at the moonlit snow-smeared land.

"You were right, J.B.," she said over her shoulder. "Must be four or five feet out there. Came down like out the back of a dump truck."

"Trader used to say that the more you wanted something, the more your judgment and common sense flew out the door," replied the Armorer, who was carefully placing a few more logs on the blazing fire.

"For once the old son of a bitch was probably right," Krysty said, smiling.

"Often was."

Doc had gone to bed, deciding an hour or so earlier that they weren't going anywhere for a while. "I think I should attempt to stoke up my batteries while I can. Good night, gentles all."

Mildred dozed on the sofa, while Jak was idly juggling with three of his knives, sending them high toward the ceiling in a weaving maze of honed steel. He had been doing it for several minutes and hadn't dropped them once.

They'd enjoyed a nutritious supper of freeze-dried mulligatawny soup and some more of the self-bake rolls, but Mildred had gone carefully through the entire larder and found very little else that she considered safe for them to eat.

Also, the hot-water system had packed up both for washing and for heating, which meant the house, despite its excellent insulation, was already beginning to drop in temperature—apart from the living room, where they were keeping the fire going. Jak had struggled out before the snow had settled in deep drifts and brought in several loads of wood, enough to ensure warmth for at least twenty-four hours.

"When do you reckon we can move on, J.B.?" Krysty asked. "Any chance of tomorrow?"

"Doubt it. You never know. Weather can change in a few hours. But that's serious snow, and nobody's going to be out there clearing the trail for us."

"You worried about Ryan?" Mildred asked.

"Course I am. What a stupe...!" Krysty closed her emerald eyes and sighed. "Sorry. On edge. If only we knew where he was. Could be safe in the school. Could both be trapped out in the open, stuck in a snow hole with no food."

"Could be storm missed him," Jak said. "Looked like we was on north edge of it."

Krysty put her head on one side, close to the pane of glass, listening. "Anyone hear that?"

"Wolves," Jak said, never missing a beat with his intricate juggling.

"You can hear them, too?"

"Course. Heard them few minutes ago. Came closer. Went away. Coming closer again."

SUPPLIED WITH TRAIL FOOD by the kitchens of the Brody School, Ryan made good time. He reached the edge of Leadville well before dusk, passing the rusted remains of what had obviously been an old predark railroad.

A battered sign told when he passed the ten-thousand-foot altitude line, though his body had already warned him that he was approaching the edge of the comfort zone. His breathing was faster and more shallow, and when he stopped he was aware of the blood pounding in his ears.

The ghost of a headache pressed behind his eye, and he felt slightly nauseous. But after eating a handful of dried apples and apricots, and taking a good long drink from a crystal-clear stream alongside the trail, he felt refreshed and carried on toward the ville.

He knew from his memory of the map he'd seen in Glenwood Springs that Leadville was only about twenty-five miles from Fairplay.

As the crow flew.

Unfortunately only a crow could make it in that distance. For humans there was the little matter of fifteen-thousand-foot mountains in the way.

The only viable route involved heading back north from the ville, to Fremont Pass at eleven and a half thousand feet, then trying to cut across to the Hoosier

Pass, above Breckenridge, at a similar height. To stick to the main highways would mean going all the way back to I-70, then heading south once more, which would be a total distance of more than sixty miles.

When he reached the fork in the road, Ryan hesitated. Part of him wanted to get on as fast as he could to reach Fairplay and meet up with Krysty and the others, who, he imagined, might well be ahead of him by now.

Evening was closing in, and the attractions of Leadville overrode his impatience. The chance of another night spent in a warm bed and some good hot food was altogether too tempting for him to resist.

He turned right, toward the distant buildings of the ville, a place that he knew well from his visit with Trader.

Back in the 1800s it had been a gold boomtown, then a silver boomtown. Its fortunes had been linked to the larger-than-life millionaire-philanderer Horace Tabor, but had declined by the middle of the twentieth century, when it had lurched from minibust to miniboom and back again.

When Ryan had visited the place with Trader and the lumbering war wags, it had been a bustling frontier pesthole with several gaudies and saloons, one of them established in what had been Leadville's very own opera house. He recalled that Doc had mentioned that a famous writer called Oscar Wilde had once traveled all the way to Leadville to perform there.

Now Ryan was back once more, this time on foot and alone, knowing that in pestholes like that, an outlander had to set his feet real careful. And watch his back.

Munching a tangy apple, he set off to walk the last mile or so into Leadville.

"MUTIES," Jak said tersely, looking out the wide picture window in the living room at the pack of huge timber wolves.

There were more than a dozen of them, rangy animals, the biggest of them standing at least four feet high at the shoulder. They had heralded their arrival by howling as they forced themselves through the powdery snow. But once they had reached the house and circled it a couple of times, they had fallen unnervingly silent, contenting themselves with sitting in a half circle and observing the humans observing them. Their shadows were crisp and clean in the bright moon.

"The brutes look half-starved to me," said Doc, who'd been roused from his bed by the noise of the pack. "Gaunt and hungered."

Krysty brushed back an errant strand of hair from her eyes. "Agree with that, Doc. Looks like they regard us as being their next meal."

"A choice selection of cold cuts," Doc said, "personally selected by our chef for your dining pleasure. I think they feel they've discovered the original boneless-chicken ranch. Look at the way their leader has his tongue hanging out. And those astounding fangs. Ah, yes, I remember them well. Fangs for the memory. Sorry."

The ferocious red eyes of the wolves glinted in the silver light, and their heads turned as one to follow any movement within the house.

Mildred had drawn her revolver and was taking aim at the animals, her finger settled on the trigger. "Bang," she whispered. "And another of the critters bit the dust. Yum, what delicious dust we have here." She laughed. "Not that I'm cracking up, friends. Not at all."

"Problem is how long they're prepared to stay out there," J.B. said.

"I don't think I'll be going out to bring in some more logs," Krysty stated.

"Chill all from upstairs," Jak suggested. "Easy target for you, Mildred."

The Armorer wiped his glasses while he spoke. "Not sure that's the best idea. Not yet, anyways. Rad-blasted animals would run at first or second death. Noise could bring more of them. Riding with Trader in northern Minnesota, we once counted a pack of nearly two hundred wolves, all running together. If that number turns up here, then we are in serious trouble."

It was a chilling thought and stopped any more conversation dead in its tracks.

A VACANT-FACED LAD WAS hammering nails into a five-bar gate as Ryan passed the first few houses of Leadville. He walked over to him. "Hey! Is there a good place to stay the night in the ville?"

The teenager turned and gave him a moonish smile. "Why, sure, mister. I know that, all right. Palace Hotel. *S-u-n* spells Palace, don't it?"

"Likely it does, son."

"Around the corner and down the hill and on your right," he chanted in a singsong voice.

"Obliged," Ryan said.

Around the corner and down the hill brought him into the ville's main drag. The sun had almost set, and lights were on in many of the buildings. A number of saloons and gaudies were open for business. The Palace rooming house was where the boy had said it would be, and Ryan went and booked a room, paying with a little of what remained of his once-substantial amount of jack.

He didn't meet any sort of formality: pay the jack, get the key, go to the room, which looked out over the desolate back of the main street, and lock it behind you.

The bed was narrow but comfortable, and the sheets were remarkably clean, making him guess that he'd arrived on washing day at the Palace.

There was a dining room in the place, but Ryan decided to check out the quality of some of the other eateries, walking along the left side of the street, down past the opera house, where a sign said that public donations were requested to carry out some urgently needed repairs and renovations. Ryan had the feeling that there had been a similar sign when he'd first come through the ville with Trader, a good twenty years earlier.

He crossed the street, waiting for a few seconds while a gas-driven wag rumbled slowly by, carrying a huge load of hewn logs on its flatbed, then headed for an eatery called Carl and Joanna's Diner, which looked to be pretty full for so early in the evening. Ryan hoped that the number of diners meant the place was good.

He pushed open the door and a bell jingled.

A middle-aged man with an apron tied over his ample stomach appeared, beaming, and offered him a handwritten menu. "You got the reading, stranger? Or one of the girls can tell you what we got on tonight."

"I read, thanks."

"Table for yourself, or do you mind sharing?"

"Prefer my own company."

The man put his finger to his lips. "Nod's as good as a wink to a blind man, friend. This way." He pushed between the tables, exchanging banter with his customers. "You passing through?"

"Yeah. Come up from Glenwood Springs. Meeting some people in a few days." Ryan was impressed with the incredible speed at which he'd gone from being a stranger to becoming a friend.

The menu offered what sounded like real good cooking. There was duck with a sauce made from oranges; turkey stuffed with cinnamon apples; breast of goose with mushrooms; steaks of all shapes and sizes with a range of about eight different vegetables.

Ryan picked the duck, choosing sweet corn and creamed potatoes with butter and mashed carrots and snow peas, selecting iced lemonade to go with the food.

The place was three parts full. There were several locals, probably storekeepers and folks working in offices, as well as a scattering of miners and trappers.

Carl was rushing around, busier than a one-legged man in an avalanche. The thin-faced woman with glasses visible in the kitchen had to be Joanna. She caught Ryan looking at her and gave him a distracted smile and a half wave of the hand.

The food was brought by a chubby young woman in a flowered print frock and a checked apron, who unloaded her tray with professional expertise, reeling off what everything was as she did so.

"That everything, mister?"

"Lemonade?"

"Sure. On the way. Enjoy your meal."

Ryan did.

Everything was delicious, cooked to perfection. As he was polishing off the last mouthful he again caught Joanna's eye and gave her a double thumbs-up, getting a broad smile in return.

"Couldn't have been better, Carl," he said, as he was settling his bill.

"Sure you can't make room for a dessert? You seen the special list?"

"I don't even have the room for a single grain of chocolate rice, thanks."

"Not the key lime pie? Or the French almond silk pie? The black cherry cobbler? The blueberry meringue with vanilla ice cream or fresh cream? The strawberry *gâteau* with a brandy syllabub? Grapefruit sorbet with a sweet raspberry liqueur? There must be something to tempt you, brother.''

Now he'd gone from friend to brother.

Half the things on offer were alien to Ryan. ''I don't think that I could... Mebbe a small, and I mean small, portion of the black cherry cobbler.''

''We got five other kinds of cobbler. There's...''

Ryan held up his hand. ''No. Don't push it, Carl. This may be a mistake and I'll have to go lie down for an hour to recover. But bring me the cobbler.''

The small portion hung over the side of a large dish, soaked in thick cream.

Ryan was three parts through it, when he felt the coldness of steel against the back of his neck.

''One move and your face ends up blown into your plate, stranger. We want to talk to you about what happened to some friends down the Glenwood Trail.''

From brother straight back to stranger.


EVERYONE IN THE HOUSE had finally gone to bed, leaving the fire piled high with enough wood to last most of the night.

And the half circle of panting wolves still sat patiently outside the big window.

Krysty lay on the sofa beneath a couple of blankets. Most of the bedding had gone to the upstairs sleepers, where the cold was beginning to bite.

She had lain awake for some time, plagued with worry that something had gone wrong for Ryan and

Dean, finally slipping into an uneasy sleep, only to be jerked awake by a dull thumping sound.

There was nothing to see when she looked around, the bright flames dancing off the reflecting glass. Jak was still asleep across the room from her, his white hair tinted pink by the fire.

Another thump, much louder, made the room rattle.

Jak woke, blinking. "What was that?"

Krysty was up on her feet, walking toward the window. "Something knocked against..." she began. "Oh, Gaia!"

It was the wolves.

One of them was just moving away, limping a little, and now the pack leader was coming at a rush. He charged through the snow, jaws wide, eyes flaring, straight for the glass.

It weighed at least three hundred pounds, and Krysty knew instantly that the window wasn't going to stop it.

# Chapter Twenty-Three

A mirror on the wall opposite Ryan enabled him to see the three men behind him. He cursed his lack of caution, lulled by the excellent food.

Three men. The one holding the short-barreled revolver at the base of Ryan's skull was average height. His face was lean with oddly thick lips. A deep scar seamed his left cheek. He looked to be around thirty, and his two companions were both much younger.

They put Ryan in mind of the gang of three that had ambushed them on the trail.

"You come from Glenwood, mister?"

Ryan continued to eat the last few forkfuls of his cherry cobbler, using his fork in his left hand to shove some of the final crumbs of pastry together.

He glanced up, trying to make a combat judgment of the trio. Neither of the younger men had blasters drawn, though they were wearing revolvers in holsters. They were obviously content that their older companion had the situation well under control.

Ryan took a sip of lemonade, laying the spoon down for a moment. "Glenwood. Yeah."

"When?"

"Three, four days back."

"How come it took so long? Was you on foot?"

"Yeah. I was with my young son. Taking him up to the school over yonder."

"Brody's place?"

"That's the one."

"You see anything of some good friends of ours? Some good, good friends?"

"They got names?"

"Joey. And a couple of kids."

He turned his head. "What was their names?"

"Eddie and Manuel."

"Right. They went off to try and get some…supplies and stuff. And they don't come back."

"Been plenty of snow behind me. Could be they got caught in that."

One of the younger men nodded in the mirror. "That might be right, Gordy."

"I don't know. Looks like this outlander's the only person come up in the last week. There was that old man and the girl going down with their burro."

The kid on the left giggled. "But we know they weren't going to make it to the Springs, don't we, Harve?"

The other teenager laughed, showing a strange dental arrangement where every other black and rotting tooth was capped with gold, reminding Ryan of a piano keyboard.

"Should be back," Gordy insisted, pressing the muzzle of his blaster harder against the back of Ryan's head. "And this son of a bitch is going to tell us about it."

Carl had spotted the disturbance and bustled over, wiping his hands on his apron. "What's going on here?"

"Butt out, asshole!" Gordy snarled, his eyes still locked on Ryan's face in the mirror. "Got us some business with the outlander here."

"It's all right," Ryan said quietly. "Let it lie or you'll likely get yourself hurt."

"I can help."

"No." Ryan shook his head warningly. "You run a great eatery, but I don't see you as a shootist. Let it lie. Best all around to do that."

Gordy laughed, licking a thread of spittle from his bulbous lips.

"Don't want to make a mess, huh? Specially inside your pants. Then let's go outside and talk this over."

"Right." Ryan had let his shoulders slump, knowing the importance of body language, allowing the three killers to think they had him cowed and totally at their mercy.

He started to stand, pushing himself up with his right hand, so they could see he wasn't doing anything foolish, such as reaching for his SIG-Sauer. The muzzle of the blaster moved from his nape, and he was able to see what it was—a Llama Comanche Model II with a four-inch barrel, chambered to take a big .38 round. It was enough blaster to spread Ryan's skull all over the mirror.

"Watch the rest of the crowd, in case there's any folks want to turn into a dead hero."

The two teenagers turned away so that Ryan could see only their backs. They dropped hands to holsters in a parody of a menacing gunslinger.

Gordy had also turned away for a moment, checking out the other tables.

That moment was *the* moment.

Ryan had kept hold of the three-pronged fork that he'd used to finish off the delicious cobbler. Now he swung to his right, slapping the Llama away from him with his free hand, lunging with the fork at Gordy's astonished face.

His target had been the right eye, but the man reacted more quickly than Ryan had expected, starting to turn and pull his head back.

But the fork still caught him, gouging a deep wound beneath his right eye, burying itself in the side of his nose, near the top. Blood gushed down over his mouth onto the floor, and he began to yell.

Ryan left the fork where it was, jammed into the cartilaginous flesh. At the same time as he'd begun the offensive, he'd pushed back, shouldering the two teenagers hard away from him, using his own chair to knock them both off-balance.

The place was instant bedlam, with everyone yelling and starting to try to escape the fight, tables going over and glasses and crockery smashing.

Ryan was totally oblivious to all that, his mind focusing coldly on what he had to do.

His right hand already had the SIG-Sauer clear of leather as he spun, now facing all three of the enemy.

Gordy had pulled the trigger on the Llama, firing wildly, the bullet splintering the mirror behind Ryan, missing him by a couple of feet at point-blank range.

He never got a chance to fire a second time.

The SIG-Sauer boomed, deafening in the low-ceilinged room, the 9 mm round catching the man through the upper chest, exiting in a welter of torn flesh and splinters of bone. It hit a fat man behind him in the right shoulder, sending him down, as well, screaming like a stuck pig.

Gordy took two staggering steps backward, dropping the blaster, hands clutching at the mortal wound.

"Burns like ice," he said in a normal, conversational voice, the fork wobbling grotesquely from his nose. Then his knees went, and he folded up on the floor.

Ryan wasn't listening or looking.

Knowing that it had been a perfect killing shot, he was concentrating now on taking out the two teenagers, neither of whom had yet managed to draw his blaster.

Carl was moving in behind one of them, reaching out to grab at the boy.

"Leave him and get down!" Ryan yelled, leveling the SIG-Sauer. He shot the lad through the side of the head, the powerful full-metal-jacket round bursting the skull like a ripe melon, showering walls, ceiling and customers with a thick gray-pink grue of brains, bone and blood.

The other youth had just recovered his balance, his right hand snatching desperately at the butt of his pistol. His gaze was fixed on Ryan's face, reading his own doom there.

"Don't" was all he managed to say. Then the 9 mm bullet hit him through the mouth, smashing teeth and ripping his tongue to flapping rags of bloodied flesh, burying itself in the core of his brain.

In less than six seconds, all three men lay dead on the restaurant floor.

"It's over!" Ryan shouted at the top of his voice, overriding the panic. "Hold it, folks. The chilling's done."

Gradually the hubbub abated, the customers who remained standing still, their faces white with shock, many of them dappled with blood. The wounded man had fallen to his knees, crying quietly, tears streaming down his chubby cheeks.

"You took them all," Carl said, breaking the silence.

"Had to. They were going to take me."

"Sure," Carl agreed, nodding like a porcelain Buddha. "We all saw that. I tried to..."

Ryan holstered the automatic. "I know you did. And I truly appreciate it. Just sorry for all the mess in here."

Carl waved his hands. "Don't worry. Soon get it cleaned. And folks'll come packing in once word gets around."

"Best settle my check."

Carl managed a smile. "Don't mention it, brother. This one's on the house."

KRYSTY HURLED HERSELF sideways, diving behind a padded armchair, shielding her face from the explosion of shattered glass.

The picture window had been reinforced, but it wasn't designed to withstand an impact like the huge mutie timber wolf.

The noise of the crash was deafening, and was accompanied by a rush of freezing air from outside. Krysty was aware of her own voice, screaming out to the others, and Jak also yelling to J.B., Mildred and Doc to come running.

She couldn't help being aware of the snarling of the pack leader, its breath frosting in the air, and the howling of the rest of the animals as they readied themselves to follow. Krysty also noticed the rank smell from the wolf, harsh and feral.

She had no idea where her blaster was, guessing that it had to be on the floor close to the sofa.

The room wasn't that dark, with the bright light of the burning logs, and Krysty pulled herself to hands and knees, the breath locked in her throat with the terror of the massive brindled animal, standing only a yard from her. Its shoulders and coat were patterned with blood, and shards of glass continuously dropped to the carpet from its heaving flanks. Its eyes were like saucers of molten gold, burning into her.

Her only hope was that Jak would be able to get at his own .357 Colt Python. His throwing knives would be of little use against an animal with such a thick pelt.

Out of the corner of her eye she saw that the window had been smashed apart, leaving a gaping hole at its center, with cracks running from top to bottom and from corner to corner. Even as she watched, a second wolf braved the gap and landed clumsily in the room, its paws slipping on a loose Navaho rug so that the creature fell against the piano.

Despite her fear, Krysty drew together the rags of her Earth Mother training, remembering about panic and about facing wild animals.

She stood suddenly, spreading her arms, her eyes never leaving the yellow orbs of the wolf. "You better leave me alone, you dumb fuck!" she said firmly.

Mother Sonja had told her that a positive response would chase away some animals and slow any attack from the rest. That was what she'd said, but Krysty had never tried it on anything like a giant timber wolf.

For a few heartbeats it hesitated, as though its murderous brain couldn't encompass such a helpless creature trying to stand against it.

During that brief stasis, a third and fourth wolf crashed into the room, all of them standing and looking at the woman and the white-haired man. Their eyes turned to the pack leader, as if they were waiting for instructions.

Jak had reached for his blaster, holding it in both hands, trying to decide what was his primary target. The pair of wolves that were menacing him, or the huge leader that threatened Krysty?

For several more racing beats of the heart, nothing moved in the warm room.

"Going to charge me, Jak," Krysty whispered, seeing the way the wolf was crouching, its powerful hindquarters quivering with suppressed tension, its eyes still fixed on her face. A thread of saliva dripped from its fangs.

The albino leveled the blaster and squeezed the trigger, the explosion releasing all the coiled, pent-up action.

Though Jak was probably the finest knife man in all of Deathlands, he would have been the first to admit that he wasn't in the top ranks of shootists.

The big .357 round hit the wolf, but missed any of its vital targets. Just as it began its spring, the bullet smashed into its hindquarters, near the top of the left leg, sending it spinning in midair. It landed clumsily between Krysty and the sofa, falling on its left side, howling at full power and turning to snap at its own bleeding wound.

The brief delay that Krysty's stand had brought them was utterly crucial.

It gave J.B. and the others time to wake and rush downstairs, carrying their own blasters.

The Uzi clattered, instantly knocking over the three wolves that had followed the leader in through the broken window, while Mildred, standing calm and foursquare in the doorway, shot a fifth animal through the head at the very moment it crashed in after the others.

But the giant mutie wolf was still very much alive, heaving itself upright, though the shattered leg made any rapid movement impossible.

Krysty backed slowly away from it, its looming shadow thrown ahead of it by the flickering flames.

The whole pack was coming now, bursting through the remnants of the broken picture window, two and three at a time, seeming to fill the room with their noise and rank stench. Jak managed to shoot another one, but the dying animal knocked him sideways, stumbling as it died, finally falling into the fire. Its bulk practically extinguished the burning logs, and the whole place was plunged into almost total darkness. There was still the filtered silver moonlight from outside, and the snarling, raging animals, filling the room.

The staccato sound of gunfire added to the confusion and carnage.

Krysty had good night sight, second only to Jak, and she could see the grim outline of the leader of the pack, dragging itself toward her as she backed away—backed away until she felt her shoulders touch the corner of the room and knew there was nowhere else to go.

She could feel the hot carnivorous breath of the wolf, less than a yard away from her. In the chaos, everyone was too busy with their own problems to worry about her. The corpse on the fire was already beginning to burn, filling the cooling air with smoke and the taste of roasted flesh.

Krysty had already decided to try to gouge out the wolf's eyes when it came at her, and bite it on the ear or the muzzle, though she also knew that the odds lay long and hard against her.

"Come on, then," she whispered, trying to boost her own failing courage, aware from things that Peter Maritza had told her back in Harmony that a wolf that size could take her arm off at the shoulder in a single crunching bite.

"Aid is at hand, my dear!" Doc yelled, stumbling across the room, tripping over the twitching corpse of one of the animals, holding the Le Mat in his right hand.

"Watch yourself, Doc!"

The mutie leader of the wolves had turned at the interruption, its attention wrenched away from the woman. It opened its great jaws and bayed defiance at the intruding man.

Doc might have been a few cards short of a full deck, but he had never lacked courage.

He stopped a scant yard from the creature and leveled the Le Mat, pointing it so that the railroad-tunnel muzzle was inches from the angular skull.

And pulled the trigger.

The hammer fell on the 18-gauge scattergun chamber, exploding the burst of grapeshot.

At point-blank range it didn't just kill the wolf, it destroyed it, blowing the head apart, covering Krysty with hot blood, peppering her with fragments of bone.

The animal never moved, simply slumping dead to the carpet.

"Gaia!" Krysty said, as she wiped her sleeve over her face. "God love you, Doc, for that."

*"Courage, mon amie, le diable est mort!"*

"What?"

"Means no more Mr. Wolf, little Red Riding Hair. We can all live happily ever after."

The shooting had stopped.

One of the wolves was whining as it lay beneath the window, but Jak stooped and carefully slit its throat.

The place stank of burned meat, scorched hair, hot blood, cordite and excrement, where a number of the animals had fouled themselves in dying. And the temperature had already dropped twenty degrees.

J.B. went to drag the body off the fire, fanning the air with his hand. "How many came in and how many stayed out?" he asked.

Mildred stepped carefully to the window, reloading the Czech blaster as she did, and peered through the shattered glass at the trampled winter landscape outside.

"All gone," she reported, turning back to the room. "And it looks like about eight or nine dead ones in here."

He nodded. "Everyone all right? Good work, my friends. Well, we were going to leave in the morning. I think we might as well go now. Anyone object? No? Then let's go."

# Chapter Twenty-Four

Ryan had spent a quiet night in the Palace Hotel, Leadville, waking once at the sound of a drunk noisily puking in the room next door. And once he thought that someone tried to turn the handle on his door, but the bolt was secure.

He woke early with the first shafts of dawn light breaking through the jagged tears in the thin curtains. As was his usual practice in most places, Ryan hadn't undressed, contenting himself with taking off his combat boots and unbelting his pants. He rested the Steyr by the side of the window, the big SIG-Sauer P-226 in its habitual location, tucked under his pillow.

He peered into the deserted dining room of the Palace, disturbing a gray rat that was busily gnawing at a cooked pork chop. Another rodent was lapping at a saucer of ketchup that stood on one of the dusty tables.

"Rain check time," Ryan muttered easing the sling of the rifle on his shoulder and walking out into the cool fresh morning.

An oil lamp already glowed outside Carl and Joanna's place and he went in, sniffing appreciatively at the scent of fresh-baked bread and frying bacon.

Carl greeted him from the swing door through to the kitchen. "The best of good mornings," he called. "See that we cleared away the mess left by those cold hearts?"

"Yeah. Must've taken all night."

Joanna appeared from inside a walk-in closet, holding a string of sausages, smiling at Ryan. "Didn't take all night, did it?" she asked her husband. "We were in bed by four-thirty."

Ryan sat at a round table by the window. A couple of miners were the only other diners, and they barely looked up at him from their breakfast of well-done steaks with eggs, grits and hash browns. A steaming jug of coffee stood on the checked cloth in the center of their table.

"I'll have what they're having," Ryan said. "But I'd like the steak done less well than that."

"I'll just carry it very quickly through a warm room," Carl said with a smile.

WHEN THE FOOD ARRIVED, it was piled high on the plate, the four eggs, sunny-side up, glistening gold.

"I put on three or four of the sausages and a few rashers of the bacon," Joanna called. "Looked to me like a man about to hit the trail again."

"Yeah."

He turned to Carl. "Never got around to asking you last night. I'm due to meet up with some friends. Wondered if they'd passed through here in the last day or so."

"We get lots of folks through here, brother."

"You wouldn't have missed them. Tall woman with the reddest hair you ever saw. Teenager with snow hair and ruby eyes. Old-timer in knee boots. And a small guy with glasses, wearing a battered fedora and carrying a shotgun and an Uzi."

"Sounds like I'd know them if I'd seen them anyplace," Carl said. "But I don't. Any message if they pass through here in the next few days?"

"Yeah. I'm Ryan Cawdor. Heading back north a ways, then cutting east over the tops. Down onto the trail above Breckenridge, if all goes well. Then up the pass to Fairplay. If they haven't caught up with me, I'll wait for them there."

Carl nodded. "Heard a lot of talk of trouble that way. This gang of norms and muties. Can you believe that? Been a load of chilling and burning. None of the miners or trappers or hunters go that way alone now. Stay together in armed groups." He paused. "If at all."

"Woman with red hair's my..." He hesitated, not sure of the right word. "She's my partner. She was reared up in Harmony and wants to visit again. Hasn't been there for years."

Carl smiled. "We've seen folks from there, every once in a while. Could be the gang's active that way."

"I figured that. No hard news?"

The man shook his head. "No. Used to be a wise woman up there, years ago. Never met her. Man I saw most was the same name as me. Carl."

"Carl Lanning?" Ryan asked, dredging the name from the back of his memory.

"Yeah. Blacksmith like his father before him. Decent kind of a man, but a few nails short of a horseshoe, if you get my meaning, brother."

"Yeah." He finished his second cup of coffee and sighed appreciatively. "Best be hitting the trail. Thanks again. To both of you. For everything."

"Take care," Joanna called from the kitchen. "Y'all come back and see us, y'hear?"

THERE HAD BEEN FROST during the night, and Ryan's boot heels rang out on the road bed as he walked back through Leadville, heading north for a while.

The same young lad with the round moony face was painting the gate he'd been working on the previous day, and he gave Ryan a wave and a broad smile.

"Lords, but I know you, mister."

"You told me how to get to the Palace Hotel."

"Right, I did. Where you headin' now, mister? Nothing that way but snow and mountains. Why, yes, *s-u-n* spells snow."

Ryan grinned, touched by the lad's good nature. "I'll take care. You have a good day now."

Another wave of the hand and he walked on, past a ruined building, reaching the point where the highway forked.

It was a lovely morning, bright and crisp, and he whistled to himself, stepping out in time to the music, a rousing old marching tune.

A recently erected wooden sign pointed left to Redcliff and the interstate, right to Climax and the pass east.

As he turned right, he segued smoothly into "She Wore a Yellow Ribbon," breaking into song as the road climbed. "'She wore it for her lover who was far, far away.'"

RYAN HAD THE DETAILS of the map firmly in his head, and he knew that he would soon have to strike off right, toward the east, and hope to find his way into the next valley across. That would then bring him up to Fairplay.

Before leaving Carl and Joanna's eatery Ryan had bought some food for the journey: a couple of crusty new-baked rolls, filled with egg, salted beef and tomato, a thick slice of some deliciously moist walnut bread and some small peaches, with a flask of fresh milk.

He stopped and sat on a ridge of bare rock, enjoying the warmth of the sun, eating lunch, admiring the beauty of the mountains that circled him. It had been easy walking, despite the elevation of eleven thousand feet.

A large crow, its feathers so shiny black they shone blue-green, had perched on a rock a few paces away from him. It watched the man with its head on one side, yellow beak ajar, button-bright eyes staring intently at him.

Ryan broke off a corner of one of the rolls and flicked it underhanded at the bird, which hopped sideways and effortlessly caught it. Throwing back its head, it then pecked urgently at a few spilled crumbs.

"You must be the bird when people talk about a distance being as the crow flies," Ryan said.

The crow saw there was no more free lunch coming, and it flapped ponderously away, giving out a melancholy cawing sound as it circled a hundred feet above Ryan, eventually flying off toward the south.

THERE WASN'T MUCH LEFT of Climax. A few stone chimneys still stood, and a couple of pack-rat cabins, thrown together from the ruins of other, grander buildings. There was little sign of life.

As Ryan passed the last of the wretched dwellings, a half-naked barefoot child of indeterminate sex ran outside, holding a stone as big as its fist. The child heaved it toward Ryan with an expression of such extreme malevolence that he recoiled and half drew the SIG-Sauer. But the rock fell short of him, rolling into a narrow gulley.

"Fuck away, outlander," the child screeched, giving him the finger.

Ryan returned the gesture. "Yeah, and your mama too," he snarled, lifting the dark eye patch to reveal the raw, weeping socket. He looked so frightening that the child started to bawl and ran back into the hut.

The incident kept Ryan in good spirits, and he walked at a fast clip toward the cutoff to the east.

RYAN ENCOUNTERED a fair amount of snow as he plodded on, finding it harder going. A dusting lay over everything, including the narrow, winding trail, as well as larger and deeper pockets in the shadows where the sun never shone.

He kept checking the trail, trying to see whether Krysty and the others might have looped around him, possibly avoiding Leadville in the night. But it had rained within the past twenty-four hours, and it had been heavy enough to wash away anything except deep wag ruts from the highway.

He walked on through the afternoon, feeling relief as he crossed the highest point of the ridge and began to descend slowly, with the valley that was his destination opening before him like a magnificent flower.

There was no sign of life anywhere around him, except for the prolific marmots that kept popping up from burrows as he passed, standing on hind legs like large prairie dogs, and the birds, mainly crows and some blue-breasted jays, that wheeled high above him.

The sun was already out of sight behind him when he smelled the bitterness of smoke.

THE SUN WAS creeping behind the mountains that lay to the west as the companions entered the outskirts of Leadville. The township seemed deserted except for a tall, chubby teenager who was painting the hinges of a big five-barred gate.

"Hi, there, strangers," he called out.

"Hi," Krysty replied, walking off the blacktop toward him. "You wouldn't have seen a tall man with one eye passing this way, would you?" She covered her left eye with her hand to try to show the soft-faced boy what she meant.

"Lords, yes!" A broad smile spread almost from ear to ear. "One eye, lady. Sad eye, lady."

"When did you see him?"

He looked worried. "Now, I don't remember times and days and months all that good. But I think it was this same day we got now. He spoke to me, real kind. Went off that way." He pointed behind them.

"Real kind," J.B. said, hearing the conversation. "Doesn't sound much like Ryan."

"The retard sure it was Ryan?" Jak asked.

"Don't call him that," Mildred snapped. "Like saying someone's a crip."

"Tall with black hair. Carrying a rifle over his shoulder. And one eye."

The boy nodded eagerly. "Lords, yes. Sure as sunshine it was him."

Krysty patted him on the arm and he blushed deep crimson with delight. "Thanks a bunch," she said. "You've been really helpful to us."

WHEN THEY FOUND Carl and Joanna's Diner there was even more information for them.

While they shared an enormous fish pie, made from fresh salmon and covered in golden-brown pastry, with fluffy whipped potatoes and buttered carrots, Carl told them what he could about Ryan's time in Leadville and the message he had left behind.

A young blond woman with heavily made-up eyes was sitting at a nearby table, listening to the account.

"There was blood and brains all over," she said, interrupting at the point where Carl had reached the three would-be killers. "Prettiest whirly patterns you ever saw." She spoke slowly, quietly and hesitantly, as though she were a long-term jolt user. She pointed at Doc's cane. "My daddy got a walking stick near as pretty as that."

Carl pointed to his forehead with a circling motion. "Long gone," he said quietly.

"And he left a message?" Krysty asked.

"Sure." Carl folded his hands in front of him, like a child about to recite a lesson that he'd memorized. "He was going to cross over the high country between the two passes. Down onto the trail above Breckenridge. And—"

Joanna had come out of the kitchen with a jug of creamy white sauce. "And he was going up to Fairplay and he'd wait for you there," she said. "That was all."

Krysty felt as though a great weight had been lifted from her heart. Ryan had obviously been to the school and been happy enough to leave Dean there. Now he was on the way up to Harmony, just part of a day ahead of them. And he had successfully survived a vicious attack on him.

"We'll stay the night here in Leadville," she said. "And get going after him in the morning. When do you think we'd catch up with him?"

"Take the better part of two days to reach Fairplay," Carl told her.

"Mebbe longer," Joanna added, looking significantly at Doc.

"Make no mistake. There may be a little snow on the roof, madam," he replied. "But I can assure you that a fire still glows deep in my belly."

She laughed. "Sure admit you can put away the food all right. Leave a space for the baked apples with cloves and cinnamon sugar, won't you?"

"Indeed I will." He stood and bowed to her, oblivious of the large trailing linen napkin that dangled from his collar. "And I should say that you are a genius among cooks, Joanna." He kissed the tips of his fingers to her.

She snorted with amusement and flounced delightedly back into the kitchen.

THEY TOOK TWO ROOMS at the Palace Hotel, ready to start soon after dawn, though everyone agreed that breaking their fasts at the diner was an essential prelude to the day.

The night was quiet and uneventful, though heavy clouds were gathering toward the north.

# Chapter Twenty-Five

The light was fading fast, and Ryan picked his careful way down the steep trail. The path wound and doubled back on itself, so that it wasn't possible to see the source of the smoke that was coiling skyward from some distance farther on.

A highway was just visible at the bottom of the valley. It was in deep shadow, but Ryan paused in the stillness and thought that he saw riders heading toward Fairplay. And he thought that his ears caught the high-pitched sound of a small armawag running at full throttle.

But he couldn't be sure of that, and the shadows grew deeper by the minute.

Behind him he heard the rumble of far-off thunder, turning to see the silver pattern of chem lightning streaking across the western sky.

Night seemed to sweep around him like a horseman's cloak.

The moon was obscured behind banks of cloud and he slowed to minimize the risk of taking a tumble on the rutted trail. The smell of burning grew stronger, and he thought that he could hear human voices.

Around the next sharp gooseneck bend Ryan finally saw the flames.

A Conestoga wag blazed brightly in the middle of the track, with a small group of men and women clustered helplessly around it. He was able to approach within fifty yards before anyone noticed him.

"They're back!" a woman screamed.

Ryan stopped where he was, his hand resting on the cold butt of the SIG-Sauer, holding up his left hand in a gesture of peace.

"I'm alone!" he shouted. "All right with you if I come ahead?"

There was frantic conversation, then a white-haired man moved to the front of the group. "If you're one of them, mister, then I can tell you that we flat got nothing left for you to take. Exceptin' for the poor lives of us that's left."

There were four men and two women alive. Only one of the men was under the age of fifty. The women were both well into their sixties.

Scattered around the blazing rig were eight corpses: five young males, two little children and a young woman with the back of her head blown away. The muzzle of a small revolver was still clenched between her teeth.

The white-haired man spoke for the others.

"We're Quakers from back east, coming into the mountains to bring the word of God to outlying communities. Been on the road for close to a year. Had some hard times in the past couple of weeks. Provisions ran low, and we got the rig bogged down to the axles in mud.''

Ryan had never seen such a sorry lot. All of them were gray-faced and haggard, eyes sunk in sockets of wind-scoured bone, prominent teeth and fingers crooked like claws.

''Then the murderers came on us like wolves on the fold. We were helpless. Sister Rosalind there chose to take her own path from this vale of tears. She also slew her own children to spare them being taken.''

Ryan looked across the valley into the blackness. ''Thought I saw some men on horseback and heard a small armawag. Was that the gang?''

The old man nodded. ''A mix of normal men, though some looked from south of the Grandee. And several stickies among them. I had never heard of such a racial mix before.''

''They were degenerate scum, Brother Angus,'' one of the women said.

''And they took what little you had left?'' Ryan said. ''Anything else?''

Brother Angus nodded slowly. ''There were five women of a younger age. One was barely into her teens. The filth took them all and gunned down anyone who tried—'' He looked at the bodies. ''One was my son. They took Sister Persephone, who had agreed to be his bride.''

Ryan looked around him, stone-faced. It was a total and appalling disaster for these people. Yet it was a scene that he'd come across too many times in his life, particularly in the days with Trader. The old man had talked about wolves on the fold. Not a bad description of the callous cruelty of the attackers and the helpless vulnerability of their victims.

"Thee wouldn't have any food, would thee, mister?" the other old woman asked.

Ryan hesitated. He had one roll and one of the peaches, plus a couple of mouthfuls of milk, enough to keep him going on into the next day. It wasn't enough to even scratch the surface for just one of the starving group.

"No," he said. "I'm sorry."

"What can we do?" Brother Angus asked, wringing his hands. "Where can we go?"

"Best go back to Leadville," Ryan said. "Nearest place I can think where I know there'll be food."

"We're jack-free. They took it all. We must throw ourselves on the charity of strangers."

Ryan sniffed. The charity of strangers wasn't that common a commodity in Deathlands.

"Still . . . Leadville's closest. You got to pick between a small chance and no chance."

"The Lord will provide for us," one of the other men said, falling to his knees, hands clasped in prayer. "He will provide for his humble servants."

"Not done much providing so far," Ryan replied, looking at the corpses and the wag, burning now to the flatbed. Another five minutes and that would be gone, and the survivors would be left in the dark and cold.

He hunched his shoulders, feeling the first pattering of rain on his back.

ONE OF THE TRADER'S most deeply held beliefs was that when you could help someone, you did. But if you couldn't help at all, then you didn't waste time on hanging around.

Ryan couldn't take on the job of guide for the ragged survivors of the raid. The only sound advice that he could give was to strike out immediately for Leadville. Despite their frailty, there was a chance that most of them could make it back to the township and a better than even hope of living.

But Brother Angus consulted with his fellow Quakers and they all agreed that they wouldn't move on under any circumstances without burying their dead comrades. Ryan's guess was that they'd be lucky to finish that chore by noon the next day. And by then their strength would be hugely diminished and most, if not all, of them would then die.

Before leaving them to their own devices, Ryan found out what he could about the gang.

It seemed that there had been between twenty and thirty of them. About a third had been stickies. Proof was marked on two of the bodies, which showed where the suckers of the stickies had ripped away patches of skin and flesh.

None of the Quakers was any help when it came to the weaponry of the gang, though one of the old women had noticed that the armawag had been towing a small trailer that she thought probably held cans of gasoline.

"You don't know where they were based?" Ryan asked. "They didn't mention any names?"

Brother Angus shook his head, his face a pale blur in the streaming darkness of the rainstorm. "Wasn't like we'd have heard, friend. Too much yelling and cursing and chilling. Like something from hell."

The brighter of the old women had been standing at his side, listening. "From hell! Truly said, Brother Angus. From the deepest circle of icy, fiery hades they came, grinning and shooting and slashing. Devils from hell."

There was nothing more that Ryan could do.

It seemed more than likely that it was the same gang that he and his friends had been hearing about since they arrived in Colorado, the gang that was reputed to have its headquarters somewhere farther up the valley to the southeast.

Up beyond Fairplay.

Toward the ville of Harmony.

THE RAIN CAME DOWN ceaselessly, and Ryan was quickly soaked to the skin. There was a great deal of thunder and, for about an hour, a ferocious chem storm with violent shocks of pink-purple lightning. Out on the exposed flank of the mountain, with a rifle slung across his shoulders, Ryan felt vulnerable and quickly sought cover, ending up crouched among the blue spruces that lined the trail.

While he waited out the storm, he tried to guess whether Krysty and the others were ahead or behind him. The odds seemed to be that they were behind, which meant there was a temptation to hole up for a day or so and wait for them. Perhaps when he reached the little ville of Alma that was marked on his mental map?

But if they'd shortcutted him and got ahead, then every hour he waited would be another hour he'd fall behind.

If they were behind him, then they should be safe from this killing gang. If they were ahead, then they could easily run into them. Despite J.B.'s firepower—aided by the others—they would still be vulnerable to twenty or more armed killers.

Ryan felt the hairs standing on his nape, and he crouched lower, laying the rifle flat in the pine needles. He smelled ozone moments before he experienced a flash of lightning so close that it blinded him for several seconds. The thunder was on top of the lightning, making the marrow of his bones vibrate and the ground tremble beneath his boots.

"Fireblast!" he whispered, his voice sounding faint and far away.

It took him a few moments to collect his scattered, shattered thoughts. Krysty and the others. The gang. One other possibility was that the gang had split into two or more parts in order to raid a larger area.

But that made the range of imponderables so vast that it was a waste of time thinking about them.

As the rain eased a little and the storm passed across the valley, Ryan shouldered the rifle and set off down the slippery trail.

DAWN COINCIDED with his reaching the end of the track, down at the valley bottom, with the highway leading left to right in front of him. His path lay to the right, to the south, more or less toward the rising sun that was just showing behind the high peaks.

Eight miles would take him to Alma, and a further six or seven to Fairplay.

But it was going to be steep walking, and he figured he'd do well to cover the distance to the top before the middle of the afternoon. He finished all his food and the last swig of milk, then filled the canteen with fresh meltwater from the river that crossed his trail.

Before going on he glanced up and behind him, trying to trace the track down from the head of the pass, among the dense blanket of spruce. He wondered if he might catch a glimpse of Krysty and the others, but knew what a long shot that was.

Ryan turned and began the haul up the road, which glistened wetly in the dawn light.

ALL THE COMPANIONS were well filled, and J.B. had ordered some trail food for the hike.

Outside the steamed-up window of the diner, the morning looked bleak and miserable. There was no sign of any letup in the grim weather. Rain streamed from a dark sky, forming rivulets along the blocked gutters at the edges of the highway through Leadville. It had poured all night with spectacular thunder and lightning that had awakened all of them—except Doc, who claimed that he would have slept through the San Francisco earthquake.

"Could have caused some double-bad damage out on the high trails," Carl said worriedly.

"Ryan can look after himself," J.B. said. "If anyone can."

"Don't tempt Providence," Krysty touched the wooden leg of the table for luck.

"Sure he can." Jak spoke through a mouthful of sweet roll, splattering the table with crumbs.

"Wish him all the best, when you see him," Joanna said, leaning on the serving counter. "And if any of you ever pass this way again, you'd be rightly welcome."

"We will. And thanks." Krysty looked out at the dreary morning. "Let's go."

THE FRESH-PAINTED GATE swung silently to and fro on its greased hinges as they passed the house at the edge of Leadville. Krysty turned as they walked by and caught a glimpse of a round face peering at them from behind lace curtains. She lifted a hand to wave, but there was no response.

In less than a quarter hour, the township had vanished in the driving rain and the five friends headed into the high country, toward Fairplay.

# Chapter Twenty-Six

Ryan had made the steep climb up toward Alma, seeing no trace of life for several hours. Then the first sign that he saw of life was death.

A telegraph pole on the right side of the road had been rigged into a makeshift crucifix, and the body of a naked woman hung from it.

The rain had finally eased, but there was still a persistent drizzle. Ryan blinked up into it, looking at the corpse, suspecting that it might well be one of the kidnapped Quaker women. Not that anyone would ever have recognized her.

It was impossible to tell at what point death had come to the poor wretch. The probability was that she'd still been living when they'd strung her up, using thin baling wire around wrists, elbows and ankles to hold her in place. The wire had cut into the flesh, leaving deep, white-lipped gashes.

The bruises around her breasts and across her thighs told their own tale of how viciously she'd been abused before death, and the circular torn patches of skin showed the rending hands of stickies had been involved.

The hair on her head and on her body had been burned away, which also indicated stickies. Nothing in Deathlands loved fires and explosions like stickies did.

After they'd used her to satisfy their own sexual lusts, the gang had crucified her, then used her for target practice. Her right hand had been blown off at the wrist, and there were other devastating wounds all over the body. What remained of her face was unrecognizable. What blood there had been had long washed away in the downpour and the corpse was as white as marble, the various wounds showing dark purple.

Ryan stared blank-faced at the sight.

If he'd had any doubts of the sort of gang they were going to deal with, then this would have removed them. It was a brutal mob with no sense of the dignity of life.

A few pebbles and clods of earth clattered down the hillside, making him jump and draw his blaster. But it wasn't repeated, and he guessed that it was a result of the heavy rain.

As Ryan started to walk on, boots splashing through the watery mud, the drizzle grew stronger, turning into full-fledged rain.

"SOMETHING'S LYING at the side of the trail," Krysty said, pushing back threads of soaking red hair from her forehead. "Looks like a body."

The light was very poor, more like evening than noon, the visibility diminished by the curtains of rain that swept across the top of the pass.

"Dead one," Jak said.

"Man or woman?" Krysty had already quickened her stride, feeling a lump like cold lead in her heart.

"Can't... Got white hair."

It was an old man and he wasn't dead. But he wasn't far off, his breathing shallow and rapid, his pulse barely there. He was sodden and looked as if he'd been lying faceup at the side of the road for some hours.

Mildred had carefully checked him over, kneeling in the muddy pool where he lay. She looked up at the others. "No chance," she said quietly. "Hypothermia's way too advanced. If I had a hot bed and a warm room within a hundred yards, and skilled nursing staff, then maybe I could just save him." She stood. "That's only a maybe."

"What do we do with the poor old fellow?" Doc asked, water streaming down his stubbled cheeks, matting the silver hair to his leonine head.

"Nothing," Mildred replied.

"We cannot just leave him! By the Three Kennedys! He is our brother."

J.B. shook his head. "No, he isn't, Doc. He's a stranger. Help him if you can. If you can't, then you might as well move on. Sympathy won't help him. He's dying."

He turned to Mildred. "Is that right, Millie?"

"I'm afraid so, Doc. A bullet would best put him out of his misery."

"Butcher him?"

"Truth is, the old man's in no pain. He's in a deep coma and he'll never come out of it. Weather like this'll take him off in an hour or so. He's that close to the dark ferry. Believe me, Doc, there isn't a single damned thing we can do for him. Can't even ask if he's seen Ryan.''

Doc stooped and plucked a scarf from around the dying man's throat, folding it carefully over his face. ''Least it'll keep the rain from his eyes,'' he said.

RYAN HAD FOUND another body, tossed by the side of the winding blacktop like a discarded toy. He guessed that it was one of the children kidnapped from the Quaker train. She lay huddled on her back with her throat slit, both arms broken. Her body hadn't been so badly mutilated as the woman.

''Building up a good blood score,'' he said to himself. He straightened the little body and placed it gently beneath a broad sycamore tree, standing and looking down at it. ''Wasn't your day, was it, kid?'' he said.

BECAUSE THERE SEEMED little evidence of serious danger, J.B. hadn't felt it necessary to order them into a strung-out skirmish line.

He walked along with Mildred, while Krysty had found herself taking the point position. Behind her, Jak and Doc were deeply involved in an argument of extraordinary complexity about what happened beyond space.

''You say space started with big bang from nothing. What was before nothing, Doc?''

"Fields, dear boy. Fields of potentiality. Thirty-seven of them, according to what was the latest thinking when they pushed me forward to Deathlands."

"But how can something come from nothing?"

"You have to be able to wrap your brain about particles that have no mass and can be in two or three places at the same time. Difficult, I know."

Krysty had been half listening to what she could catch above the ceaseless plashing of the rain on the trail. But half of her mind was fixed on Ryan. At least they knew that he was roughly a full day ahead of them.

For a moment the rain stopped altogether, and shafts of silvery sunshine broke clear across the valley, showing them their destination, a thousand feet or more below, and the ribbon of highway that wound back up to their right, toward where she knew Fairplay and Harmony lay.

Everyone stopped to stare at the beautiful view.

"Worthy of the painter Turner at his mystic best," Doc said.

"We can almost see Ryan from here," Mildred stated. "If we knew just where to look."

Krysty was following the snaking trail down below them when her eyes were caught by what looked like the wreckage of a burned-out wag, and some people. Although none of them seemed to be moving.

"BROTHER ANGUS went for help," breathed the elderly woman who was crawling steadily, head down, knees raw and bloodied, about two hundred yards from the scene of devastation. "I just decided to go after him but...can't make it."

They had made her as comfortable as they could. Mildred and Krysty went to check the others.

A snow-haired man and another old woman were still clinging by their fingernails to the ragged edge of life. Beyond the wag, on a flat stretch of the tundra before the first of the remorseless lines of blue spruce, were some graves.

Some were completed, some half-finished and some barely started. One was full of water and held the floating corpse of a child and the body of a man, who looked as if he'd been digging, had slipped and fallen in headfirst and drowned.

Mildred returned to where Doc was sitting in the dirt, cradling the head of the old woman in his lap. "She said they were attacked by a gang that included stickies," he said. "And Ryan passed by them in the night. She can't remember more than that, but it must've been him. Tall, one-eyed man, who tried to help." He sighed. "Her mind wanders, and I fear that she is also a candidate for that dark ferryman."

Mildred checked her over, confirming Doc's informal diagnosis. "Yeah," she said, straightening and looking around. "She say anything else?"

J.B. answered her. "They're Quakers. Got attacked. Lost all their food, which was little enough. They were all close to starvation. Ryan told them to go back to Leadville. They insisted on trying to bury their dead. She says that's what pushed them all over the brink."

Krysty sniffed. "Ryan had an ace on the line. Time's gone and it's too late. If they'd struck off for Leadville straight away, most of them could've made it. As it is..." She shrugged.

"What we do?" Jak asked.

J.B. had been about to speak, but he looked instead at Krysty and Mildred, hesitating. "They're all dying. We don't have the food or the facilities to help a single one of them."

Mildred nodded, the beads in the wet plaits whispering softly. "Goes hard against the grain, but like John says. There isn't a thing we can do. Except stop and hold hands until they let go."

"How long would that be?" Doc asked. "It is grim to leave a fellow human being to a lonely passing."

"Afternoon now," Mildred said. "They'll all be gone by moonrise."

Doc rose, carefully laying the dying woman's head in the dirt. Her eyes had closed, and she seemed to have slipped into unconsciousness.

"If we are to go, then it were best that we go quickly," he said. "Before I allow my heart to take precedence over my head. I know that we must leave them. But..." He allowed the sentence to trail away into the gray drizzle.

THE GANG MEMBERS HAD BEEN using their victims for their pleasure along the road, stopping, sometimes, to light a small fire to keep themselves warm and to inflict a little pain and torture. Then they moved on, higher up the trail, leaving the corpses discarded by the roadside.

Brother Angus had told him that the bandits had taken five women from the wag.

Before he reached Alma, with the sun well down, Ryan had found all of them.

Ryan had two kinds of anger.

One was the sudden flaring rage that he had always found difficult to control, which dated back from when he was a young boy. The veins would throb in his temple and the scar across his cheek would pulse like a disturbed snake. A crimson mist seemed to filter across his mind, sometimes snatching away his combat senses.

It was something that seemed to happen much less often than it used to, and Ryan could now, generally, bring it quickly under control.

And there was the other kind of anger, the kind that was slow to be triggered but gradually gathered its own murderous momentum. It was like a cold flame that burned with a terrible clean light.

The short-fuse anger would come and go within a minute.

But the kind of rage that now seeped through Ryan's mind and body would be extinguished only when he'd taken revenge on the gang of mindless, brutish murderers.

THERE WAS MORE of their handiwork to see when he eventually reached the site of what had once been the attractive little ville of Alma.

With the steady rain it was impossible to tell when the fires had been set, but the smell still lingered. The cracked and blackened timbers streamed with water, and every last spark was long extinguished.

At least there weren't too many bodies. It looked as if a lot of the inhabitants of Alma had gotten wind of the raiders and managed to make their escape, possibly down the trail toward the old interstate.

A row of four men had been crucified to a barn wall, with long steel nails that had crushed through their palms and ankles. One had been hung upside down and a fire lit beneath him, so that little remained of his charred skull and torso.

Once again, it was cruelty for its own mean sake, tainted with the vicious sickness of the stickies in the gang.

Most of the township had been fired, with every building on the main drag either destroyed or seriously damaged.

Night was closing in, and the endless rain showed no sign of abating. Twice in the last half mile Ryan had come across evidence of serious earth slips, where the dirt had absorbed all the water it could and had given way in a wall of streaming mud.

"Best get shelter," he said to himself.

Glancing around through the gloomy drizzle, he could see that some of the side streets of the little ville seemed to be untouched by fire.

Movement caught his eye, and he saw what looked like a dozen or more tiny mice scurrying across from one building to another, their little legs powering through the spray.

Ahead of him he could make out a row of wooden shacks, some of them already tumbled, built against a steep slope that held some stunted pines. He thought he could see the remnants of an ancient mine a little higher up the hillside, but it was getting too dark to be sure.

Ryan picked his way through the muddy puddles, trying to decide which of the cottages looked the most solid. Four or five of them seemed to have been inhabited, with unbroken glass in windows, curtains and decent front doors. One had a few scrubby rosebushes tangled around a white picket fence, and a hand-painted nameplate on the gate. Pong-de-rosa, it was called.

Ryan took a last look around the dead township, checking that he wasn't being watched, then walked up the narrow path and pushed at the front door. After a momentary resistance, it gave, and he stepped into a dark hall.

There wasn't the usual dead, flat smell of a long-empty building and he hesitated. Food had been cooked within the last day or so, and he could smell lamp oil.

The woman's voice from the shadows wasn't all that much of a shock.

"You got three seconds to tell me why I shouldn't blast your cock clean out your ass."

# Chapter Twenty-Seven

A note of raw panic ran through the woman's voice like a hacksaw through a sheet of plate glass.

She was crouched in the doorway of what Ryan guessed was likely the kitchen. The voice came from low down. Just as she spoke, his keen hearing had caught the click of a shotgun hammer being thumbed back. So it probably wasn't any kind of a bluff.

"Could use ten seconds, if you don't mind," he said. "Three's not enough."

"Three's plenty if you're the murdering bastard that I take you for. Speak out, quick. I can see you silhouetted against the front door real good. Not going to miss with my 12-gauge, old Betsy here."

"Sure you're not. Name's Ryan Cawdor. Come from out in the Shens. On my way to Fairplay to meet up with my wife and some friends. Came across a party that had been attacked on the trail. Said it was a gang of norms and stickies. Seen plenty of their work. They fire the ville?"

"Course they did, stupe! Hadn't been for the heaviest damned rain I've known in fifty years of living in Alma that put out the flames."

"Most folks get away?"

"Yeah." The tension eased just a little from her voice. Now that his eye was becoming accustomed to the semidarkness, Ryan could see her, kneeling on the floor, about fifteen feet in front of him.

"They been gone long? The killers?"

"Half a day. I'm not sure I believe your story, mister. You took a gamble coming in here."

"Didn't know anyone was left in the ville."

"Still a gamble. You a gamblin' man?"

"Best I know is not to hit seventeen when you bet against the dealer," he replied.

There was no response, though he could see the woman had shuffled a little, as if she were uncomfortable.

Outside, he could hear the rain sweeping against the door, slicing into the narrow hall. He stood still, not wanting to make any move that might leave him on his back, staring at the ceiling, with a bellyful of buckshot.

"You still there, lady?" he asked.

"Yeah. I can't see why you'd have come back on your own if you were one of those devils. They only go around in gangs."

"Comes down to you believing me and letting me in. Or you don't believe me and you gut shoot me and that's the end of the line. Up to you. But it's cold and wet waiting here."

The woman stood, sighing, helping herself with a hand on the frame of the door. "Damned arthritis creeps up in rainy weather," she said. "Best close the door, mister. What did you say your name was?"

"Ryan Cawdor." He pushed the front door shut. "You wouldn't have some light, would you?"

"Lamps attract the wrong kind of interest, Mr. Cawdor. Some of my friends found that out when the gang hit us."

"I believe that they've moved on. Higher up. Toward Fairplay and Harmony."

She nodded, just visible. "Stand still, so you don't knock over any of my valuables. I'll tug the curtains closed and we can risk a light."

He could hear her moving slowly in the front room and the whisper of the curtains being drawn shut. Then came the rasp of a self-light and the golden glow of an oil lamp.

"Come ahead, Mr. Cawdor. But remember, I still got Betsy here in case you got fancy ideas."

"My only idea is to try and get dry and warm. Don't even know your name."

He walked into a neat parlor, with a pedal harmonium in one corner and the remains of a fire glowing in the hearth. A copper scuttle held some cut logs. The main impression was of a comfortable clutter of ornaments.

"I'm Elvira Madison."

She looked to be around forty, with a mop of bushy hair tied with a red ribbon. She had a perky face and bright eyes, but her heavy body, swollen legs and twisted

hands showed the extent that the arthritis had her in its
thrall.

Elvira was wearing a skirt of handwoven wool and a
blouse of embroidered cotton, and she was holding a
single-barrel Model 94C Stevens shotgun as if she was
still ready to use it.

"Seen enough, Mr. Cawdor?"

"Sorry. Didn't mean to stare. Just that this part of
Colorado seems flooded with death, and it's good to see
someone as alive as you."

"Flattery gets you everywhere. Oh, I can't keep hold
of old Betsy. You look like a hard man, Mr. Cawdor,
but not a vicious one. Hope I'm right in that."

She uncocked the blaster and leaned it against the side
of a well-worn armchair.

"I was going to put on some stew. How's that sound?
And there's a pile of blankets in the spare room. Probably damp with all the rain, but they'll dry out. You can
strip off and get your clothes dry." She saw the look on
his face. "Doubt you got anything that I haven't seen
before, Mr. Cawdor. I'm a widow with three husbands
in the graveyard yonder. You can peel bare naked and I
won't blink." She made her careful way to the hall,
pausing to smile back at him. "Might not blink, but I
might ask you to jump my bones later. Been a while."

She cackled with laughter and went into the kitchen.

Ryan intended to take her advice about getting himself and his clothes dry, but he walked around the room
first, letting some of the day's tension ease away.

Elvira kept her little home in bright, new-pin condition. He ran a finger over the top of a mahogany bureau, finding it spotless. There were bits of china and glass all over the place. Taking pride of place in the center of the mantel was a porcelain figure of a swarthy man in a white-fringed jumpsuit with a jeweled buckle. He had long sideburns and carried a guitar. Ryan wasn't absolutely sure, but he thought it was probably a statue of the legendary Elvis Presley.

An ornate ormolu clock on a side table chimed the hours. Six o'clock.

There was a strange groaning noise that made Ryan stop and look around. It had sounded as though a very large dog had leaned against one of the walls of the house, but it wasn't repeated.

Elvira reappeared, hobbling with the aid of a stick. "Couldn't hold this and Betsy, as well." She grinned.

There was a strong gust of wind that rattled the catch on the window, and a fresh burst of heavy rain dashed against the front of the house.

"Have to be getting hold of some cubits of gopher wood and building me an ark if this goes on," Elvira stated. "I never knew the like."

There was a faint and distant rumble, and some of the glass animals on the shelf by the fireplace started to chink against one another.

Ryan turned to the woman.

The house moved, carrying Elvira toward him, her mouth open in shock. Pictures fell off walls and the door cracked down its center. The rumbling grew

louder, as if a war wag were roaring into the middle of
the room.

Ryan's last glimpse was of the ceiling falling, splintering apart, and seeing the dark sky beyond the tumbling walls. There was a blow to the side of his head
and...

Darkness.

# Chapter Twenty-Eight

Krysty stopped walking through the evening darkness, almost doubling over, both hands snatching at her forehead, pressing at her eyes as though they were bursting from their sockets. "Oh, Gaia!" she gasped.

Doc was alongside and he reached for her, putting an arm around her shoulders, supporting her, saving her from dropping to her knees in the watery mud that covered the trail. "My dearest lady!" he exclaimed. "Have you turned your ankle?"

"No." Her voice was thin with shock. "Not that. Just got a dreadful jolt to my mind."

J.B., Mildred and Jak had gathered around her, barely visible in the streaming drizzle.

"Is it Ryan?" the Armorer asked.

"Yes."

"What?"

Krysty straightened, still leaning heavily on Doc for support. "I don't know. Something bad. Something real bad. Hit me like a lightning bolt in the brain."

"Any idea what it is?" Mildred asked. "Or where he is?"

Krysty swallowed hard. "Not too far away. It was so triple strong." She laughed nervously. "About the most powerful 'seeing' I ever had."

"Dead?" Jak probed.

"I don't…can't… He was falling, and the world was spinning about him. Like he was lost in space." She shook her head. "I don't know, friends. Just that it's serious, and I don't believe it's chilled him outright."

"We're at the bottom of the valley," J.B. said. "Should be finding somewhere for the night. Do you want to push on up the grade?"

Krysty hesitated. "Could easy pass by whatever's the trouble in the dark," she finally decided. "Let's try and find somewhere out of this rain, then get moving at first light. And hope we find him."

WATER DRIPPED remorselessly into Ryan's open mouth, making him choke and bringing him back to a sort of consciousness.

For several long seconds he was totally disoriented, not knowing where he was or what had happened. He struggled to bring back the memory of the last few seconds before the world fell in on him.

Elvira Madison. The woman living alone in the ruins of what had once been the pretty little ville of Alma. Middle-aged and spunky, sorely disabled by arthritis. Neat little house with a harmonium and lots of ornaments.

Ryan blinked, aware of a ringing pain behind his left ear, becoming aware that something was pinning him down below the waist, holding him immobile.

"House fell . . ." he mumbled.

Now it came back to him: the noise like a large animal leaning clumsily against the frame house; the woman hurling toward him; walls cracking; the ceiling coming down, opening up the roof to the dark sky; jangling and wheezing from the tormented harmonium and the splintering of china and glass all about him.

"Earth slip," he concluded.

Ryan tried to work out how he was, the extent of his injuries.

His right hand was free, but his left arm was trapped beneath him. By feeling, Ryan could work out that the floor had opened and he'd dropped into it, leaving him caught around the ankles and thighs by a tangle of jagged beams and joists.

Some torn carpet was bulked up and wrapped around his waist, preventing him from getting at either the SIG-Sauer or the panga.

It was almost full dark, but there was a faint glimmer of ragged moonlight breaking through tatters of high cloud, enough for him to see a pale blur of white only a few inches from his face. Above the sound of the ceaseless pattering rain, Ryan realized that he could hear ragged breathing.

Not his own.

"Elvira?" he croaked, coughing out a mouthful of dirty water. He tried again. "Elvira? You hear me?"

There was no response.

He made an effort to move his legs and kick himself free. Something moved down below, pinching his left ankle, making him yelp at the pain. A rumbling seemed to come from everywhere at once, and Ryan had the sensation that everything had settled a little more firmly around him. He suddenly realized that his legs, to the knees, were also immersed in watery mud, thick and clinging like ice-cold gravy.

He wriggled his head sideways, trying to locate the moon, but it had vanished. The woman's face was barely visible, just in front of him, and her breathing seemed to have become slower in the past few minutes.

"Elvira? You hear me? Hang on in there. Got friends..." He succumbed to another coughing fit at the tightness of the wreckage around his waist. "Friends on the way. Could be here some time after dawn. Just hang on."

The wind rose for a time, finally carrying the last of the rain away with it, clearing the sky, bringing a watery moonlight.

Ryan was able to see his wrist chron, finding that it was only a little after midnight.

He could also see the way Elvira was lying. A large roof timber had her pinned to the ruined floor. She was flat on her stomach, hands out of sight, hair dark with black, congealing blood, eyes closed. A deep cut dripped more blood from the side of her mouth, exposing the broken end of a denture. There was something sticking into her throat from beneath, which Ryan finally decided was the headless statue of Elvis Presley.

ELVIRA STOPPED BREATHING at 1:15 a.m. There was no drama, as there rarely was, simply the unmistakable cessation of everything.

It was a short while after her passing that the first of the tiny rodents appeared, the same breed that he'd spotted scampering through the puddles when he arrived in the heart of the burned-out ville.

They reminded him of the notorious cuddlies, furry little golden bears that looked like every child's bedtime ideal. The unbelievably vicious creatures had left young Jak Lauren with two deep scars on his face, near his mouth, that he would carry with him to the grave.

He was aware of them pouring over the wreckage like a black tide, none of them any larger than his thumb, with tiny dark eyes and miniature razor teeth. For several minutes they paid him no attention at all.

When one of them came close and began to climb up onto Ryan's jacket he gave the loudest roar he could and the mutie mice vanished.

They didn't reappear until a few minutes after three in the morning. There seemed to be even more of them, as if they'd been enlisting reinforcements from the whole of the devastated little township.

It was about then that Ryan also became aware that the watery mud was rising around him and had reached his groin.

"Fireblast!" The familiar expletive was so quietly and resignedly said that the absurdity struck Ryan and produced a ghost of a grim smile—a smile that vanished at a pricking pain in the back of his trapped left hand. He flexed his fingers, looking down to see that the mutie rodents were turning their attention to him. Some of them were also making good time with the dead, staring face of Elvira Madison.

They covered her skull like a shifting hood of dark hair, with occasional glimpses of bloody skin beneath.

Ryan shouted and batted his right hand at them, disturbing them for a few moments. Only this time they didn't all vanish. They just withdrew and regrouped, hundreds of microscopic eyes watching him fixedly.

The moon showed him all too well the danger from the furry mice. In less than a half minute they'd virtually flayed the skin from Elvira's skull, less than a yard from him, also removing eyes and lips and much of the nose. Even as Ryan stared at the horror that she had become, a blood-sodden rodent emerged from her open mouth and dropped off into the wrecked timbers.

He shouted again, his voice echoing around him in the stillness. As he waved his fist threateningly at the creatures, he felt some of the beams shifting, pinning him even more tightly, sucking him lower into the watery trap.

If they could swim below the surface, then he was instantly, irrevocably doomed. But he had noticed that their fluffed-up fur held so much air it was impossible for them to dive. Indeed, it was almost impossible for them to drown unaided.

The timbers around him creaked and groaned under increasing pressure.

And the horde of tiny rodents edged closer again.

DOC WAS SNORING, and she could see in the moonlight that Jak, flat on his back, was also fast asleep. J.B. and Mildred had been whispering for some time, snuggled together, but they'd finally fallen quiet.

Only Krysty remained awake, lying in the corner of the ruined cabin just off Highway 9.

She kept remembering something that Ryan had said a few days earlier, how the thing he hated most was vermin. Rats and mice. Any kind of rodent.

But Krysty couldn't understand why she kept on recalling that conversation, eventually deciding that it had to have something to do with Ryan's current predicament.

Krysty prayed to Gaia and to the forces of the Earth Mother that she was wrong.

Despite all her skills, she still wasn't able to embrace sleep, lying with emerald eyes open, staring out at the starry night, worrying about Ryan.

The only bright spot was that it had finally stopped raining, though water still thundered down the wide streambed behind their cabin.

RYAN COULD FAINTLY HEAR the roaring of the swollen stream that ran clear down the valley toward the north.

It crossed his mind that Krysty might also be listening
to it.

He had been watching the seething army of vermin,
turning his head to try to check that they weren't coming at him from behind. Two or three hundred had
edged closer, until they were within his reach.

His hand shot out like a striking rattler, grabbing a
fistful. He plunged them below the scummy surface of
the water around him, holding them there while he
counted to twenty, figuring that would be long enough
to flood their tiny lungs.

Ryan held tight, ignoring the biting, until the wriggling stopped. When he opened his hand a dozen or
more little corpses bobbed into sight. One or two had
struggled free and were climbing out of the water onto
the ruins of the house.

"One for me, you little shits," he said, breathing
hard with the tension.

The icy floodwater was now over his waist, and he
started to worry about snakes. But he pushed that particular thought to the back of his mind. There were
three possible ways that he was going to die: crushed if
the beams slipped any more; drowned if the water continued to rise; eaten alive if the rodents finally massed
and attacked him all at once.

The way things were going, his best guess was that
one of the three would have happened by dawn.


As soon as Krysty touched J.B.'s shoulder he started
awake.

"What?"

"We should go."

"Now?" He sat up, whispering so as not to disturb Mildred or Doc. Jak, in the corner of the ruined building, had also awakened, his senses razor honed.

"What is it?" he said. "Danger?"

Krysty shook her head. "Not here. But I have this triple-strong feeling that Ryan is in deep trouble."

"Dawn in an hour or so," the Armorer said. "We could wait until then."

"Move faster in light," Jak agreed.

"Could be too late then." She gripped J.B. by the shoulder, hard enough to make him wince. "Now."

RYAN HAD LOST COUNT of how many of the mutie vermin he'd crushed and drowned. All that he was really aware of was the undeniable fact that they kept on coming. And each time there were more of them and each time they were bolder.

Twice in the past half hour his own violent reaction to the rodents had caused the timbers around him to slip, tightening their embrace on his legs and left arm, squeezing and crushing his chest so that breathing became more and more difficult.

Though it hadn't rained again for four hours or so, the level of water around him had continued to rise steadily until it was now across the top of his chest, scant inches from his face.

A raft of little furry corpses bobbed around him on top of the dull surface, and he waved them away with his free hand. Breathing was becoming much harder with the compression around his chest, and he had lost all sense of feeling below the waist from the icy flood.

There were fifteen or twenty minor cuts and bites on his right hand and arm, but nothing serious. Ryan knew that it wouldn't be long before the diminutive rodents gathered themselves and made a concerted rush at him. Hundreds would cover his head and chest and swarm over his eye and mouth, suffocating and blinding him.

He watched them in the moonlight. Making a high cheeping sound like newborn chicks, they were moving restlessly all over the ruins of the house, occasionally coming down to feast on Elvira's corpse.

There was enough illumination for Ryan to see the progress of their ravenous devouring. The dead woman's skull gleamed white, with ragged patches of matted hair and threads of gristle dangling from it. Despite their tiny size, the rodents were voracious eaters, and he could hear the noise of an infinity of small teeth tearing at the cooling flesh.

Dawn was still a good half hour away.

Ryan sensed that the ultimate attack from the mutie rodents was about to begin, and he readied himself to go down fighting into the last darkness and take his final ride on the wall of death.

# Chapter Twenty-Nine

The first tremulous gleam of the false dawn lightened the sky with its promise of light to come. But the trail up toward the outlying houses in the small ville of Alma was still in darkness, rutted, muddy and treacherous.

Krysty had encouraged the others along in her wake, with poor old Doc struggling with the cold, the dark and the altitude, panting and wheezing at the rear.

"Got to get there," she kept saying. "Come on, guys, we got to get there. Ryan needs us triple bad."

"But we don't know where he is," J.B. said. "Could be up at Fairplay by now."

She shook her tightly bunched hair. "No. Closer than that. Much closer."

"Suppose cold hearts still around?" asked Jak, who had kept up effortlessly with Krysty, over the steepest part of the old highway.

"Can't feel them," she replied, breathing hard. "No smell of fresh fires. No lights. I'm certain that they're well ahead of us up the mountain someplace. Probably in Harmony itself. That's my feeling."

"Feelings!" Doc snorted. "Feeling appealing while the dealing is reeling. Peeling apples and pealing bells. Congealing like the faint aroma of performing seals. If we don't stop soon then my *feeling* is that blood will begin to gush from my mouth, nose, ears and eyes. I am certain sure that I can feel a nosebleed just waiting to begin.''

Krysty stopped and swung on him. ''Doc, there's plenty of times I find you real cute. This isn't one of them. Ryan's life is on the line and we need to get there. Faster we go, the better the chance. Even our fastest might be too fuckin' slow. Right?''

Doc nodded, the moon glinting off his silvery hair. ''Right,'' he repeated. ''I am properly chastened. Let us proceed and I shall strain every nerve and fiber to get there with you.''

RYAN HAD MANAGED to beat back yet another attack.

But now he had blood streaming down his cheeks and over his good eye from a score of bites from the mutie rodents. As he thrashed about, fighting them off with his right arm alone, there had been a sonorous crunching sound and he had felt himself starting to slip down, water splashing in his face.

The furry mice had retreated, leaving another forty or fifty of them crushed or drowned.

But Ryan had reached the end of the line.

When they came again he would have to let go of the room joist that he clung to with all his failing strength. Then the shifting, sliding rubble of the building would quickly tug him below the surface.

Of the optional ways of dying, he was now certain that it was going to be drowning.

''Better than being rat food,'' he muttered.

"BANDITS CLEARED this place," the Armorer said as they paused to look across what remained of Alma. "Must've been the endless rain put out all the fires and saved some of the houses off the main street."

"Soon be dawn," Mildred added, huddling her shoulders against a cool wind that was blowing up the valley from the north, behind them.

"Another day, another dollar," Doc mumbled, running fingers through his thinning hair.

"You think this place is where Ryan's trapped?" J.B. asked.

Krysty nodded, looking around at the burned-out buildings and the rivers of water and mud that seemed to run everywhere. As J.B. had said, several of the buildings at the back of the main street were all right, though she could see that there had been a major earth slip to one side that had felled a solid block of four houses, reducing them to tangles of matchwood.

"How we find him?" Jak said.

Krysty looked around, almost as though she expected to see a celestial finger of blazing gold pointing to her lover, or a column of living fire and a glittering angel beating on a sounding gong of brass.

"Close, that way," she said hesitantly, pointing over toward the ruined homes.

"Best way's to shout for him," the Armorer stated. "Spread out a little and all walk through yelling out his name. Best I can think of."

Krysty chose the side street that held the tumbled houses, her blaster drawn and cocked, calling out at the top of her voice for Ryan.

IT WAS VERY DOUBTFUL that a single person in Deathlands could have survived as long as Ryan under such appalling, life-threatening circumstances.

But everyone had a breaking point, a point at which hope ran out and the senses became numbed and the muscles could no longer hold on.

Finally, even Ryan reached that point.

The massed vermin had attacked him once more and, against all the odds, he'd beaten them away.

Now he was stretching every sinew to hold his head strained back, the oil water lapping at his mouth. Every breath was a desperate struggle, and every single breath was more painful than the one before, with the increasing pressure around his ribs that was crushing his lungs.

He could make out a lightening in the sky, the glow reflected off the hundreds and hundreds of tiny black eyes that were all fixed on his weakening struggles.

It crossed his mind that at least he was going to die in daylight and not in the blackness of night.

"And with my boots on," he whispered to himself.

For a moment he relaxed and his face dipped under the water, making him cough and splutter.

When he broke the surface again, his ears were filled with the high-pitched squeaking of the mice. Something, probably his own submersion, had disturbed them.

Ryan was suddenly conscious that the ordeal had affected his mind. It seemed to him that the mutie rodents' cries were mouthing his name, mocking him, as death crept inexorably closer, by an echo of his name.

"Ryan! You here?"

His mind was instantly crystal clear. "Here! Over here in the ruins of the house. Quick!"

He couldn't help noticing the high thread of ragged panic in his own voice, but he didn't much care about that.

"I hear you, Ryan."

"Krysty! This way."

Boots scrabbled among the wreckage and a shadow appeared between him and the rising sun.

"Gaia! Go away, you little bastards!" A hunk of wood landed among the massed rodents, finally sending them scurrying back to their dark holes.

"Be careful. Whole place is like a booby trap. One wrong move and it'll take me under."

Krysty reached down and touched him on the cheek. "Hang on, lover. Soon have you out."

She raised her voice. "Found him! Over here, but step careful."

"Everyone all right, Krysty?"

"Sure. Don't talk. Can I help?"

"Support the back of my neck if you can. But watch where you move."

"Don't worry. Couple of minutes and we'll get you free. That's all."

But it wasn't all.

DOC HAD SCRAWLED figures in the mud with a pointed stick. "It is a simple problem in three-dimensional physics and mathematics. There are disparate stresses acting here...and here, with the weight being transmitted through the longitudinal cross section of the roofing timbers. As far as we can tell, below the water, there is a similar maze that holds Ryan trapped by the legs and waist."

They had been there for over an hour.

It had been possible to take only one positive step to remove the immediate risk of Ryan drowning in the muddy water that was flowing into the retaining bowl of the wreckage.

At Doc's instruction, J.B. had fired a dozen rounds with the Uzi into one of the walls of the ruins, opening up a small hole through which the rain spillage poured, lowering the level to around Ryan's chest.

The other thing that Jak and Mildred had done together was to drag the ragged corpse of the woman from the shambles, so that Ryan no longer had to stare at the grinning memento mori.

"Think should drop other beams along Ryan. Take weight off of him." Jak looked at the others. "We try and move timber it'll all collapse like house cards."

Doc nodded. "I believe that our ivory-headed young companion might have deduced a possible solution. Try and build a sort of cage, as it were, around Ryan. If we can find something strong enough to use as a lever."

"This could take us days," Mildred said. "I know he's not in immediate danger from drowning anymore, but most of his body's been immersed in freezing water for about ten hours or more. Hypothermia's becoming more and more of a reality to steal his life out from under our eyes.''

"We could get a fire going and boil plenty of water,'' J.B. suggested. "Pots and pans all over the ville. Then we could pour it in around him and take off the biting chill.''

Mildred kissed him on the cheek, making his sallow face blush. "Brilliant! Hot water and plenty of it.''

"You ladies can undertake that.'' Doc grinned, showing his wonderful set of teeth. "John Barrymore Dix and Master Lauren and I will work on the lad's scheme. Come gallants all, and let's away, to try our fortunes on this happy day.''

RYAN WAS AWARE OF the sun moving steadily across the bright blue sky, visible through the cracks and holes in the wreckage that surrounded him. Noon came and went.

The hot water helped a little in taking off the chill, and he could actually feel life returning to his numbed lower legs and feet. Krysty stayed close to him, making sure the miniature mutie rodents didn't return, keeping up his spirits while they brought each other up-to-date with their news.

They agreed that the prospect of finding Harmony untouched by the murderous gang of norms and muties was remote. They had both seen too much evidence of the brutal murders committed by the thugs.

"Part of me wants to get you out and then turn around and head back for Glenwood Springs. Up into the hills to the redoubt and jump out of here," Krysty said. "And part of me wants to go ahead and look. Just for my peace of mind. Whatever we find up there in Harmony won't be any worse than my imagining what might've happened."

Ryan nodded, reaching up to hold her right hand in both of his. Jak had managed to work away the timber that had trapped his left arm.

"We'll see what's there. I got me a big blood score against these swift and evil bastards," he said. "Seemed you couldn't turn a corner of the trail without coming on another violated, crucified corpse."

Jak appeared, carrying a length of tubular steel scaffolding across his scrawny shoulder. "Think this could do trick." He moved cautiously, feeling timbers shift and whisper under his weight. He looked down into the dark depths of the water and slid the end of the tube down, angling it between Ryan's trapped legs, through a gap in the timbers.

"Watch what you're doing with that," Ryan warned. "I have hopes of fathering more children."

He felt the steel easing between two of the main roof joists that kept him helplessly trapped.

Jak grinned proudly. "That'll do it."

He called to Doc, Krysty and the others to come quickly and lend their weight. "This'll do it."

With both arms free, Ryan himself was able to give them some help, bracing his feet against the bottom of the pole, sensing where the snarled, twisted mass of broken wood was weakest.

The others had all managed to find a platform for their own pushing and pulling, standing and waiting, gripping the steel pole, until Jak gave them the word to start.

Mildred suddenly laughed, breaking the tension.

"What's funny?" Krysty asked.

"The way we're all standing here. One of the most famous war pictures in American history was the Marines raising the flag over Iwo Jima after it had been captured from the Japanese in the Second World War. It occurred to me that we look exactly like that photograph."

Jak knelt on the slick planking of what had been the floor of the attic. "You ready, Ryan?"

"Sure. Let's do it. If I feel things breaking up, I'll be the first to yell."

Jak stood again, finding a place on the steel for his own white hands. "Now," he said.

Ryan was at the heart of things, his whole body sensitive to the slightest movement of the gripping timbers. The scaffolding pole was firmly grounded, and everyone's weight made it bite hard into the wreckage. There was a squealing sound, and one of the joists snapped with a report like a revolver shot.

"Hold it!" Jak yelled. "You all right, Ryan?"

"Sure. Some of the pressure's gone off of my chest. Try and tilt it a bit more that way... yeah. Bit more. That's it. Now go for it again."

Once again everyone strained. Doc's knee boots slipped and he fell sideways, splashing himself with the water. "By the Three . . . ! Sorry, people . . ."

"Shifting something," Ryan said.

The weight on his chest was much easier, but something was still gripping his left ankle like a mantrap. More wood split and cracked, and he could finally take deep breaths.

"Done it?" Jak asked.

"Nearly. Lot easier and I could almost climb out. Except for my foot. Left foot."

Jak slapped the cold steel. "Easy all," he said, then knelt and peered into the murk. "Need to get down there and slide end of pole into exactly right place."

"I could do that," Krysty said.

Jak grinned at her. "No. Me. Smallest. Agile. Slip down easy."

"You could get yourself caught," Ryan protested. "No way anyone could rescue you from that tangle down there."

"Take chance." He drew one of his throwing knives. "When right place I'll rap with this. Listen for it. Then shove with all strength."

Without another word he slipped down into the dark water and disappeared, though Mildred, leaning over, could still see the white flare of his hair, floating like a baby's caul around Jak's narrow skull.

Ryan could feel the teenager's lithe body, twisting sinuously around his legs, while the end of the steel scaffolding pole also moved from side to side.

"Listen for the sound," he whispered to the others.

"Been down there close on a full minute," J.B. warned. "Can you signal to him to come up, Ryan?"

"No."

Jak seemed motionless and the tip of the pole was no longer moving.

"Eighty seconds," J.B. said.

Simultaneously there was a swirl in the water, as though a large fish had passed by, and there was the clearly audible chinking of the steel blade on the tube.

"Go," Doc roared, and everyone threw their strength against the twenty-foot length of steel.

Ryan felt the pressure slip off his ankle and he kicked out, reaching to pull himself up onto the section of planking, looking behind him for... "Jak!"

The young man erupted from the water in a froth of bubbles, a blade gripped in his teeth, his hair flattened against his face, eyes wide, panting with the effort.

"By the gods!" Doc exclaimed. "You look damnably like Israel Hands from *Treasure Island*. Well done, young man, wonderfully well done."

Ryan embraced the albino, feeling his own body still trembling from the tension of the experience. "Thanks, Jak, thanks."

"We've got a fire going, lover," Krysty said. "Let's all get ourselves dry."

"Best offer I've had in days," he replied.

# Chapter Thirty

They reached the Brown Burro diner in Fairplay just as the sun was setting.

The small ville seemed untouched by the ravening gang, with smoke coming from several chimneys and the smell of cooking drifting from open windows.

Ryan was little the worse from his ordeal, though Mildred insisted on bathing his many cuts, bites and scratches with boiled water, as hot as he could bear it, to try to remove the risk of any infection. He'd quickly walked off the stiffness of being trapped.

The eatery was completely empty except for a middle-aged woman wearing a spotless white linen apron. She had looked up as the six strangers walked in, her face a mask of apprehension, tinted with fear.

"Yeah?" she said. "You looking for a meal?"

"This is a diner?" Ryan asked.

"Sure is. Best in town. Brown Burro's been goin' since way back before skydark."

"You looked like you might have been expecting different company," J.B. said, leaning the scattergun in the corner of the room and sitting at a rectangular table.

"Been some bad ones around here in the…" Her eyes flicked nervously over the group. "You ain't them?"

"Gang of stickies and norms?" Ryan said. "Seen their bloody leavings all over the Rockies. No, we aren't them."

The relief could almost be touched.

"Figured you wasn't them."

"We came through Alma," Krysty stated. "They took the ville apart. How come Fairplay isn't touched?"

The woman sniffed, eyes looking past her, through the curtained window at the cool evening. "Some folks think they're just waiting for the right moment. Some folks run to do their bidding. Brown-nose bastards! Nobody'll stand up to them."

"Many people prefer the option of living on their knees to dying on their feet," Doc intoned.

"Right there, mister. Fairplay's useful to them. Get all the stores they want on the slate here. Not that they'll ever pay their dues."

"They eat here?"

She looked at Jak, clearly unhappy at his white hair, pale face and ruby eyes. "You sure you ain't...? No. Eat here? Sometimes. I make them pay. Jack up front for what they want. Don't like to think where that jack comes from. Blood money is what I reckon it must be."

"They likely to stop by tonight?" Ryan asked, walking and opening the door, looking and listening all around.

"Hardly. Always get back to their camp up in Harmony before full dark."

Krysty had sat beside the Armorer, running her fingers over the odd covering on the table, which was lots of predark coins, set in thick, clear plastic.

"They taken Harmony?"

"Sure have. Hear they did some chilling and raping. Usual story. Most of the living are too scared to run now. One or two got out in time. They hide around here. Now, they could look in for some supper tonight."

Mildred was reading the chalked menu. "Reckon I could start at the top with your potato-and-leek soup and work my way through every single thing until I got to the coffee at the end. Sure sounds real good."

"Brown Burro prides itself on giving folks value for money," the woman said. "You all sit yourselves down and I'll take your orders."

It didn't take long for them to make up their minds, and they waited, mainly in silence, while the woman went into the kitchen to pass their orders to her cook.

Krysty was restless, shifting in her seat, glancing out as the darkness folded itself around the little ville. "So close..." she said.

Ryan called out, asking if there was accommodation to be had in the ville.

"Sure. A few empty cabins. I'll tell you which ones to try when you're ready to go. They belong to some of the locals who've done a runner, ones who reckon the gang'll pay us in blood when the markers fall due. Seems pointless to me. Up and running. About as much good as waving a lantern at a runaway train."

She turned as a bell rang from the kitchen, telling her their food was ready. Moments later she reappeared with a tray in each hand, the dishes jostling each other.

"Venison stew with creamed potatoes. Same with roasted potatoes and peas and beans. Steak-and-bacon pie with wild rice and chicken gravy. Breast of chicken with french fries and sliced tomatoes in oil. Trout we got was so big I've divided into two portions. With cress and lettuce and a side order of fries. Sourdough bread and our own salted butter. Got some blueberry jelly I made myself if anyone's interested. There's some red currant sauce for the venison and onion sauce with the pie and the chicken. Fish has its own white sauce with pepper and some of my own herbs. That everything you ordered?"

Ryan looked at the mountain of food, passing half the trout to Krysty, taking the other half himself. "I reckon it'll keep us going for a while."

"We got some good desserts, as well. Take some pride in my pies, I do."

"What you got to drink?" J.B. asked.

"Mostly beer. With beer as a second choice. And milk as the third choice."

They all chose beer.

Doc broke the munching silence. "The trouble nowadays is that food is killing the art of conversation."

Mildred laughed through a mouthful of steak-and-bacon pie. "Last few days have been either feast or famine, haven't they? Eating in two good eateries. And in between living off rocks, gravel and rainwater."

"Prefer beer to rainwater." Ryan grinned.

At that moment the door of the restaurant inched open, making everyone look around. A heavily built, middle-aged, unshaven man peered in, blinking at the bright light from the oil lamps, staring at all of them, his eyes returning to Krysty.

"Little Krysty!" he exclaimed hoarsely. "My first-est and bestest girl."

She stood, hand dropping in an automatic reflex to the butt of her Smith & Wesson 640. Then her green eyes widened in surprise, recognition slowly dawning.

"Gaia! It's Carl. Carl Lanning. Herb's boy."

The man shut the door quickly behind him, after a glance to make sure that nobody was close by or watching him. He walked over to sit at the table, ignoring Ryan and the others, holding out a hand for Krysty to shake.

"Little... By the gods! Never thought I'd ever set eyes on you again, Krysty. That's..."

The sentence trickled off into stillness. The woman who ran the Brown Burro had appeared from the kitchen, and then spun on her heel and vanished again.

Ryan studied Carl Lanning. Krysty had told him how, when she had been an adolescent girl in Harmony, under her mother's tuition, she had decided that the time had come for her to lose her virginity. And Carl Lanning, about her age, son of the blacksmith, had been the chosen candidate.

She had seduced him, using him for her own purposes. But it had affected Carl and he had jumped to the conclusion that they were as good as engaged. Almost married. He followed her everywhere around the ville and neglected his chores until she'd finally driven the message home that she was going to leave Harmony one day and would leave it as a single woman.

Carl was a year or so older than Krysty, but he appeared at least twice that. His face was weathered and his eyes had the floating dimness, like watery eggs, of heavy drinkers. His features looked as if they were set in stone and he had a nervous tic, a nerve twitching beneath his left eye. It was possible to see behind the rapid aging that he had once been a handsome youth. Ryan's guess would have put him on the scales now at the two-fifty mark. He reckoned that Carl probably stood around five feet nine inches tall.

The handsome youth had vanished under the weight of far too many glasses and bottles.

"So," Krysty said. "After all these years. To meet up like this. Let me introduce you to my friends, Carl."

"Sure thing. I guess I knew you'd come back one day, Krysty. Folks said you'd flown the coop forever and a day. But I told them no. Knew that one day Harmony'd pull you back. Though there's been changes."

She nodded. "We can talk about that in a moment. First off, this is Ryan Cawdor. Mildred Wyeth and—"

"Yeah, good to meet you." He interrupted her without even a token nod to the others. "Changes, Krysty. By the gods, but that's true enough!"

Krysty persisted with the introductions. "John B. Dix, Jak Lauren and the old guy's Doc Tanner."

"These changes all started—"

But Doc wasn't going to let Carl get away with such rudeness. "I fear that I have no time for any man who uses vulgar words and vulgar language and vulgar manners, Mr. Lanning. But I assume that you are under stress and I will make allowances. I am pleased to meet any friend of Miss Wroth."

He stood and offered his hand across the table. After a few seconds' delay, Carl stood and shook hands, finally doing the same with everyone.

"Sorry," he muttered, eyes downcast. "You was right to slap me on the wrist, Doc Tanner. My pa would have whaled the tar out of me for bein' so rude. Specially to friends of the daughter of Mother Sonja."

Krysty was still standing. But now the color leached from her cheeks and she sat quickly. "Mother..." she said, barely audible.

"Why, sure. You won't have heard nothing about Harmony, will you? Unless folks here in Fairplay told you. Which way did you come, anyway, Krysty?"

Seeing Krysty's distress, Ryan answered the man. "From Glenwood Springs to Leadville and across the tops. Then down and up again through Alma. Put my son into Nicholas Brody's school. You heard of it, Carl?"

"Guess I have. So you seen some of the work of the gang of killers we got landed with? By the gods, but there are some triple-sicko sons of bitches there. I'm on the run from them. Been after me for days. Just because I stood against them. Laid one cold with Pa's old hammer. Busted his skull like a ripe melon."

He looked toward the kitchen. "Any chance of some pan-fried chicken with hash browns and grits? And..." His voice took on an unpleasant wheedling tone. "Mebbe some whiskey?"

The woman reappeared. "Told you we'd give you the basics, Carl, until you got yourself together. Doesn't include giving you jack-free liquor to muddle your brains."

"Just a glass?"

"One."

"Thanks a million."

"I'll go get the food and let you talk private to your friends."

She went through the swing door into the kitchen, and there was an uncomfortable silence that nobody seemed to want to break. Until J.B. spoke.

"How many in this gang?"

Carl turned to him, narrowing his eyes as though he'd already forgotten who the Armorer was. "The gang? There's fucking stickies in it, you know? What kind of a man rides with mutie shitters like that?"

"How many?"

"Stickies?"

"All of them."

"Around twenty or so norms and half that many stickies. Too many for you and your friends, Krysty. Even with all those pretty blasters."

"Tell me about Mother Sonja and Tyas McCann and Peter Maritza. What happened in Harmony after I left?"

CARL TOLD THEM how his father, Herb, had died a few years earlier of a bloody flux after the wheel of a cart had shattered and the rig had fallen on him.

Peter Maritza had been killed the previous year. He'd gone hunting and vanished. The spring thaw had revealed his desiccated corpse with both legs broken.

"Think it was an accident," Carl insisted.

Uncle Tyas McCann had gone into a decline after Krysty had run away from Harmony ville.

"You was always his sweetheart among the whole family," Carl said, wiping his stubbled chin after draining the quarter glass of whiskey in a single gulp. "Broke his heart, Krysty. Broke mine. Most of the young fellers in the ville. But Uncle Tyas sort of lost interest in everything. Faded away and dried out like a leaf in the fall. Got one of them coughs that bring out the red roses. Know what I mean?"

"When did he die?" asked Krysty, who'd been sitting with her eyes fixed to the patterned tablecloth as Carl poured out the sorry news of the decline of Harmony.

"Two years after you went."

There was a long silence, while Krysty tried to summon up the courage to ask the one question she was frightened of hearing answered.

Despite his lack of sensitivity, it was obvious that Carl knew what the question was and he was backing off from responding to it.

"My mother?" The question was asked in the faintest whisper, yet everyone in the diner heard it.

Carl had been eating his meal while he spoke. Now he gestured with the empty glass to the woman who stood by the kitchen door. Slowly and grudgingly she poured him another slug of the home-brew whiskey.

"Mother Sonja. By the gods, Krysty, but I been dreading meeting you one fine day and having to be the one told you about what happened."

"She's dead?"

"No. Yeah. I mean, we don't know."

She was on her feet again, pointing an accusing finger at the fumbling man. "You may have turned into a fat old drunk, Carl, but you better just tell me what happened, clear and careful. Now."

To everyone's surprise and embarrassment, the blacksmith's son put his head in his hands and started to cry, sobbing, his broad shoulders shaking, tears trickling down his cheeks and dripping onto the table.

The woman owner of the Brown Burro went and patted him on the back. "There, now, Carl, there now. It wasn't your fault. You weren't the one up and ran away and broke the heart of a whole ville," she soothed, staring angrily at Krysty.

Ryan was also standing, hands braced on the table in front of him. "Fireblast! Will someone just tell us what exactly happened to Krysty's mother?"

"Nobody knows. Few months after you left her, it seems she left Harmony in the mid of the night. Abandoned her home and all her possessions. Left no note. No message. No word. Nobody seen or heard from her since."

"Nothing?" Krysty's face was carved from living marble, showing no trace of any emotion.

"Nothing," Carl said, wiping his nose and eyes on the back of his sleeve.

"Oh, Gaia help me," Krysty breathed, sitting again and closing her eyes.

IT WAS A SHORT TALE, simply told.

Sonja Wroth had walked out of her life and walked out of the ville and nobody had seen a glimpse of her. Nor had there been any word of a sighting. She had disappeared off the face of the earth.

"Not even a whisper. We asked packmen and traders and travelers to look out. She was kind of distinctive to recognize. But we never got a word. By the gods, Krysty, sweetheart, I'd have given all the jack in all the villes in Deathlands not to have been the one told you this."

"I wanted her to be alive," Krysty said haltingly. "So I could make it up to her for... Or, if she'd been dead, then I could have mourned her and made my peace that way. But with her gone. Just gone..."

Nobody spoke for several long seconds. Finally Ryan broke the silence.

"Least we can do something to clean Harmony ville from its plague of rats. You want to do that, lover?"

Krysty sighed and smiled. "Yeah. I think I'd like that very much."

# Chapter Thirty-One

As the woman from the Brown Burro had told them, it was easy to find unoccupied cabins in Fairplay.

Carl showed them to one that he'd been using since he fled Harmony, which had enough space for Jak and Doc, while the place next door had two double rooms, ideal for J.B. and Mildred, and Krysty and Ryan.

There had been no argument that they'd start off toward Harmony, about a half day's brisk hike, as soon as the first light reached Fairplay. Carl would act as their guide, getting them as close as possible to the ville, where they would do what was necessary against the gang of killers.

"Remove them with extreme prejudice," was Doc's comment, when they talked over their plans.

RYAN HADN'T BEEN SURE whether Krysty would feel like making love and he held off, knowing how deeply distressed she had been at the news of her mother's bizarre disappearance.

But she had moved close to him as soon as they were between the slightly damp sheets, with a half-dozen thick blankets piled over them.

Her hand reached for his hand, holding him tight in silence. Then her leg moved against his, over his thigh, her knee nudging at his groin.

Ryan reacted instantly, and he could actually feel her smile at him.

"Ever-ready, lover?" she whispered. "I wasn't sure you wanted to."

"I thought you might not feel like it. After the news of all the deaths and... of your mother."

Her other hand danced across his chest, pausing to tweak at his nipples, then moving lower, across the flat, muscular wall of his stomach, grasping him.

"One of the great things that Mother Sonja taught me, from her store of wisdom, was to try not to allow yourself to be loaded with guilt over something you couldn't help. Leaving when I did was the right thing then. It's still the right thing. What happened doesn't alter that at all."

He kissed her, his lips butterflying over her cheeks, until he reached her mouth. The tip of his tongue probed gently between her parted teeth, then pushed harder as she responded to him.

"I don't believe she's dead," Krysty whispered, pulling away for a moment. "Like it was with Trader. Everyone figured he'd bought the farm, then he was back, almost as good as new. I think it'll be like that with Mother Sonja. I do, lover. I honest and truly do. One day we'll find her."

That was the end of the talk. Then the loving began.

THEY LEFT FAIRPLAY so early in the morning that the Brown Burrow wasn't even open for breakfast.

Carl Lanning had been difficult to rouse, rolling over irritably and pulling blankets up over his head like a fretful child who didn't want to go to school, complaining that it wasn't near dawn yet. J.B. had to threaten him with a bowl of meltwater before he finally struggled up and got dressed in jeans, a patched shirt and work boots.

"How about letting me have one of your blasters, Ryan? You got two, so has the skinny little guy with the glasses. You could give me one."

Ryan shook his head. "No. We all carry the blasters we do because they give us balance. Take anything away and the balance goes. Look after your blaster, and it'll look after you."

He had a momentary flash of when he'd been talking to Nicholas Brody about Dean's stay with the school. The headmaster had commented that the boy hadn't wanted to be parted from his beloved 9 mm Browning Hi-Power automatic. "But rules are rules, Mr. Cawdor." Brody had suggested strongly that Ryan should take the gun away with him but had finally agreed to keep it secure in the school's safe, against the time that Dean was finally ready to leave.

Now they were finally moving away from Fairplay.

Carl told them it had once been called South Park or Bayou Salado or Salt Creek, and it had been a summer hunting and trapping ground for the Utes.

"Bigger than all of Rhode Island, this valley," he said proudly. "Tyas McCann told me that."

Doc grinned. "That is somewhat akin to saying that someone is a very tall dwarf," he said.

Ryan noticed that the blacksmith's son kept glancing at Krysty as they followed the trail toward Harmony. And he twice brushed clumsily against her at places where the track had grown narrow. It was all too obvious that Carl still carried a blazing torch for Krysty Wroth.

Ryan filed the fact away, with the knowledge that it could prove potentially dangerous.

HARMONY LAY IN A shallow bowl of fertile land, around the ten-thousand-foot mark. They came around a bend in the overgrown blacktop and saw the ville spread out ahead of them.

"Gaia! I've come back," Krysty said, standing with hands on her hips, staring down into her old home.

"Someone coming," Jak warned. "Two men on mules. Think might be stickies."

The albino teenager's eyesight in the cloudy half-light of the morning was impeccable.

Everyone took shelter among the large boulders that were scattered on both sides of the highway, watching as the two unsuspecting figures drew closer, both riding spavined burrows, their long legs angled out, heels almost brushing the muddy trail. They were stickies.

Their clothes were ragged and torn, showing the sickly gray pallor of their skins beneath. They were both male, with stringy hair that seemed pasted to their bony skulls. Typically they both had weeping sores all over their faces, with clusters of yellow spots around their thin-lipped mouths. Each had a large handblaster strapped to his waist. As they drew closer, it was easy to see the circular suckers that marked their hands and fingers, giving them their Deathlands name of stickies.

One was singing a tuneless dirge as he rode along, his companion passing the time by practicing hawking up phlegm and spitting at rocks in the road.

Ryan had warned the others that it could be helpful to chill the first one silently, and take the other prisoner to try to extract information on the dispositions of the gang within Harmony ville.

Silent killing meant Jak and his leaf-bladed throwing knives.

The teenager waited until the stickies had passed him, then rose from his hiding place and let fly with one of his concealed blades. It whirred through the air like a loosed arrow, striking the second of the stickies through the side of the throat, just below and behind the right ear. It severed the artery, sending him toppling off his donkey, hands grabbing at the sharp pain of the wound, unaware that he was already dying.

Blood fountained high in the air, pattering in the mud as the mutie crashed to the ground.

His comrade was starting to turn, a sickly grin strung across his face as he thought his comrade had simply fallen from the back of the burro.

"Wrong move and you get to be dead," Ryan said, appearing in front of him, holding the rifle at his hip. J.B. came into sight on the other side of the trail, the Smith & Wesson scattergun covering the stickie.

Krysty, Mildred and Doc also showed themselves, as did Carl Lanning, a few moments later. He was gripping a short-handled sledgehammer that he normally carried tucked in his broad belt.

The mortally wounded mutie was kicking and scrabbling in the dirt at the side of the trail, the flow of blood already eased to little more than a trickle.

"Why you chill Jimbob?" the other stickie asked, looking puzzled. "You gonna get chilled when word gets to rest of us." He spit in the dirt near J.B.'s boots. "Triple stupes all soon chilled like Jimbob."

"Get off the burro," Ryan ordered. "Want to ask you some questions."

For a moment it looked as if the stickie was going to ignore the command, sitting negligently on the back of the burro, hands holding the dangling reins. Finally, slowly, he dismounted.

"Sit down there," Ryan said, pointing with the rifle to a shelf of rock set among the bracken and heather. "Look after the animals, Jak."

"You chill me?"

"Mebbe. Depends on you telling us what we want to know about the rest of your friends."

"Friends?" The brutish face showed bewilderment. "I ain't have no fuck friends."

The rest of them gathered around the prisoner, Carl standing just behind him.

"The rest of the gang. Where they're living. Where you keep the gas wag. Weapons. That kind of stuff."

The stickie's hands were knotting and fumbling at each other, the tiny suckered circles in the palms and along the strong fingers opening and closing like nervous mouths.

"I don't tell you that."

Without warning, Carl hefted the hammer and struck the mutie a single cracking blow across the back of the skull. There was the unmistakable, unforgettable sound, like a large apple being crushed underfoot. The stickie slumped forward, rolling onto the trail, the looseness of his hands and feet the sure sign of his death. A thread of crimson blood oozed from his right ear, from his nose and mouth, and leaked from the corners of his watery eyes. One hand tapped on the cold, mud-slick pebbles for a few seconds, then became still.

Ryan turned the Steyr toward Carl, filled with one of his sudden murderous rages, his finger tight on the trigger of the rifle.

"You...! I said not to hurt him."

"We was goin' to chill him anyways. Bastard had it coming, didn't he?"

"Sure he did and sure we would," J.B. said, sensing Ryan's rage, stepping in close. "But we all knew he wasn't to be harmed until we'd questioned him. Now..." He gestured at the corpse with the scattergun.

"You dumb bastard," Ryan snarled. "I should gut shoot you and leave you like a dog in the dirt. One more stupe move like that and I swear..."

Carl had backed away, his drinker's eyes swimming with fear, hands in front of his chest. "I just thought—"

"Thinking was what you didn't do!"

"You haven't seen what those...bastard chillers been...doing around these parts," he said, stammering with fright.

"I've seen the dead and I've seen the dying and I'm going to make sure that the cold hearts don't get away to do it again. I mean it, Carl..." His temper eased a little. "One more step out of line, and you either leave us or you end up dead as a beaver hat. Understand?"

"Yeah, sure. Sorry. Got carried away, Ryan." He wiped his sleeve across his mouth. "Wouldn't nobody have any drinkin' liquor, would you? Krysty?"

She shook her head and turned away from him, looking at Ryan. "So, what do we do now, lover?"

Ryan shouldered the rifle. "Now we have to get in close and careful and have a good recce. Mebbe go in during the night hours. Can't go walking in shooting. They'll butcher us from hiding. Have to find out where they are."

"And go in at dawn?" the Armorer asked.

Ryan rubbed the side of his nose with his index finger, looking down into Harmony. They were too far away to make out any details, but they could see the smoke of cooking fires and hear a dog barking.

"Likely dawn'll be the choice. Best turn the burrows loose and drag this scum off the trail, out of sight."

"Animals might find their way back to town," Carl said hesitantly.

Ryan suddenly spun, making the blacksmith's son start. "You're right. Good thinking. I hadn't... Getting careless. The animals come from Harmony?"

"Believe so," Carl replied.

"Cut their throats, Jak."

"Oh, surely they could..." Doc began, stopping as he saw the flickering flame of anger still smoldering in Ryan's eye. "Perhaps you're right."

A WIDE DRAW RAN in close to the northern flank of Harmony and Ryan led them along it, guided by Carl at his shoulder. They kept well out of sight of the ville, until they reached a stand of cottonwoods within a couple hundred yards of the nearest house.

"What time is it?" Jak asked.

"Little after three." Ryan sat down and lay back, closing his eye. "Might as well all take a rest. Won't be moving for a good while."

# Chapter Thirty-Two

They split up for the recce.

Jak went with J.B. and Mildred, while Doc accompanied Ryan, along with Krysty and Carl, whose local knowledge of Harmony, so Ryan hoped, should prove vital in their attack plans.

It was around eight o'clock at night when Ryan gave the word for them to start off. The moon was veiled behind banks of low cloud, and there was the threat of more rain.

Despite Carl's begging for a firearm, Ryan had refused to let him borrow one.

As a result of this rejection, Carl had led the way in a silent, sulky mood.

They moved around the outskirts, toward the south, while J.B. and the others circled north. It was agreed that they would all meet back in the cottonwoods in four hours.

At midnight.

ENOUGH LIGHT FILTERED through for them to make out the main features of Harmony, most of them familiar to Krysty.

"Church," she said, pointing to the spire. "Where we took Sunday services. That's the school next to it, with the bell tower. Our house was up on the bluff. Can't see it."

She turned to Carl. "Why can't I see my old home?"

"Got burned down. Lightning strike. Years ago now. Came in a dry spell, and there weren't no chance to get water to it. Few other houses went that evening."

"Where's the gang holed up?" Ryan asked.

Carl hesitated. "Spread in different places. The gas wag and the fuel for it's locked away in a barn out back of the sheriff's office."

"Who's sheriff of Harmony now?" Krysty asked. "Used to be big Ed Fisher."

"He got bad cancer in his back," Carl said. "Last sheriff's a guy called Ludlow Thompson. Don't know if...?"

"Sure, I remember him," Krysty said. "He's only a kid. Sign of getting old when lawmen get younger."

"Well, Ludlow won't be gettin' no fuckin' older. One of the stickies ripped out most of his throat, day before I upped and run away. Hope you won't mind if I off some of the fuckheads with my hammer here."

Ryan ignored the attempt at sarcasm. "I'd be happy to sit out here and let you chill the lot, Carl. Except it doesn't seem like you've had much success in that line."

"And you smartass outlanders goin' to come in hootin' and hollerin' and shootin' off them fancy blasters. And stop the gang?"

"Yeah," Ryan said. "We are."

IT WAS EASIER than Ryan had feared.

For starters, the gang of killers didn't seem to have any worry of being attacked, either from within the ville or from outside. There were no sentries posted, and they had mostly congregated in the ville's one saloon, the Pot O'Gold.

Ryan was able to crawl close to the back of the place, lurking invisibly in the shadows near the outhouses, watching and listening to the singing, the shouting and the breaking of glass.

Most of the norms in the gang seemed content to stagger off to bed around eleven, though the stickies remained longer at their funning.

But there was time enough to pinpoint where all of them were sleeping. It was noticeable that norms and muties kept apart when it came to living quarters, which wasn't surprising when you considered the vile habits of the stickies.

The local folk of Harmony were keeping very much to themselves. Apart from those working in the Pot O'Gold and in a couple of cheap-jack diners, the streets were deserted by nine.

Krysty waited with Carl while Doc joined Ryan on a recce along the backs of the houses, marking them carefully for their attack the following morning.

Despite his clumsiness and cracking knee joints, the old man did his best, working hard at establishing a mental plot of where the various gang members were staying—and which ones had local women entertaining them.

"I fear there could be the blood of innocents spilled on the morrow," he whispered hoarsely.

Ryan nodded. It was getting colder, and he had tucked the weighted ends of his silk scarf around his throat. "Could be, Doc. Wasn't there some old pre-dark saying about having to break some eggs before you could cook an omelet?"

"Something like that, Ryan. Will we succeed?"

"Sure."

"Your confidence is powerfully uplifting, Ryan. Back in my days you could have wowed them as a river-crossing preacher offering redemption and salvation from hellfire. A positive Elmer Gantry, my dear friend."

RYAN LED DOC BACK along a narrow alley, his SIG-Sauer ready. He nearly shot off a round as a large black cat seemed to erupt from the ground under his feet, clawing at his legs before darting away into an overgrown orchard.

"Supposed to be good luck," he muttered.

He'd left Krysty with Carl, figuring that they might appreciate the chance to talk over some of the old times that they shared.

When he drew near where he and Doc had left them, Ryan was surprised to hear raised voices.

"That was then and then was a long ways ago."

"I always hoped you'd come back."

"Get your hands off of me, Carl. It was a good moment, and you're just souring up the memory."

"Only want a quick—"

"Quick what, Carl?" Ryan asked quietly, finding the heavily built man was gripping Krysty by the shoulders, shaking her, his drink-dulled face swollen with anger, inches from hers. Spittle was hanging from his puffy lips.

At the return of Ryan and Doc, Carl let Krysty go and spun, his fingers clenched. "Nothing to do with you, Cawdor. This is personal for me and Krysty. You don't have what we got."

Ryan took a half step in. "That right, Krysty?" he asked. "Carl got an ace on the line, does he?"

She pulled away, brushing at her clothes, as though something unpleasant had been smeared on her. "It's all right, lover. Just that good old Carl kind of forgot where he was and *when* he was. It'll be fine."

"I hope so," Ryan said, staring grimly at the man.

"Easy to talk big with a cannon in your hand, ain't it, outlander?"

Ryan never hesitated. He holstered the big automatic with his right hand, then stepped in close to Carl, slapping him hard with the left hand, palm open, the sound cracking in the quiet, sending the bigger man staggering back several paces.

"Son of—"

Ryan punched him once with the right hand, deliberately pulling the blow so that it only landed with a fraction of the force that he could have used. It hit Carl in the midriff, just below the rib cage, driving the air from his lungs. He tumbled to his hands and knees, fighting for breath, making strangled, puking noises.

"Get up," Ryan ordered, his voice as cold as Arctic pack ice. "Get up now."

"Can't . . . Broke somethin' inside me. Bastard!"

"You get up or I'll cut your throat where you are. You have to realize how much out of your league you're playing here, Carl. Now, for the last time, get up."

Slowly, holding himself tightly as if he feared his guts were going to spill in the dirt, Carl drew himself erect. "Could've chilled me," he said quietly.

Krysty spoke for the first time. "Wrong, Carl. If Ryan had planned on chilling you, then he'd have done it without making a mistake. Your mistake was thinking something that happened so many years ago was so important that it still had a meaning now. It doesn't."

"I see that now." He managed a watery smile. "Figure I've made a double stupe of myself. Like to say sorry to both of you. Won't happen again."

Ryan nodded. "Stick to that, Carl. We'll all get along fine. Now we best get back to meet up with the others."

The blacksmith's son took the lead, picking a route between some abandoned cabins, toward the distant stand of cottonwoods. Krysty walked along with him while Doc and Ryan brought up the rear.

"Do you trust the village smithy?" Doc asked quietly. "I am minded of the saying about talk being cheap and the price of action colossal."

Ryan nodded. "Know what you mean. Seems to me that Carl might be a good man under the liquor and the self-pity. Seeing Krysty again's stirred up feelings he thought long-buried. Could be he'll be all right in the morning." He grinned at Doc. "But I'll be watching my back."

THE RECCE HAD GONE WELL.

As far as they were able to tell, they knew the nighttime location of virtually all of the gang, both stickies and norms. Some of them had taken up residence in the homes of the good folks of Harmony, living in uncomfortable proximity. But most were in small groups in empty houses.

With a little help from Krysty, and a lot from Carl, they were able to draw up a map of the settlement that showed the network of streets and alleys, and the placement of all the main buildings.

Jak had built a small fire in the heart of the trees, having checked that the wind would blow any smoke away from the ville. By its light they were able to draw up their final combat plans for attacking the murderers.

Ryan borrowed Doc's swordstick to point out who would go where and what they would try to do there.

Krysty suddenly interrupted him. "Sorry, lover, but...?"

"What?"

"Got a question for Carl."

"What is it, Krysty?"

She hesitated, closing her eyes for a moment and taking a deep breath. "Been thinking about visiting Harmony for... for too many years. Now I'm here and it's really too damned late. The ones I loved best are all gone."

"There's still some that would recall you," Carl said. "Dozen or more still living in the ville."

She shook her head and patted him gently on the arm. "Past is past, Carl. We'll do what we can to purge away the infection that's destroying the place."

"What was your question, Krysty?"

"Where's the graves? Tyas and Peter."

"On the hillside. Catches the morning sun. Real beautiful. Want me to take you there? Time to do it now, if you wanted. It's way from where the killers are living."

"I remember the cemetery. I just wondered if it was still there and if that's where they rested. Now I know, then I can sort of feel easier about it."

"You don't want to try and find some of the older folks and ask them... ask them if there's any clues about what happened to your mother?" Ryan cleared his throat. "Like Carl said, there's time. Not moving until close to dawn."

Krysty smiled, her teeth white in the semidarkness by the small fire. "Thanks, lover. Coming home's never like you imagine it. Hills aren't as steep and the roads aren't so long. Church steeple's shorter and the school looked a lot smaller than I remember it. Not the same."

"There is a belief that you should never go back," Doc said.

"True." Krysty rubbed her hands together as if she felt the cold. "It's true."

THE PLAN WAS TO SPLIT into three pairs.

If the gang had all been in one central location, then Ryan would have gone in leading a full frontal attack. But they were scattered in several different buildings, including church and school. So the best bet was to hit in a coordinated series of lightning raids.

"If all goes well, then it should all be over and done in fifteen minutes," J.B. said.

He was going with Mildred.

Jak and Doc were going to circle to the north and come in that way, picking up any of the gang who might try to escape on the highway out.

Ryan and Krysty would set the ball rolling, along with Carl.

"Best check our chrons," Ryan said. "Moment the shooting begins, it'll be like gasoline on an ants' nest. We all move on the stroke of five. Just be enough light to see our way around by then. And make sure the blasters are all loaded. Anyone got any questions?"

Nobody spoke, except for Doc.

"Would it be in order for us to try and catch up on a little lost sleep?"

Ryan nodded. "Sure. All do the same. And we leave here at four-thirty."

# Chapter Thirty-Three

At least five of the cold hearts were sleeping together in the church. They were the first of the targets for Ryan, Krysty and Carl.

They waited in the lee of a stone wall to the east of the building. Harmony was as quiet as death, with not even a distant howling coyote to disturb the silence.

"What's time?" Carl was breathing hard with tension, and Ryan could almost taste his sweat.

"Two more minutes. You all right?"

"Sure. Want to get started is all."

Krysty was sitting cross-legged, hands flat along her thighs, eyes closed, looking as serene as a Buddhist statue of calm. The calm before the hurricane.

Ryan checked his chron again. "Right," he said. "Carl, take that side door and chill anyone coming out of it." He gripped him by the shoulder. "Anyone, Carl. Hold back for a moment and you'll be buying the farm."

"Don't worry," he replied hoarsely. "You wouldn't have a small jug of drinkin' liquor anywhere around, would...? No, I guess you wouldn't."

He vanished into the opalescent dawn light, creeping through the dew-decked grass.

"Ready, lover?" He kissed her softly on the cheek, seeing her eyes open.

"Ready. Let's go do it for all of the dead and for Harmony."

THE OAK DOOR WAS STUDDED with heavy iron nails. The handle was cold and damp as Ryan carefully turned it, his eye half-closed, wincing against the expectation of squeaking hinges.

But the door swung open quietly, revealing a small porch with a pair of muddied boots in one corner. The door into the body of the church was partly open and Ryan ghosted through it, the SIG-Sauer drawn, the rifle across his shoulder. Krysty was at his heels like an avenging angel with hair of living fire, holding her own Smith & Wesson blaster.

The church was white and wooden-framed, with a stained-glass window facing the east. The first weak shimmering rays of the dawning lit up the picture of the blessed Saint Buebo of Ishmailia, smiling beatifically while defeating the great worm of Salonika with a fiery trident.

There was enough light in the building to show Ryan and Krysty the sleeping men, sprawled between pews, one of them lying drunkenly across the stained top of the altar. Most were wrapped in blankets, making it difficult to tell if they were norms or muties.

Ryan counted and held up six fingers, looking around to see if any others slept in the shadows.

Krysty shook her head. She held up seven fingers, pointing with the barrel of the Smith & Wesson 640 toward the pool of darkness between the pulpit and the covered font.

"Yeah," Ryan whispered. "Got him."

The chron's dancing digital figures glowed as he checked them again.

It was nearly time.

IT WASN'T A FIREFIGHT, not at all at the start, and not very much at its ending. It was simply a straightforward series of executions, carried out with clinical efficiency.

Trader used to say that it was always better to slay a sleeping enemy rather than one wide awake.

Ryan catfooted to the man on the altar and brought the barrel of the SIG-Sauer to his nape, angling it toward the occipital bone at the rear of the skull. He looked behind him to see that Krysty had taken a similar position, kneeling by one of the sleeping gang of killers.

Four fifty-nine and fifty-seven seconds.

Eight.

Nine.

Five o'clock.

Ryan pressed the blaster against the warm skin and pulled the trigger before the man could lurch out of sleep. The 9 mm round drove through into the deeps of the slumbering brain, bringing death before wakefulness, giving a dark mercy that the killer had done nothing to deserve.

Once that first marker had fallen due, it was quickly on to the second, before the muffled echo of the shot had traveled around the building. His heavy booming SIG-Sauer was followed immediately by the lighter, flatter crack of Krysty's 5-shot, short-barreled revolver.

The murderers died without waking, with the exception of the one who'd been sleeping near the pulpit. Ryan was still a step away when that figure started to throw back the blankets, the beginnings of a scream birthing in his throat.

Ryan pulled the trigger of the SIG-Sauer, and the bullet smashed through the front of the killer's head, exiting into the base of the font in a welter of blood and brains, drilling a hole clean through the carved wood. The body slumped down, the holy water leaking all over it, streaming darkly down the center aisle of the church.

As the corpse rolled clear of the blanket, there was enough light for Ryan to see that he'd killed a middle-aged woman with short, curly hair.

Krysty walked across to join him, the heels of her Western boots ringing on the stone flags, carefully avoiding the spreading pools of dark blood.

"Done?" she asked, pausing as she saw the last victim. "Gaia! That's Martha Pachelbel. I knew her when I was little. Lived next... How come you...?"

"Just another person in a blanket," Ryan said, swiftly replacing the empty rounds.

"I guess if she was sleeping in here with them then... Hear more shooting."

Ryan nodded. "Others getting on with the business. Let's move. Every second's precious."

They left the building by the front door, calling for Carl to join them from his watch on the side entrance.

"You get them all?"

"Yeah. Seven. Never felt a thing." Ryan didn't mention the woman. Time for that later.

J.B. AND MILDRED had been given the school. It seemed that this was one of the centers for the muties, and the firepower of the Uzi and Mildred's uncanny accuracy with her Czech revolver could prove vital.

J.B. took the back, slipping in past the outhouses into a small cloakroom, lined with benches and rows of pegs. Mildred walked along the grass at the side of the gravel path to the front door, which stood slightly ajar. There was the strong smell of smoke, and she could make out the remains of a big fire still glowing in the grate, which was another pointer to the presence of stickies with their notorious love of flames and explosions.

She entered the single classroom at the same moment J.B. appeared from a door at the side of the teacher's desk. The first dawn light was just enough, as Ryan had said it would be, for them to make out the sleeping enemies.

The Armorer started to check his chron, but his keen hearing caught the sound of shooting from over toward the church and he knew that it was time to start.

There were six sleeping figures, mostly snoring through open mouths. All were unmistakably stickies, with eroded, corrupt features, scabbed skin and the tiny circles of the suckers on their hands and fingers, opening and closing rhythmically, in time with their breathing.

J.B. had the Uzi on single shot and walked briskly between the sleeping muties, killing each of them with a single bullet in the brain.

The shots came at three-second intervals. The fifth stickie was partly awake, sitting up, rubbing at his eyes as the Armorer shot him through the suckered palms, straight into his skull.

Only one woke enough to make any sort of move, and Mildred shot him smack in the center of the low, brutish forehead, the impact of the big Smith & Wesson .38 round knocking him into a scrabbling heap, where his thrashing legs kicked over a predark globe of the world.

"So far, so good," J.B. said, reloading the Uzi, his scattergun still slung unused over his shoulder.

JAK AND DOC ALSO HAD their primary target.

It wasn't one of the larger buildings in Harmony, like the church or the school. The recce had identified the old sheriff's office, where Ludlow Thompson had once enforced the law, as a place where several of the norms in the gang were staying during the night.

Neither Doc nor Jak had superaccurate comp-controlled digital wrist chrons like Ryan and J.B., but the albino had an uncanny sense of time passing and he had been mentally counting down toward the five-o'clock mark.

"Is there long to go, dear boy?"

"Four minutes, I make it."

"We should hear the shooting once the others open fire, should we not?"

"Should. Your blaster full ready?"

Doc's commemorative gold-plated Le Mat J. E. B. Stuart special had been fieldstripped, oiled and cleaned, unloaded and reloaded by the Armorer while they waited for the dawn to draw closer, with some scabrous comments about Doc's neglect of the beautiful weapon.

The .65-caliber grapeshot round was devastating and had saved the old man's life on several occasions. But it was a one-off shot and, once fired, it was fiddling and perilously time-consuming to alter the hammer to make it engage on the nine chambers of .44s.

So it was going to be the .44s spitting from the weighty cannon.

They waited in a narrow alley at the rear of the building. The curtains were open, and Doc could see that there was an oil lamp still lit in the back, where Carl had told them the cells were situated.

"Think that the ungodly are still awake?"

Jak shrugged. "Find out three minutes."

Doc took a long deep breath and did several knee bends, though the explosive cracking of the joints made Jak look worriedly at him.

"Sorry, dear lad, sorry," he whispered. "Presume not that I am the man I was."

"Two minutes."

A shadow passed across the face of the lightening sky, swooping low over the sheriff's office, its great eyes staring down at the two men. Doc ducked under its whispering feathers.

"Barn owl," he said. "I assume that it is returning to its nest after a night's hunting. I hope it has been successful. I hope that we shall be successful."

"Know soon."

"Time is passing. Should we not ready ourselves closer to the door?"

Jak nodded, his stark hair burning like a mag-fire in the first dawning. "Let's go do it, Doc."

Harmony still slept as the ill-matched couple, the old man towering over the teenager, made their way up the path to the back of the sheriff's building.

Jak went first, stepping lightly onto the porch and testing the door handle. He looked back to give Doc the thumbs-up as it eased open. Light spilled out past the slim youth, reflecting off the satin-finish Colt Python with its six-inch barrel. He gestured with it for Doc to go around the front, where he could cover any attempts to escape.

Doc nodded and walked along the side, past a barred window, to find himself on the shadowy main street. Just as he reached a position to cover the front door, he heard shooting erupt from two different places in the ville.

"All done in the tying of a cravat," he muttered to himself. "Time, gentlemen, please."

Jak slipped in through the door, seeing that a game of cards had been in progress, though all but one of the players had fallen asleep, slumped facedown among the tumbled bottles, stained cards and half-empty glasses. The stink of liquor and sweat was heavy in the room.

Only one was still awake, but drink had totally fuddled his brain and he blinked at the apparition. He was fat, in his fifties, with thinning hair pasted across his scalp. His fingers were covered in cheap rings.

"You brought the breakfast for us? Well, it's way too fuckin' early, so you can go away and stick it up your ass, kid." He giggled. "Less you want somethin' else up your early-mornin' ass, kid?"

"Don't call me 'kid,' asshole," Jak said, shooting him through the upper chest, knocking him backward out of the chair. His legs kicked the table over, waking the other three members of the gang.

Knowing his limitations with blasters, Jak aimed for the safe, broad target of the upper chest, not risking the head shot. He put the other men down and dying with three bullets, leaving himself two more rounds.

Doc heard the muffled rumble of the rapid gunfire and a single yell of terror, and transferred the Le Mat to his left hand, propping the swordstick against a hitching rail. He wiped the sweat from his right hand before taking up the heavy blaster again.

He was just in time as the door was flung open and two men raced out, one wearing only a shirt, the other in a pair of shorts, both barefooted, neither armed. One of them was screaming at the top of his voice.

Doc hesitated for a moment, then remembered the crucified bodies and the raped girls. He leveled the Le Mat and squeezed the trigger, cocking it and firing it again. At less than twenty feet, both the .44s were perfect aces on the line, tumbling the fleeing thugs like shotgunned rabbits.

A half minute later Jak appeared in the door. "Nobody else here," he said, looking at the two corpses leaking dark blood into the dirt. "Got them both? Good."

"I heard more shooting, Jak."

The boy paused, head on one side, the light breeze blowing his long white hair back off his chiseled face. His red eyes darted around the ville. "Be out and running any second. Be some more shooting."

NINETEEN WERE DEAD, or down and dying, in the first minute and a half of the raid.

Roughly ten norms and a couple of stickies were left alive in Harmony, all of them jerked from deep sleep by the sound of shooting, broken by the occasional scream.

Ryan hesitated outside the church, looking at the ville, wondering how the others had done so far.

The first chillings were just the beginning.

# Chapter Thirty-Four

Ryan watched as a window opened in the second floor of one of the houses that they'd marked down as harboring gang members. A breed with a heavy mustache appeared, looking both ways, not seeing the one-eyed man in the shadows. He climbed out onto the top of the porch, followed by a companion. Both were partly dressed, holding bundles of clothes and both with unidentifiable revolvers in their hands.

Ryan waited until both of them were preparing to jump before bringing the Steyr rifle to his shoulder. The light was growing stronger every minute, but the night scope was still useful, the laser image enhancer making everything easier.

The SSG-70 barked and Ryan worked the bolt action, readying another of the 7.62 mm rounds, squeezing the trigger a second time, watching through the scope as the two men rolled lifelessly off the porch onto the ground.

THE PLAN HAD BEEN for everyone to separate after the first flush of the butchery, going to other properties where they believed other gang members were staying.

Doc was nearly caught by a stocky man with a bush of gray hair and protruding teeth who suddenly jumped down from a low roof, knocking the Le Mat from his fingers, sending him staggering into a green-painted picket fence.

"Whodafuckyou?" The snarl turned the phrase into a single word. The man had a bowie knife in his right hand, and he gestured toward Doc with it.

"We are the lily white boys, clad all in green," Doc replied, giving a twist to the silver lion's-head hilt of the swordstick, letting the ebony sheath fall to the alley, exposing the blade of the slim rapier.

"Fuckin' swordbastard!"

He came at the old man in a grinning, clumsy rush, the blade held low in the classic knife-fighter's pose, ready for the lethal cut upward at the unprotected belly.

Doc extended his right arm, wrist flexible, keeping the needle point moving in a small circle. "Cursed be he that first shall cry 'Enough,'" he chanted.

The man feinted to the left and came in at Doc from the right, hacking away with the long blade of the bowie knife.

Only Doc wasn't there.

He'd ignored the feint and moved toward it, drawing back the rapier and lunging with all his strength, aiming at the point where the man's throat melted into his broad chest.

"A hit, a palpable hit," he whispered, smiling with delight as the Toledo steel slid into the killer like a hot needle through butter.

A turn of the wrist shredded the lungs, opening up the artery in the neck. The blade, blood slick, was withdrawn as the man dropped his knife and staggered back, hands to the pumping wounds, eyes open wide with shock at the cognition of his own imminent passing.

Doc stopped and resheathed the sword as his opponent sank to his knees. He picked up the Le Mat and turned away, looking back at the dying wretch.

"Goodbye cruel world," he said, and moved on.

MILDRED SHOT TWO of the desperadoes as they were running for the livery stable, trying to get mounts to escape the slaughter. Ryan had told her to go there when she split from J.B., and she stood in the center of the main street of Harmony, legs slightly apart, holding the butt of her ZKR 551, looking two-eyed along the barrel of the target revolver.

"Hey!" she shouted, halting the fleeing killers in their tracks, about eighty yards away from her.

They turned, both holding single-shot cap-and-ball muskets, and started to laugh when they saw a stocky black woman in her thirties, with beads in her plaited hair that caught the rising sun, wearing a quilt-lined denim coat over reinforced military jeans tucked into calf-length boots of black leather.

The woman held a small hand blaster, and seemed to believe it threatened them.

"You got us real scared, sweetheart," yelled the man on the left. "Little toy blaster might reach about halfway."

Mildred shot him through his open, laughing mouth, the full-metal-jacket .38 blowing the back of his head all over the street.

His companion turned and gaped at the mist of blood and brains that hung in the air around his friend's skull as the man began to spin and topple.

Mildred shot him through the right ear, the bullet tumbling and taking out his left eye, part of his nose and most of the left cheek as it exited.

The woman turned and moved into one of the side alleys, continuing the hunt.

KRYSTY AND CARL STAYED together. It had been his idea, pointing out that he knew the ville better than anyone and could take her along safe shortcuts.

But when they reached the neat house, with its swinging sign offering Bed and Breakfast, they discovered that the pair of stickies they'd hoped to find had already fled, leaving the married couple who ran the place lying dead in a lake of blood in the kitchen with their three young children. An attempt had been made to fire the house, but the wood the stickies used had been green and it only smoldered.

Carl had been nervous while he stamped it out, gripping his hammer so hard that his knuckles were white.

"Where do you reckon they've gone?" he asked, his face pale. "Think Ryan and any of the others are still alive?"

J.B.'S NEXT DESTINATION was the garage where they knew the small armawag was kept, along with the two-wheeled trailer that held spare cans of gas.

He used the stock of the scattergun to break off the brass padlock, swinging the Uzi on its sling across his back. He started to pull the door open, when a bullet crashed into the woodwork eighteen inches from his head.

The Armorer spun, seeing that two of the gang had the same idea as him, realizing that the wag might give them their best chance of escaping from the massacre that seemed to have taken most of their comrades in the ville.

They were half walking, half running toward him, one of them unarmed, the other holding what looked like a remade Model 669 Taurus revolver. He fired again as J.B. turned to face them, the bullet this time hitting much closer. If the killer had stopped and taken careful aim, it was likely that the first shot would have hit J.B., but he was in too much of a hurry.

There wasn't a third chance.

J.B. fired the M-4000 from the hip, using the folding butt. One of the eight Remington flechettes burst from the 12-gauge muzzle, all twenty of the inch-long darts ripping into the murderer with the Taurus blaster. They tore his chest, lower stomach and groin to tatters of ragged sinew. The whole of the front of his body seemed to turn into a huge sponge, filled with blood, that was squeezed dry in a single soul-stopping moment.

His companion skidded to a halt, looking in amazement and horror at the devastated, leaking, whimpering, twitching thing at his feet, which had been his friend only a moment earlier.

J.B. aimed the weapon a second time, firing another burst of flechettes that sent the surviving man staggering backward, identically wounded, until his feet got tangled together and he fell in the street.

The Armorer calmly inserted another round and waited a few moments, before turning back to investigate the armawag in the garage.

JAK WENT to the trim house that Carl had assured them was the bordello in Harmony, and that was believed to harbor three of the norms. It stood in a neat side street off the main drag, bordering a narrow stream.

As soon as he cautiously worked the back door ajar, he could smell the bitter scent of jolt, hanging in the air like a forgotten promise.

He recognized it immediately from a dozen frontier pesthole gaudies. For some reason that Jak had never been able to understand, gaudy sluts were among the most addicted users of the heroin, cocaine and mescal mix.

The occupants of the brothel were all together in the big front parlors, four women, mostly edging into middle age, and three members of the gang of murderers. All of them were deep in a drugged sleep, oblivious of the shooting and yelling that had been going on in the ville for several minutes.

They were all partly dressed, and a potbellied iron stove was still throwing a lot of heat into the room. There was a round mirror, a pair of syringes and some white powder on a small table, along with three empty gin bottles. One of the gang had fallen asleep in the act of copulating with a fat, bleached gaudy slut from behind and he was still draped across her, snoring loudly, pants around his ankles.

Jak holstered the blaster, reaching into the small of his back and drawing one of his beloved throwing knives. Holding it by the taped hilt, he went silently from man to man, as gentle as a surgeon, and opened the carotid artery in each of them with the leaf-shaped blade.

As the blood spurted ceiling high, one of the men moaned in his drugged slumber, swatting at the neat, deep cut as if he dreamed he'd been stung by a skeeter.

Jak went last to the gang member who'd been overcome by the jolt while still in the sex act, cutting his throat with the same professional expertise. Something penetrated through the drugged darkness. The man muttered a few inaudible words and tried to push himself off the woman, sliding down over her buttocks, his limp penis flopping to one side as he fell bleeding and dying onto the flowered carpet. The sudden movement made the woman blink awake, her head turning from side to side as she tried to puzzle out what was happening.

The albino teenager wiped the reddened steel of the knife on a cushion and resheathed it, smiling to himself and walking out into the brightening morning.

He'd gone nearly a whole block before he heard the start of the screams from the house.

BY THEIR COUNTING, that was the end of all the norms in the gang, nearly thirty human lives snuffed out in the center of a beautiful ville in old Colorado, all done for in less than ten minutes.

Ryan met up with Jak, Doc and Mildred outside the main store of the ville. J.B. quickly joined them, reporting that the armawag was gassed up and ready to roll.

"Carry all of us back to the redoubt with a bit of a squeeze," he said.

There was no more sign of any threat from the gang, though a few of the honest citizens of Harmony were beginning to appear in the dawn-lit streets, looking like shell-shocked victims of a savage war.

"Where's Krysty and Carl?" Ryan asked. "Anyone see them?"

"They were supposed to be out to the south, by the park, weren't they?" Mildred said. "Haven't heard any shooting or noise from over that way."

IT SEEMED like it was over.

Neither Krysty nor Carl had heard shots for a minute or more, though a group of women screamed somewhere off the main street, and several dogs barked hysterically throughout the ville. A light wind rustled gently through the trees and bushes.

"You going to stay here for a while, Krysty?" Carl asked, sighing and sitting on a bench at the edge of the park.

"No. I wish I hadn't come at all, Carl. Like I said before, you can never go back. Not really. Good to see you. Wish you well. Truly."

"Some folks'll want to see you."

"Just tell them hi from me and that I had to get back on the road."

She had sat on a bench facing Carl, studying her old friend, seeing in the stark morning light the ravages that time and liquor had wrought in him. She was saddened that such a handsome boy had become so weary and defeated. Krysty ran her fingers through her bright red hair, feeling how tense and coiled it was, responding to the danger that still lingered in the air.

"Wish I could get away from Harmony and go on the road like you and Ryan and the others," he said, toying with his short-handled hammer.

"It wouldn't work. But you could get away from here. Find a new ville and a new life. Get a good woman and settle and have kids. That's what you should do, Carl."

He looked up and grinned at her, revealing a flash of the teenager that had once made love to her. "That'll be the day, pilgrim."

"You could—" She stopped in alarm as Carl leaped to his feet, his face contorted into a mask of hatred and rage. He moved toward her, the crushing hammer lifted in his right hand.

# Chapter Thirty-Five

Krysty staggered sideways and fell over as Carl pushed out at her with his left hand, his lips peeled back from his teeth in a feral snarl of anger.

Her hand was reaching for her blaster, ready to try to take him out when she suddenly realized what was happening.

The last two stickies from the gang of killers had escaped from their safehouse and had been hiding in the shrubbery behind her, waiting their chance to strike.

Carl had stopped them just as they were emerging at Krysty's back, their suckered hands reaching for her.

The lead mutie was grappling with Carl, while his skinny partner was groping toward Krysty, lying helpless on her back in the middle of the overgrown path. There was a hideous smile of triumph on its suppurating face.

The fight was short.

Carl managed to swing the heavy hammer at his adversary, breaking its upper arm as if it were a dry branch. The stickie squealed and lurched clumsily away from him, the limb dangling helplessly. Belying his bulk, Carl was after it, striking again, this time the blow glancing off the hairless skull and snapping the right shoulder.

"You dirty fuck!" Carl panted, swinging again and again, aiming at the stickie's head. Krysty heard the noise, like a thick bowl of soup being crushed, and the creature went down, blood seeping from its open mouth.

But the second attacker wasn't done. He had drawn a straight razor from under the ragged shirt and flourished it at Krysty, missing her face by a scant couple of inches. She felt the whisper of its passing and smelled the exhalation of rancid breath from the threatening mutie.

"Got your friend, now I'll get you!" Carl roared at the top of his voice, stepping toward the stickie with the clubbing hammer raised.

In his newfound pride, Carl failed to look where he was setting his foot and he stepped into the oozing trickle of blood from the dying stickie, his boots slipping, throwing him off-balance for a moment.

"No..." Krysty breathed, seeing the horror before it had happened.

The surviving stickie gave a high-pitched cackle of laughter and swung the razor at the man, catching him across the front of the neck, the steel cutting deep into the flesh, slicing through the sinews, veins and arteries, so that Carl's head drooped forward and blood jetted out, vivid scarlet, into the bright early sunlight.

He staggered and made a last effort to strike at the gloating mutie, but the shock to his system was too great and he dropped the hammer with a thunk on the path.

"Die easy..." the mutie hissed, turning away from the doomed man toward the woman.

Krysty had her Smith & Wesson half out of its holster, but she couldn't tear her eyes away from her dying friend. Carl had dropped to his knees, hands clutching at the gaping white-lipped wound, trying hopelessly to stanch the torrent of blood. His eyes were turned to Krysty, and his mouth opened and closed soundlessly.

The stickie stood over Krysty, his thin cotton pants showing an obvious erection at the thrill of chilling, his gray tongue flicking out like a reptile's to lick withered, sore-crusted lips. The watery eyes were flooded with hatred and lust.

Krysty dragged at the butt of the short-barreled blaster, knowing with a sick certainty that she was too slow and her race was well run.

The razor angled toward her face, and she had the gun clear.

There was the sound of a shot, and a neat black hole appeared in the chest of the mutie, a little to the left of center. A spray of blood erupted from the creature's back.

He took two teetering steps away from her, still clutching the razor, face puzzled. "Blaster didn't shoot..." he said, tripping over the corpse of his colleague, and sat down in the path. He waved the razor a couple of times and then simply died, still sitting upright, head dropping onto his breast.

Krysty struggled to her feet, seeing Ryan standing motionless, a hundred yards away, the Steyr hunting rifle still held to his shoulder. The others were grouped around him.

Krysty closed her eyes for a moment, muttering thanks to Gaia that they'd all made it through again.

"Krysty..." The voice was no louder than a breath of sea fog against a stone wall.

The relief at being saved, and seeing Ryan and the others alive and well, had momentarily taken her mind from poor Carl.

Death was close, its shadowy cloak poised above the bulky figure.

Krysty dropped to her knees, lifting his head into her lap, ignoring the blood that had slowed to a trickle. The light of life in his eyes was fading, and he tried to lick his dry lips, struggling to speak.

"You saved my life," she said, feeling tears pricking at the back of her eyes, a part of her childhood dying in her arms. "I'll never forget you, Carl." She kissed him on the forehead.

His efforts to speak were futile, but he managed a final half smile before life rushed from him.

As Ryan and the others came to join her, Krysty laid him gently to the earth and stood.

"Over," she said. "All over, and we can go."

# Chapter Thirty-Six

Krysty had insisted on going straight to the armawag, avoiding any kind of contact with the people of Harmony, who had seen their ville turned into a bloody abattoir.

"There must be folks you know," Ryan protested. "Surely you could just see them?"

"No."

"But they must realize that we have saved their homes and their families from probable death," Doc said.

"The whole ville's running with blood." Krysty was on the verge of tears. "I told you, all the ones I loved are dead and gone. Or, like Mother Sonja, just plain disappeared. There's nothing left here for me."

And she climbed into the armawag and waited for the others to join her.

RYAN TRIED TO COPE with the folks who flooded out of their houses, gaping at the dozens of corpses, unable to believe that the shadow of the murderous gang had been lifted from them. Their leader appeared to be Richard Thompson, brother of the murdered sheriff, and his pleas for them to stay a few days were echoed by virtually the whole ville.

Ryan refused as politely as he could. "You don't know how it'll be. Innocent people have been harmed here and hereabouts, and the time'll come when you'll all resent us almost as much as the gang of murderers."

"No, I assure you that—"

Ryan shook his head. "Guess we're a bit like the wind that blows through and cleans away the bad things. You won't want to be reminded of us."

"Someone said they saw little Krysty Wroth, the daughter of Mother Sonja, along with—"

Ryan held up his hand. "We have to go and you have dead to bury and tears to shed."

With that he turned his back and quickly strode toward the alley, where he could hear the small armawag was already warmed up and ready.

"Take her away, J.B.," he said as soon as he'd squeezed into the cramped interior. He pulled the steel hatch closed, shutting out the noise of shouting.

The engine revved, coughing blue gray fumes into the sunny morning. The Armorer engaged first gear and the vehicle began to move steadily forward, out onto the main street of Harmony. They made a right turn and headed north back toward Fairplay and the highway that wound down the valley toward the interstate and Glenwood Springs.

Krysty was sitting in the rear of the wag, with the rear ob slit partly open, looking out of it as Harmony ville shrank away behind them.

And vanished.

WHEN THEY REACHED the ville of Breckenridge, Mildred asked if they could stop there for a break and to get some fresh air. "Like traveling in a can of tuna with the added flavor of the exhaust fumes," she said. "Like to see Breckenridge. I took place in a shooting competition here, a year or so before I . . . got ill."

J.B. parked the wag in the center of the ville, near a long-dry fountain, its base cracked by an ancient earth slip, and they all climbed out.

"By the Three Kennedys! What a relief. Perhaps it beats the labor of walking, but I am most damnably cramped. I have been shaken, rattled, bumped and bounced from pillar to post and back again. Thank the Lord for some good fresh air. This must have been a pretty place, Mildred, once upon a time."

"It was. Pay anything up to a thousand dollars a night for a suite. Look at it now. Tumbled glory."

The ville seemed to be deserted and looked as if quake damage had ravaged it, probably at the beginning of the long winters. Its triple-decker shopping mall was a heap of rotting concrete and shattered glass, and the trendy little boutiques with their fancy names were no more.

"Good country for skiing," Krysty said, looking around. "That why it was so costly?"

"Sure was. Like Crested Butte and Vail and Aspen. Lovely little villages that got themselves 'developed.' Blocks of identical condos sprouted overnight, and film stars bought blocks of land for their hideaway ranches and mansions. And now the developments have been swept away by earth slips and quakes and avalanches and the hand of Father Time, and it's all beautiful again."

"Should have asked the people up in Harmony for some food," Ryan said.

"Probably fruit here. Go look?"

"Sure, Jak. Why not. But don't go wandering around on your own."

"I would be delighted to accompany the young fellow," Doc offered.

Ryan looked at Krysty. "You want to walk some and see the sights, lover?"

"Sure. Mildred?"

"Think that John and I might take us a stroll around the ruins."

"Meet back at the wag in an hour or so. Then we can move on and get through Glenwood Springs well before sunset. Mebbe rest up in the dormitories."

"If they haven't flooded," J.B. said.

"Fireblast! Forgot about the burst pipes in all the excitement since then. Yeah, as long as the redoubt's not flooded out we could spend the night and get some rest. Then jump first thing the next morning."

"Sounds fine," Mildred agreed. "You sec locked the wag, John?"

"Yeah. Back here in an hour."


RYAN LINKED ARMS with Krysty and they walked south, along what had been the main street of Breckenridge, past row after row of ruined stores, some with their faded names still visible after nearly a hundred years.

"That's an odd name." Ryan pointed at what seemed to have been an art shop. "Yrellag Gallery. Think it's a Native American name, lover?"

Krysty smiled at him. "No."

"You're looking smug. Why's that?"

"Because I get the name. It's the same backward as forward. Uncle Tyas McCann told me about things that are like that. Called palindromes. A sentence he told me was 'Madam I'm Adam.' Another one's 'Able was I ere I saw Elba.' About Napoleon. You get it, Ryan?"

"Oh, yeah. Not so clever as I thought it was once you can understand it."

There was a store that had sold designer pants, called Ski Bums. A religious bookstore called A-pray Ski. A liquor store was named On the Piste. Children's clothing was available at Nursery Slopes.

"They just have any places called the Grocer's or the Butcher's?" Krysty asked. "Seems you had to think up a witty title before you were allowed to open here."

"Stupes," Ryan sniffed. "Just another reason why the world ended."

"Don't be a misery." She kissed him on the cheek. "How do you feel about your mother mebbe being alive?"

"Can't say. Gaia, but I wish I knew where she was."

"Could be we'll bump into her one day."

Krysty smiled again. "Could be."

"It's odd not to have to keep looking over my shoulder to make sure that Dean's not gotten himself into trouble. Hope the kid'll be all right."

"If any kid can survive, it's Dean Cawdor," she said. "Takes after his father."

"Think so?"

"I know so."

JAK AND DOC CAME BACK from their scavenging expedition with pockets filled with small sweet peaches. And Mildred and J.B. had found their way along the back of the main street of Breckenridge until they came across a clean, fast-flowing stream of meltwater from higher up the valley.

They'd washed out the canteens from the stinking armawag, opened up the ob slits to let in some fresh air and purged the stench of the killers.

Ryan sat with his back against the warm flank of the vehicle, sipping the icy water, chewing at one of the tangy peaches, yawning. "Known worse places and worse days," he said.

Doc flicked a peach pit into the bed of the dry fountain. "What I find truly bizarre about this wonderful day is that it commenced at its dawning with the legitimized butchery of hordes of the vile and ungodly."

Mildred nodded. "Agree with you for once, Doc. Our hands are smeared with blood, and yet it all seems like it was several days ago."

"Another world," Krysty said, running her fingers through her mane of flaming hair, now uncoiled and free across her shoulders. "Far away."

Ryan was aware of movement and spun, seeing an elderly woman standing watching them from the bal-

cony of a house, a little way up the hill. She was wearing a stiff black dress with a string of jet beads around
her neck. And she held a black parasol to protect her
from the sun.

"Good day to you, ma'am," he called, waving a hand
in greeting, but the woman ignored him.

Everyone turned and saw the strange sight. Doc
cleared his throat. "By the Three Kennedys! She is like
a portrait from an ancient lithograph." He stood and
bowed, receiving a slight inclination of the head toward him. "Some apparition from the pages of Mon-
tague James."

The woman watched them as they finished their al-
fresco picnic, once more returning a final bow from
Doc as they readied themselves to leave.

"Think all right?" Jak asked. "Need help?"

Ryan shook his head firmly at the teenager's question. "Looks fine to me, Jak."

He raised his voice. "Anything we can do for you,
ma'am?"

The woman almost smiled and slowly moved her
head from side to side, the afternoon sunshine flickering off the polished jet of her necklace.

"There. She's fine. Everyone finished eating and
drinking? Then we can get going again."

Krysty was last into the armawag and she turned to
wave farewell to the woman, but the balcony was deserted.

THEY REACHED the predark interstate close to the ville of Frisco, starting to move along west at a fair rate. A rusted sign told them that Glenwood Springs was around eighty miles away.

They stopped again for a comfort break near Eagle, having found that the interstate was buckled and destroyed by quakes, forcing them to use an older parallel road.

Doc, more prudish than the others about his bodily functions, had gone deep into a tangle of chokeberry bushes, vanishing totally from sight. They could all hear an exclamation of surprise and a thrashing around in the undergrowth.

"You okay, Doc?" J.B. called.

"I am in the very best of health, my dear fellow. Tiptop. Top of the tip-top. Top of the world, Ma. Top of the morning to you, Seamus. Spin the top…" The voice faded away to a preoccupied mumble.

Everyone else had long finished before he came lumbering out of the bushes, cursing under his breath as the tangles plucked at his frock coat.

"What you got there?" Ryan asked, seeing that the old man appeared to be holding an arrow.

A peculiarly long arrow.

"There was the body of a deer in the brush. Well, to be perfectly specific, it was little more than a skeleton. Bones and a few fragments of its skin. And this was jammed between two of its ribs. Poor animal must have been shot and fled, eventually finding its surcease in hiding."

Ryan took the arrow, measuring it against himself. "Least four feet long. And the feathers aren't goose, are they? Look more like a heron, or something like that." Realization dawned on him. "Fireblast! Course. It's like one of those Japanese arrows, isn't it?"

"That was my thought," Doc admitted. "They certainly get around, our mysterious Oriental brethren, do they not? From the condition of the deer, I would hazard a guess that it met its doom at least six months ago."

Ryan examined the arrow, which was beautifully made, far better than most of the hunting arrows that he'd seen from the Oglala and the Chiricahua, from plains to mountains. And he wondered again where the samurai came from and how they traveled so easily through Deathlands.

In all the years of riding with the Trader he'd never even heard a whisper of slant-eye killers with long arrows and honed swords.

"No sign of any others, Doc?"

"Absolutely none, John Barrymore. The deer could have run for miles before expiring. And, as I said, it was a long time ago, in another country and, besides, the wench is dead." Doc's face wrinkled with puzzlement. "What in hades made me say that? I believe it is from some play or other."

"Time we were moving on," Ryan said. "Need to get through Glenwood Springs before dark and up to the redoubt."

"No kind of shortcut?" Jak asked. "North?"

J.B. had slid behind the wheel of the small four-wheel-drive wag. "No, afraid not. Have to go right into the ville and then dump the wag. Rest on foot."

The highway was in worse condition than they'd expected, and they had to take bone-rattling detours over muddy rutted trails. By the time they saw the pale yellow lights of Glenwood Springs in the distance, the sun was already setting beyond the endless forest.

# Chapter Thirty-Seven

A strange mutie creature galloped across the road in front of the armawag, casting a long, grotesque shadow on the highway. Ryan had taken over the controls, and he swerved and braked to avoid it, staring in disbelief.

The body was a large deer, though with shortened, stubby legs that ended in furry, clawed paws. The neck was short and muscular, supporting a head that looked like a cross between a wolf and a pig, a rooting snout and a double row of wickedly curved teeth that glinted red in the setting sun.

It turned as it reached the edge of the pavement and snarled at the vehicle, glaring from the three split-pupil eyes. There was such an aura of hatred from it that Ryan flinched. Instinctively he dropped his hand to the butt of the blaster on his hip, even though he knew that the layers of armored steel that surrounded him would protect him from any attack, even from a monstrous creature like that.

"What that?" Jak asked, peering out one of the side ob slits.

"Don't know," Ryan said, setting the pedal to the metal, making the engine roar. "Just hope I don't ever meet it on a moonless night." The wag vibrated as they

built up speed and roared into the ville of Glenwood
Springs.

THEY'D DISCUSSED the possibility of trying to find
someplace to eat in the ville, but Krysty had pointed out
the serious risk that the girl, Maria, from Ma's Place,
might spot them and rouse a lynch posse against them.

"Should've strangled her, you and Doc," Jak insisted. "Trader said live enemy's bad enemy."

"And the only good Indian is a good Indian," Doc
countered. "Yes, dear youth, we do all know that. But
the taking of human life still comes hard to me. Call me
a humanitarian old fart, but I would rather spare than
take."

Mildred grinned, unwilling to miss the chance. "Sure.
You're a humanitarian old fart, Doc."

The old man nodded. "I realize that traveling the way
that we do through this blighted world of Deathlands
must inexorably weaken the sensibilities. But it will
never justify a callous disregard for the sanctity of life."

The albino shrugged. "Live like you want, Doc. Just
saying girl was vicious. Better chilled. Now can't risk a
stop here to eat. Shame."

THEY PASSED the burned-out ruins of Ma's Place,
heading a little way out of the ville, up toward the
north. They took a side trail that carried them another
mile, up a long, rising grade, past some raggedy, tumbled shacks, shortening the walking distance from the
redoubt.

The road petered out along a forest of stunted piñon pines. Ryan tried to force the wag a little farther, but the slope was too steep and it ground to a halt, the arrow on the temperature gauge sliding deep into the red.

"And that concludes the entertainment for the day," Doc said, swinging open the hatch. "Oh, my dear friends, smell that wonderful scent."

Conifers in the cool of evening, after a hot summer's day, had liberated the odors of the balsamic sap.

Everyone piled out of the sweating interior of the armawag, Ryan last of all, having switched off the engine, which began to click as it became chilled by the dusk.

"Going to leave it or blow it?" the Armorer asked. "Could just walk away. Give someone a nice present."

Ryan nodded, tossing the ignition key into the driver's seat, leaving the hatch open. "Hell, why not?"

He took several deep breaths. "Fireblast! You're not wrong, Doc. That is some good air."

"Are we going to walk on up to the redoubt, lover, or camp here?"

Ryan considered the question, glancing up at the red-tinted, cloudless sky, with the segment of silver-bright moon riding high. "Should be enough light, I reckon," he said.

BEFORE FULL DARK descended over Colorado, they covered a mile and a half, climbing constantly up a winding path among trees. Twice they disturbed small herds of long-horned goats that clattered off across the bare rocks.

Doc struggled with the climb, still not acclimated to the altitude.

"Upon my soul! There was a time in my life when I used to do this sort of madness for pleasure! Presume not that I am the man I was." He looked around. "I have the odd feeling that I have already said that, not long ago. Perhaps I did and perhaps I did not. I know not."

"Can't help you, Doc," Mildred said. "Truth is, we never listen to what you say, anyway."

RYAN CALLED A HALT when they crested a ridge, a half hour later, pausing to look down over the twinkling lights of the ville, now far, far below them.

"How's everyone? Doc?"

The familiar voice boomed from the darkness a little farther down the winding trail. "I confess that for once I shall almost be pleased to make a jump. Anything to get away from this damnably thin air."

"But it's *good* thin air, Doc," Mildred said. "You told us that yourself."

"That was then, madame," he retorted, finally joining them and slumping down with a creaking of joints, "and this is definitely now."

After a brief rest Doc was ready to carry on. "How much farther, my dear Ryan?"

"We're moving across to cut the trail we came in on. Unless there's a problem, my guess is that we should find ourselves back close to the redoubt in about another hour. Hour and a half. No more."

THE HUGE BONEYARD outside the main entrance seemed to tower higher, its sharp angles stark in the moonlight.

"Hope no more crazies," Jak said, staring up at the towering redoubt.

"Think we killed off the last of the breed," Ryan replied. "Soon find out."

He realized that he'd been unconsciously waiting for Dean to jump forward and offer to press in the triple-digit number code that would open the vast vanadium-steel sec doors, as he always did.

"You waiting for Dean to do the numbers?" J.B. asked. "Me too."

Everyone smiled as they realized that they'd all had precisely the same thought.

"Allow me," Doc said.

"No sign water," Jak stated, bending and touching the ground below his boots. "Dry."

Ryan nodded. He'd already noticed that. There was no way of knowing until they were actually well inside the ranging military complex whether the flooding that had been going on when they left had continued, or how much damage it might have caused, or how deep it might have gotten. It could have reached down into the deeps of the redoubt and affected the mat-trans complex and the gateway itself.

Far too many questions.

No answers.

"Everyone get clear of the doors," Ryan cautioned, "in case we get a tidal wave rolling over us."

"A tsunami," Mildred said. "That's what they call them in Japan."

Doc pushed a finger at the worn keyboard, peering to make sure he was hitting the right numerals in the correct order, lips moving. "Three . . . five . . . two."

There was the familiar distant grinding of gears, and the door began to move. To Ryan's relief there was no sudden gushing tumble of water.

"After me," he said, walking cautiously into the main entrance of the redoubt, his nostrils flaring at the damp smell that permeated the complex. "Keep on double red."

"Should I close the door again?" Doc called, standing inside. "Be safer."

"Sure. Let her go."

The old man pressed the numbers in reverse, two, five, three, and the moonlight was shut away. Most of the strip lights inside the complex had malfunctioned, and it felt as if the air-conditioning had also failed in the few days since they were last there.

"Damp's gotten into the heart of the place," J.B. said, pausing to wipe his glasses on a white handkerchief that he'd taken out of one of the capacious pockets of his coat.

"Just hope it hasn't done any damage to the gateway." Ryan looked around. "I think we should go straight there and try for the jump. Something here that doesn't feel good, Krysty? You feel anything?"

She touched her sentient hair, now curled tight against her skull. "See for yourself. Can't feel any life, though."

THE PLACE REEKED of stale water. There were puddles in all the dips of the floor, and a film of oil lay on top, making any movement treacherous and difficult.

Some kind of mutated lichen, a sickly phosphorescent green, had taken over some of the first floor, splashing itself over walls and doors.

Doc began to sing a song about how times were getting hard, and if things didn't get better, then he was going to leave the place. His voice echoed flat and hollow, sounding depressing. After a single verse, he fell silent again.

"Looks like the main reservoirs must've drained down," Mildred commented.

"But where's water gone?" Jak looked around, his feet slapping in a shallow puddle.

"Down." J.B. offered a hand to Mildred to help her around one of the largest pools. "It'll have found its own level and soaked away."

Ryan stopped. "Yeah. Down. To the gateway?"


THEY WORKED THEIR WAY through the levels, finding that the elevators still worked. Krysty hadn't been happy.

"Suppose they malfunction and lose power when we're halfway down in one of them. Don't want to spend eternity in a cold, wet, metal box."

"Worst comes to it, we can climb down the cables," J.B. said.

"Then let us profoundly pray that the worst doesn't come to it," Doc muttered.

"SMELL'S WORSE." Jak sniffed, head on one side, eyes glowing like stoplights in the bare overhead lights.

The deeper they got into the redoubt, the more harm seemed to have been done by the flooding. Twice they encountered long stretches of corridors where all of the strip lights had blown out, sprinkling the floor with shards of razored glass.

Ryan had stood everyone down from double red, and they had all holstered their weapons. There seemed to be little doubt that the complex was now totally uninhabited, and there was no threat from anything living.

He sniffed. "Smells more like an underground cave than a redoubt."

"Decay. Rotting." Mildred pulled a face. "Sort of stink that lies on your belly and makes you want to puke. If it gets much worse, we could have problems."

"How?" J.B. asked.

"Poisonous gases, John. Workmen who are involved in digging deep shafts and tunnels sometimes get overcome by some very nasty substances. And they die. Often get this smell, but it covers up the danger lying below."

"You get any warning?" Ryan sniffed again, trying to decide whether he was beginning to feel a little lightheaded, unable to be sure.

"No. Safest here is for us all to string out into a line and take it slow and easy. Then, if the guy out front goes down, the others get a warning and they can probably take deep breaths and drag him out to safety. The pockets of gas are likely to be very localized."

It was obviously sensible advice and Ryan imple-
mented it, taking point himself.

Now that he was aware of a potentially lethal threat,
Ryan moved much more cautiously, constantly stopping to check his own reactions.

But the air seemed breathable, though foul, and he
eventually found himself in the passage that led downhill to the locked sec door of the gateway.

"FOUND THE WATER," he said, his voice drifting back
to the others.

"Much?" Krysty called, walking second in line about
fifty paces behind him.

"Enough. Plenty."

"Safe to join you?" Mildred shouted, her voice
sounding flat, reaching him from a dark section of corridor.

"Yeah. Feel all right. Bit sick. Air's not that great."

They joined Ryan, staring at the motionless expanse
of black water that filled the corridor in front of them.

"How much farther gateway?" Jak asked.

"Close. I'm certain it's around the next bend. I remember that locked door we just passed." Ryan tested
it with his foot. "Starts shallow, but it'll get deeper as
the floor drops."

"The sixty-four-thousand question is whether it has
penetrated into the actual mat-trans chamber." Doc
whistled softly. "If it has, then goodbye will be all she
wrote."

Ryan considered options.

"If it's flooded we can't jump. Climb back. Find the armawag, if nobody's gotten to it first. And move on until we can find a gateway we've used before."

J.B. rubbed at his chin. "If it isn't flooded already and the sec door's holding it back, then we open the door and it pours in. That could be unpleasant if the electrics start shorting out while we're knee-deep in Old Muddy."

"All the consoles and the main controls are at least waist high, are they not?" Doc closed his eyes, trying to work out the problem. "All to do with liquid flow dynamics and cubic... Say there's about sixty feet. Pythagoras says that means a volume of approximately... two hundred million gallons. No, that surely can't be right. Oh, I see where my fuddled brain made..." Finally Doc opened his eyes again.

"Well?" Ryan said.

Doc looked at him. "My guess is that opening the sec door will certainly produce a flood of some dimension. Important to slide it up gently so that it doesn't come tearing in with a heated rush. My calculations indicate that the level might not reach the key controls on the gateway."

"Might!" Mildred exploded. "What the...! What does 'might' mean, Doc?"

The old man smiled and patted her on the shoulder. "It means that the game is afoot and we shall try to prove the case, my dear Doctor. I believe that no great harm is particularly likely to come to us."

"Still some water," Jak said, pointing at the sheen on the wall, where the flow still trickled down, joining the other uncounted gallons.

"Means we could get trapped, Doc," Ryan said.

"I think not."

Ryan bit his lip, sighing. "Let's try for it," he said.

THE WATER WASN'T AS COLD as he'd expected, only a little below blood heat. But it quickly grew deeper, reaching his waist as Ryan led them around the corner, in sight of the sec door to the mat-trans unit.

Mildred and Jak were both only five feet four inches tall, and the dark water rose halfway up their chests.

"Can't go too much farther without starting swimming," Mildred complained, holding her ZKR 551 revolver over her head to keep it dry.

The others carried their blasters as high as they could.

"Levels off here," Ryan said, finally reaching the doors. The green control lever was out of sight in the murky water. Only one overhead strip light still functioned, casting its insipid glow over the six friends.

"Want me to open her up?" J.B. offered, his spectacles glinting in the pallid light.

"No, I'll do it. Take your point, Doc. Do it gently. Until the level stabilizes inside and out. Then all the way and we go straight for the chamber to jump. Don't waste any more time. Everyone ready? Here we go."

IT TOOK about ten minutes.

The water started to drop, bubbling under the heavy sec door, through the six-inch gap that Ryan had left for it, dropping until it wasn't much above the knees.

"Open her the rest of the way, Ryan," Doc said. "I fear that it will not get more shallow. Only deeper."

"Right." He threw the lever all the way up, moving back as the massive weight of the sec steel lifted ponderously to the ceiling, letting them into the main control area.

The water level was close to the tops of the monitor desks, lapping at the walls. At first glance Ryan saw that about half of the comp panels were down, the screens dull and lifeless.

He waded toward the anteroom, careful not to make too great a turbulence, followed by Krysty, then Doc and Jak. Mildred and J.B. brought up the rear.

At his heels he heard a gasp, followed by a splashing and thrashing. He looked back to see that Jak had caught his feet on an overturned stool, hidden below the surface, and had fallen, sending a wave right around the chamber that broke against the tops of some of the nearer desks.

"Sorry," he spluttered, his snow-white hair pasted to his shoulders like a bridal veil.

Ryan didn't say anything. No point in warning them all to be careful. He reached the door to the small anteroom, seeing the six-sided armaglass chamber just in front of him, its pale pink walls gleaming. There was a crackling sound from behind, and half the remaining lights cut out, leaving them in almost total darkness.

"Time to go," Ryan said, easing open the door. A the water gushed in, he noticed the small smear on th floor that had once been Melmoth Cornelius.

"Have to stand," Krysty said, bracing herself again the back wall.

"Yeah. Quick." Ryan waited until everyone was in side the chamber, huddled together, all pale-faced an nervous. He reached for the door, ready to trigger th jump mechanism.

As he touched the metal edge of the door he got sharp electric shock that made him jump, and a brigh blue spark leaped across the gap.

"Fireblast!"

"You all right, lover?"

"I am. Just hope that the rad-blasted jump mecha nism is all right."

"Water still rising slowly," Jak warned.

Ryan didn't answer. He pulled the armaglass doo firmly shut, walking across and standing next to Krysty putting his arm around her.

"So long to Harmony," she said.

They waited for the disks in floor and ceiling to star glowing, the latter just visible under the water, for th mist to gather above their heads and for the brain sucking darkness to swoop down over them.

"Has anyone considered that if we fall unconscious we might drown during the jump?" Doc asked.

But the jump didn't start.

Ryan opened and closed the door again.

All that happened was a flash of silver light from the control room and all the lights went out.

In the silent dark, the water was still rising.

It's the ultimate battle between
good and bad—Made in Mexico

# THE Destroyer

## #102 Unite and Conquer

### Created by
## WARREN MURPHY
## and RICHARD SAPIR

Not that things were so hot before, but when a huge
earthquake guts Mexico, nobody wants to hang around,
especially with all sorts of demonic doings by the barbaric
gods of old Mexico, released from hell when the earth
ruptured. It's god versus god, with the human race
helpless trophies for the victor.

Look for it in March, wherever Gold Eagle books are sold.